CW01594130

The Stories of George the Hamster

Recorded, Translated and Compiled
by Lee H and Kathleen Smith

A Metro Golden Hamster Production

Shedhead Productions

The Stories of George the Hamster

Recorded, Translated and Compiled by Lee H and Kathleen Smith

A Metro-Golden Hamster Production © 2008
by Lee H. Smith
previously © 2004 by Lee H Smith
Register of Copyrights Registration Number TXu1-189-925
Dated July 23 2004

All rights reserved.
No part of this book may be reproduced, stored in a retrieval system or transmitted in any form or by any means without the prior written permission of the authors or translators, except by a reviewer who may quote brief passages in a review to be printed in a newspaper, magazine or journal.

This book is published by

Shedhead Productions,
Antioch Centre,
Copperworks Road,
Llanelli
SA15 1PY

ISBN : 978-0-9546989-3-5

Printed in Great Britain by :
Gwasg Gomer Cyfyngedig,
Parc Menter,
Llandysul,
Ceredigion,
SA44 4JL

DEDICATION

For all hamsters, past and present, who've encouraged me to write these stories that they've recited around food bowls throughout the world since they were very young hamlets.

CONTENTS

Page

A Human's Introduction 1

Acknowledgements and Thanks 7

The Hamster History of the World 9

Introduction 10
High Moon (HH2) 12
The Battle of Copenhagen (HH1) 17
Tappuwocky 21
The Virtuoso Performance of Mandy Reid (HH1) 24
The Capture of Sardis (HH1) 29
The Space Walk of Buzz Hamstrin (HH1) 33
The Great Sunflower Seed Robbery (HH3) 39
The Last Flight of Douglas Hamster (HH1) 45
The Imprisonment of Tutanhamster (HH1) 49
The Master Stroke (HH2) 52
The Big Sleep (HH2) 58
What if... (HH2) 62
The Hamster Olympics (HH2) 67
The Dark-Skinned Stranger (HH2) 73
Gerbileo 77
Voyage to the Bottom of the Duck Pond (HH3) 80
The Pilgrim Hamsters (HH3) 86
Hamster in the Lions' Den (HH3) 97
The Great Escape (HH3) 102
The Final Battle (HH3) 104
Select Bibliography (HH3) 111

An English Hamster in Paris	113
Introduction	115
Arrival	116
The Louvre	119
The Place du Tertre	125
L'Opera de Paris and Hamdini	131
Rue de Rome	142
Notre Dame and Versailles	147
L'Arc de Triomphe and the Eiffel Tower	156
Charles de Gaulle	164
A Tail of Two Hamsters	173
Introduction	175
The Journey	176
The Arrival	183
The Rest	190
The Island	199
The Truffles	202
The Celebration	210
The Observatory	220
The River	227
The Departure	232
Appendix - For a Few Peanuts More	235

A HUMAN'S INTRODUCTION

The works and writings of George the Hamster are now legendary amongst the rodents of the civilised world - even amongst the civilised rodents of the not-all-that-civilised parts of the human world (you know who you are).

His works have been translated into eighteen different hamster dialects, three gerbil and twelve grasshopper, too - and there's seldom a day goes by when human political leaders don't hold their head up high and acknowledge their debt to the legacy of George the Hamster.

Therefore, it seems appropriate to give the reader some background to this most famous and celebrated of rodents.

George was purchased from a local pet shop during February 1991. We cannot be sure where or when he was born as the owner of the shop is unsure himself - George's explanations don't throw much light on the subject, either, as he dates his birth to '...the fourth eclipse of the planet Mercury that it makes with Venus on its half-circuit around its third moon.'

As you can see, hamster dating techniques are so far removed from our own more advanced methods that his description is virtually non-sensical. However, judging from the size of George when we purchased him, we estimate that he was born approximately during the last full week in January of the same year.

He was a fast developer, lifting up items in his cage and making the appropriate squeaks that represented the object. We learnt quickly that he was trying to communicate with us and after several weeks of intense study, research and practice we grew fairly proficient in the translation and transmission of the hamster-tongue.

We never once realized that he'd turn out to be such an intelligent hamster, or that we would be able to hold intellectual conversations with him, but this is how it worked out.

The Hamster History of the World Volume One

George dictated six short articles for use in the local church's magazine within his first few months with us, but he was working on a greater work that, at that time, we were blissfully unaware of - 'The Hamster History of the World.'

He dictated the first volume to me during the early part of spring and we distributed copies to our friends at the same time.

The concept behind the publication was that human history had been written with an unfair bias - hamsters being so small, they often went undetected in the momentous events of world history and it was George's aim to correct that imbalance with six pithy short stories (including the first hamster in space, the first hamster to fly and, what proved to be one of my favourites, the story of Furatio Half-Nelson, the hamster that lived in the great Admiral Nelson's empty sleeve).

The popularity of those first six articles proved to be the catalyst that propelled him into gathering together stories from the lives of some of his relatives in the ancient and modern past and to draw spiritual truth from them.

The Hamster History of the World Volume Two

In the coming months we developed Hamscript for him to use - after all, we were getting limited sleep having to be up at all hours of the night whenever George felt the inspiration starting to flow.

Incidentally, the use of the word 'Hamscript' refers throughout this book either to the characters that a hamster uses in order to write, or else to a scroll of hamster writing as in the human equivalent, a manuscript. The context determines which meaning it should be given.

Hamscript, then, was a way for George to be able to commit to paper stories using a series of full and semi-paw prints with pronunciation marks.

Having formulated an alphabet (based on an old Hamsterglyphic monosyllabic alphabet) and having introduced it to him, there was an added complication of using paper, for hamsters have an irresistible urge to chew anything. This posed us with what we thought would be an insurmountable problem, but at last discovered that white lino was both unchewable and reusable.

Using a black ink pad, George wrote these stories in 'Hamscript,' which we subsequently translated as accurately as possible.

You will, of course, understand that the style was bound to be different, as before we'd only been able to give the sense - now a word-for-squeak translation was possible.

It was in Hamscript, then, that the second volume of 'The Hamster History' was written, subsequently translated and distributed in late spring. The thrust was much the same as the first, except that George broadened his storytelling to include events for which there are no human equivalents.

The Hamster History of the World Volume Three

(Also, more commonly, known as 'A Critical and Exegetical Compilation of Selected Ancient Hamscripts with Close Reference to Hermeneutic and Homiletic Principles'.)

Then, during late summer, George drafted volume three, which was a studious and academic work for which he received critical acclaim throughout the rodent world. He used many different ancient Hamscripts (even referring to some of those uncovered within the past decade by archaeologists at Qumran) to put together six texts, which he subsequently translated for the benefit of us humans.

Indeed, as far as we are aware, this is the first of its kind and it therefore needs a little explanation before the reader can fully appreciate the originality of this work.

In the previous two editions of 'The Hamster History of the World,' the stories had come from tradition handed down from one generation to another by squeak of mouth - hence they're called 'Oral tradition.' But, in this volume, George had been hard at work comparing ancient Hamsterglyphic manuscripts and their variations that stretched back many centuries.

As hamsters moved west and east from the Ark, both the hamster-tongue and script varied, often changing entire words and giving phrases totally new meanings. George had to study carefully each culture's native tongue, interpret accordingly and piece together, with incredible accuracy, the underlying tale to which these Hamscripts testified.

It's quite amazing that the hamscripts survived when one considers how prolific hamsters are at chewing. But, for one reason or another, there are enough extant Hamscripts available to perform a higher criticism of the text.

To present to the reader an easy-to-understand format, George disregarded technical notes wherever possible. However, on a number of occasions he had to resort to a footnote to explain a textual problem that can be pursued by anyone wishing to delve in to the waters of higher Hamscript criticism for themselves.

Although longer in writing than the other two volumes, it was well worth the wait. To mark the milestone of this achievement, both the Royal Mail and the US Postal Service issued a series of special postage stamps to coincide with the release.

For this first edition of George's works, I've taken the liberty of combining all three volumes into a single section and harmonised George's original introductions into one.

An English Hamster in Paris

Having achieved more than most hamsters do in an entire lifetime, we thought that George's statement to us that he was going to 'hang up his blotting pad for a rest' meant a permanent break from the literary world but, far from it - 'An English Hamster in Paris' was released during October '92 and distributed to a wider audience than were any of his other works.

I'd known that George was up to something when, way back during the early weeks of May, I'd found several half-chewed Hamscripts at the back of the kitchen cupboards that he'd disappeared behind one Saturday morning when I was cleaning out his cage.

I'd tried to decipher them but to no avail as they had certain characters that I wasn't familiar with. Upon questioning, George revealed nothing - in fact, he categorically denied ever having seen them and put their existence down to the 'unauthorised entry of a bunch of field mice' that he said he'd heard late one night after Kath and I were sound asleep in bed.

The meticulous planning that went into George's escape was what I had unwittingly stumbled upon - as he later revealed to me - but, having realised the impossibility of progressing any further in my investigations, I pushed all thought of the Hamscripts aside and got on with daily living.

It was at about the same time that I noticed a floppy disc to our word processor go missing. I didn't question George about this as I couldn't conceive of a hamster having any use for it, but it's evident now that he was storing it up for the day when, unbeknown to me, he would return from his summer vacation in Paris and begin to record his exploits.

Using a specially developed Brother 10/12 pitch daisy wheel in modern Hamscript, George was able to work on his own with arduous toil and fevered brow once we'd gone to bed - correcting, improving, expanding and printing (we thought that the tiny pat-pat-pat below us in the living room was George running like a mad lemming around his compound - but it turned out that it was the word processor printing out one after another of George's recorded experiences).

The text in this specific work was the result of many hours of toil that I had little to do with - by swapping the Hamscript wheel for one in standard English, a direct word-for-word translation was possible (all I can be credited with is changing the daisy wheel).

This, then, was truly George's first totally original work and must be ranked, we believe, as one of the truly great works that has ever come from the paw of a golden hamster.

An English Hamster in Scotland

Then, almost a year later, George produced another epic (well, we thought so, anyway), the record of his eventful trip to Scotland that took place early in the year.

George kept a diary while he was there and, having returned, expanded his brief notes into a fuller account of that 'fantastic voyage' in which he experienced Scottish hamster hospitality at first hand.

This was written and compiled in the same way as 'An English Hamster in Paris' and was again circulated to a wider audience than the previous four works.

And then...

What happened 'next' must be reserved for a future book but, for now, these opening five works will give the reader some basic grounding in rodent literature and the reason why, twenty years or so from now, there may be one who takes his seat in the White House.

I have reluctantly had to make the decision not to retain the original introductions and prefaces of the works as they were released in small locally produced booklets and they now simply clutter up the text. I have left, however, George's own introductions, which give the reader a quick overview of each of the five works at the appropriate points.

I've compiled the sections omitted into this article, for they show the progression of thought and give snippets of information not available to the college student who's generally only ever given the text of the stories themselves for critical analysis.

I have also used an edited compilation of George's own acknowledgements that appear in the original works and brought them together with the addition of my own thanks to people who are, today, just as deserving a mention - as George would have wanted me to.

Lee H Smith

ACKNOWLEDGEMENTS AND THANKS

Thanks are due to my masters, Lee and Kath Smith, who laboured intensively to get the early manuscripts both translated and typed, who painstakingly developed Hamscript for me to use as a vehicle by which to commit these stories to lino and who did a great job of attending to my every need.

Although they think that they were 'lucky' to stumble upon me in the pet shop that fateful day, they've still never come to terms with the fact that it was *I* who choose *them* and not the other way round.

Thanks also to Lee's mum who first put me in contact with her friend's cat, Ginger, with whom I had some wonderful correspondence - and to Lee's dad who sent me things through the post. They both continued to give me encouragement and were delighted when Lee broke the news that the book was finally to be allowed to escape into the world.

A specific mention must go to Liz in Washington and to all the hamsters of the 'Hamster for President' Campaign who continually encouraged Lee to '...get the stories published, you blockhead!'

To all those people - voices from the dim and distant past - who were specially encouraging at some point or another in the writing of these five works - but I must mention specifically Steve and Catrin (who also proofread some of the original stories and were panic-stricken when I went AWOL to Scotland), Maggie and Phil Bough (who were the people whom I escaped from to journey over to Paris), Pavel and Jaron Plasencia in Tennessee and Steve Hamblin.

Thanks from Lee to Jaime who first put these works into book format and who helped Lee see just how good this manuscript could look. And to Adrienne who produced the first cover that was all and more than I'd wanted it to be. What a shame all your hard work was swept under the carpet by forces outside both your and my control.

Thanks to Deb and all at Shedhead who had to start from scratch and bring together Lee's ideas and suggestions. And thanks for being patient with him - he *is* a strange guy.

And, finally, to you the reader - thank you for reading these articles not as a work of fiction but as a commitment to paper of what really took place.

I trust that these stories will draw you nearer to the Creator, that you might hear His voice speaking to you through them, instructing you in the way that He's prepared for you.

George

The Hamster History of the World

THE HAMSTER HISTORY OF THE WORLD
A Metro-Golden Hamster Production

INTRODUCTION

It has come to my attention that history has been recorded with a definite 'human' bias in your textbooks and classrooms throughout the world. Very little has ever been written about the role of animals - especially hamsters - in the great events of history.

However, I have decided to redress this imbalance by pulling from my own genealogy some of the events that my ancestors have been witness to.

Obviously I would find it difficult to tell you accurately the things concerning hippopotamuses or elephants for I don't have access to their archives. But hamster history has long been acknowledged as a parallel and adequate commentary on the distortions that exist in human history.

I have moved only slightly away from the restriction of limiting myself to write solely about major historical events in a few of these stories, and have recorded events that you'll not find the human equivalent for in your textbooks. It has to be remembered that hamsters often find important events to which humans pay little or no attention.

My third series of stories was deliberately written to cover new ground.

Though I remained true to my thesis that human history had been recorded with an unfair bias and sought to correct it accordingly, I endeavoured to use the writings of hamsters much older and wiser than myself who were eyewitnesses of momentous events in world history, thus eliminating any errors that may have crept into the oral transmission of the stories.

I have consigned technical comments to pawnotes where absolutely necessary but have tried to eliminate the need for them entirely by adding a Select Bibliography to which the student and lay person may refer.

For those of you wishing to know which stories appeared in each of the three previously released volumes, Lee has added special indicators to the Contents section of this book (HH1, HH2 and HH3).

HIGH MOON

The slim, dark stranger galloped down the dusty track, his whiskers shimmering in the breeze. Rusty brown clouds of earth gusted behind him as he journeyed, ever onward, ever nearer to his destination.

It was to a small quiet town deep in the heart of the midwest that he was headed. His mission, as always, to bring justice to the poor and freedom to the oppressed.

He flashed past two ladies strolling in the cool of the late afternoon summer and he heard one sigh with awe as he disappeared into the distance.

'My hero.'

They had encountered, albeit very briefly, the one who strikes fear into the heart of every bandit and terror into every robber.

It was...yes, it was...the Lone Hamster. Two miles from town he removed the black mask from his eyes and folded it neatly into his left pouch - it was time for the Lone Hamster to go incognito.

Perhaps I should explain to you what had brought our hero to this small backwater town on the edge of the mountains. You see, the Lone Hamster had heard reports though at first he thought it was only gossip. Then he saw the fear in the eyes of the rodents that had ridden through on their way east. Finally, all his worst fears were confirmed when three hamsters galloped into town to save their fur from the wild goings-on in that place.

Rats! Those most loathsome of creatures had been terrorising the hamster population and driving them, one by one, away from town. The humans suffered too - death and disease had spread throughout their ranks like vile plague engulfing men, women and children, merciless to rich and poor alike.

Rats! The hamster's enemy. The hamster's foe. And only the hamsters held the solution.

The Lone Hamster, heavily in disguise having taken off his thin black mask, rode stealthily into town looking first this way, then that, in case they'd anticipated his arrival.

Nothing.

No sound except the wind as it whispered down the main street and the sand as it brushed past the wooden walled buildings. It seemed like a ghost town.

He found the hotel on the corner of the only crossroads in town and went in through a crack in the entrance steps. In the wild west, hamsters set up trade underneath their human counterparts so it was easy for any stranger to get a soft bed of straw for the night.

The proprietor was a small hamster, grey in the ears with a nervous twitch over his left eye. He eyed him over suspiciously, not noticing that it was the Lone Hamster because of his cunning disguise.

'You new in town?' he squeaked, his eyes looking at the dusty rodent that stood before him, one paw on the reception counter.

'Room for one,' he retorted. 'My bags are out on the porch.'

The Bell-hamsters scurried off outside, pouched his luggage and carried them upstairs.

'We charge extra if yer gnaw the fittin's,' the landlord squeaked as he handed him a curiously shaped sunflower seed shell. 'That's yer key - room 48.'

The Lone Hamster pressed his face close to the landlord's, lowering his voice to a whisper.

'Where are the rats?' he said.

The proprietor's face lit up in a cross between terror and amazement - 'You looking fer the rats?'

'Can you get a message to them?'

He thought for a moment.

'I...er...well...erm...well, yeah.' He seemed nervous.

'Tell them,' he squeaked. 'Tell them they stink. And tell them I said so.'

The landlord gulped and accidentally swallowed the hazelnut that he'd pouched to eat later.

'They won't be pleased, they'll come a-lookin' fer yer,' he warned.

'Just tell them,' he spoke in a calm tone. 'Just tell them.'

Two hours later as the Lone Hamster sat curled up in his straw, a note was pushed under the door. He wasn't asleep, he was waiting... waiting for the reply.

He scurried over to the door and read the message. It was a rhyme:

'When the moon is high

In the sewer you will die.
We will tear you limb from limb
Cos we hate you whoever you are.'

'Mmmm,' he thought. 'Rats never were any good at poetry.'
He screwed up the note and ate it.
'So, high moon. Until then, rats, I wait.'
And, with that, he curled up and fell fast asleep.

High Moon! The time had come! The Lone Hamster, still heavily in disguise, paid his bill, found the nearest toilet and descended into the sewers.

The main sewer ran north to south underneath the road. As the Lone Hamster fearlessly, courageously pawed his way step by step to the confrontation, he noticed first one hamster, then another, joining behind him, cowering in fear and trepidation. Then it seemed like the entire population stood with him. Frightened - yes - but, nevertheless, standing with him. Word had got round.

'Good!' he thought. 'Let them stand and watch!'

The rats approached from the south, inching their way towards him like a grey mass of slime that swallowed up the earth before it. Death and disease were in their wake. You could hear the maniacal laughter as they came, biggest and bravest first, to stand ten inches from the Lone Hamster.

'You scared, hamster?' they mocked. The menagerie of rats gurgled with intimidation.

The Lone Hamster, still in disguise, said nothing.

The rats weren't expecting that, it took them by surprise so that some began to wonder what 'secret weapon' he might have concealed in his pouches. The younger ones began to whisper, 'Do you reckon it's a sharpened sunflower seed?'

'No,' came the answer, 'more like a loaded hazelnut.'

'You've had long enough, hamster.'

The biggest and meanest rat came forward and stood before them all, towering over the Lone Hamster, eyes glittering with intent, paws fastened tightly on a sharpened twig - 'You draw first.'

He didn't need a second encouragement.

In a lightning movement that took everyone by surprise, he flashed from his pouches a small black object and, unfolding it, placed it across his eyes.

The mask! The Lone Hamster had put on his mask!

The rats went silent, immovable.

Then one whispered, 'It's the Lone Hamster!'

Then another.

They looked around for support and encouragement but it was gone. The Lone Hamster had struck fear into their hearts.

Before long, the entire pack were screaming, 'The Lone Hamster! It's the Lone Hamster! Take for the hills, flee for your lives, it's the Lone Hamster!'

The rats scattered everywhere, falling over themselves, screaming for mercy, shouting in terror. In the space of a few short minutes, the rats had disappeared, never to return.

The town hamsters rejoiced.

And rejoiced.

And rejoiced.

They danced, they sang. Some wept, others laughed.

Then they remembered the Lone Hamster and looked round to lift him high upon their shoulders to carry him through town, but all they saw was a cloud of rusty brown dust in the distance.

The Lone Hamster had gone.

Another town awaited him.

Now let me explain the meaning to you.

The Lone Hamster had learnt that it isn't natural strength that wins the fight but who one is. And, similarly, it isn't so much what you do that wins the battle but who you are in the Creator.

Overcoming the enemy is all about position and not verbal formulae. When you come into conflict, my friend the Believer, remember who you are - what He's made you to be, where you are seated, what He's put under your feet.

And then, from there you'll see all that stands in your way overcome because of it.

THE BATTLE OF COPENHAGEN

Furatio Half-Nelson, that most intrepid of all sea-faring hamsters, lived in the empty sleeve of the great Admiral Nelson. He was there, directing the attack of the rodents against the Danish fleet on board HMS Elephant at Copenhagen in 1801 (for those of you not accustomed to the 24-hour clock, 1801 is just after six in the evening).

Admiral Nelson (though he wasn't 'Admiral' in that battle) never realized throughout the entire campaign that Furatio lived in his empty right sleeve. This was partly due, of course, to the nocturnal habits of hamsters - he'd dart out to visit his fellow sailors at night when Nelson was fast asleep in his cabin.

But, you must realize that, in the thick of battle, it was necessary that he leave the sleeve in order to command his crew.

It was on these occasions that Furatio came out on Nelson's blindside, shot down his right trouser leg and away, below deck, to where the crew awaited his command.

Furatio and his men had campaigned in many previous battles and it was this band of comrades-in-arms that strengthened their commitment to each other. Furatio saw in them a devoted fighting force, ready to lay their lives down for the sake of ultimate victory - they saw in him a master tactician who wasn't too proud to take up a pin in his paw and fight alongside when the battle grew especially tough and fierce.

Let me give you an example of their bravery before I tell you about the battle of Copenhagen.

It was long before Furatio lived in the empty sleeve of Admiral Nelson, and the crew slept huddled together below deck directly under the captain's cabin, in an English frigate called HMS Hamster (history doesn't record that there was a ship by such a name, but this line of tradition I quote is particularly reliable).

The Hamster had engaged a Spanish man-o-war, full of able-bodied soldiers bound for some military campaign in some far-off land, but fires from the first broadside had seriously charred the navigational tackle and the man-o-war's only hope was to draw alongside the Hamster and board her.

Learning of the plot by overhearing the captain of the frigate and seeing the man-o-war approach in a plume of thick black smoke - much of the fire having already been extinguished - the hamsters ran as one to the sailors' quarters and pouched as much straw and hay as they could find. When the man-o-war began to pull slowly alongside they cast it on the smouldering timbers, re-igniting the ship and thus preventing them from boarding the disadvantaged frigate.

Furatio lost his left paw in this conflict and, having previously lost a right eye and rear foot in past campaigns, his crew changed his name from 'Nelson' to 'Half-Nelson' because there were so many bits of him missing. It was a term of endearment that he both recognized and accepted.

But, I digress. Let me return to the Battle of Copenhagen and the part that the Hamster crew of HMS Elephant played in the amazing battle that was won that day in 1801.

In the evening of 1st April, Nelson anchored south of a shoal known as Middle Ground, hoping that by daybreak the wind would veer round to the north to enable him to attack in the early hours of the morning. Furatio spent the night with his crew, encouraging them to be fearless in the coming battle, to '...fight with all courage and boldness in the face of this awesome adversity, laying down our fur for one and all that those left alive may extol the bravery of the dead'. And with many other words he lifted their morale.

Daybreak came and, with it, the much-needed change of wind direction. Nelson hoisted the signal and the fleet sailed into war. The hamsters sat in a row in front of the mainsail, blowing with all their might to force the Elephant to sail faster into battle.

Gradually they picked up speed, the hamsters sitting back on their rear paws, waiting for the command of their fearless leader.

The battle was joined.

Now what I am about to tell you may sound fanciful and you will find it in no human history book - but that illustrates my point that history has been recorded with a human bias.

Furatio, resting comfortably in the empty sleeve of Nelson, was listening intently to hear how the battle progressed. Shortly after the commencement of the firing cannons, Nelson was heard to say 'We're firing short, we're missing the enemy!' but, as no-one stood by him, no-one heard it except Furatio. He quickly ran out of the sleeve on Nelson's blindside, down his right trouser leg and leaned over the side of the ship.

He couldn't believe his eyes.

Every salvo from the British fleet fell twenty feet short of its target. His mind raced with mathematical calculations - 'twenty feet short...er...a distance of four hundred yards. That means...er...that means...Yes! That means that if the cannons fire at a one-degree higher trajectory, they'll hit their target.' Then, as if to confirm his course of action, he squeaked loudly, 'We have to raise the trajectory by one degree.'

Furatio hopped down from the ship's side and scurried across the deck to the main mast, climbing frantically sailwards to his crew who were sitting, resting, after their long continuous blow.

'Crew!' he shouted as he raced up the rigging. 'Crew!'

They swung round recognizing his voice.

'We've got a problem, we're not reaching our target, we've got to elevate the cannons.'

'How do we do that?' they questioned among themselves. Then turning to Furatio said, 'What do we do?'

Of course, Furatio knew.

But before they could carry out the strategy, they formed a hamster chain and suspended themselves from the top of the highest mast. They had to signal the hamsters on board the other ships to let them know what action to take. Finally, every ship acknowledged the signal and Furatio led his crew down the mast.

Meanwhile, the British fleet were still firing and still missing while the Danes sliced through the British ships one after another. The port side was taking a pounding (for it was this side that lay broadside to the Danish fleet), the human sailors frantically making repairs to shore up wooden walls that held the sea at bay and the rigging in place.

'Into action!' shouted Furatio, the hamsters dispersing below deck. Each of them ran to the port side, pouched as much as they could, then ran starboard and put all that they'd gathered there.

Minute after minute they continued, the port side being lifted gradually out of the water until the cannons finally found their target.

One by one the British fleet hit their mark. One by one the Danish ships were being reached and destroyed. One by one the hamsters slapped each other's paws and congratulated themselves.

Furatio and his crew had saved the British fleet from defeat and Nelson won the Victory.

Courage in the face of adversity - that's what Furatio's life epitomised. Courage is not the absence of fear but the pressing on through regardless.

When Furatio found himself on the Elephant the evening before battle was to commence, he didn't run away - in fact, there was no place for him to run. He either had to stand and fight or throw himself over the side and swim for shore (of course, hamsters can't swim so the latter suggestion was not a viable alternative).

He faced up to the crisis and won through it. Even so, his paw shook!

In your life, sometimes it will mean repelling the enemy or standing your ground. Other times it will mean just surviving. But in everything it will mean ultimate victory and the overcoming of all that stands against you and your life in the Creator.

TAPPUWOCKY

Tappu the hamster loved apples.

For him, they were the ultimate prize in his search for food. It didn't matter whether they were green or red, small or large, deformed or perfectly symmetrical - even if they had the tell-tale signs of maggot-entry on their peel (that just meant added protein) - the point was that there was nothing, in his opinion, that compared with the complexities of the taste that varied from an early seasonal sourness through the sweetness of the ripening flesh to the warming sensation that fermenting juice brought.

Just as well, then, that Tappu lived under the trunk of the best producing apple tree in the entire county and had done so since he first spotted the spreading branches from his night-time excursions when he was very young.

And the season of the first ripe apples was fast approaching when a difficult and lengthy ascent up the outside of the bark repaid the effort with an endless evening of satisfaction.

Tappu spent the day time in excited anticipation, keeping one ear open for the occasional thud of an apple as it fell to earth and rolled down the short incline at the trunk's base. With each sound he became increasingly excited until, scarcely able to contain his eagerness, he decided to sleep at the burrow entrance with his nose protruding into the air to tell at an instant when the sun had gone down.

Although it seemed like a week of waiting, in just a few short hours, it was sufficiently dusk for Tappu to leap like a hart from the protection of his nest to attach himself to the bark and gingerly climb upwards towards his own unique paradise, feeling for pawholds in the cracks and rings that littered the trunk.

By the time the sun had fully disappeared below the horizon and darkness had engulfed the land, he'd made it to the summit, carefully pacing his way along a branch where a particularly large and succulent fruit reflected the moonlight, the gentle breeze wafting the fragrance into his overly sensitive nostrils.

As he approached the apple, Tappu forgot about safety - as he very often did at this time of year - and saw only the prize hanging by too slender a thread to be attempted with no branch beneath that could take the weight of his fall should it snap.

Fogged by his own desire, he securely gripped the twig in his rear paws and slithered down the stalk until his front legs, head and entire upper body lay over and round the prize. The stalk held firm as he sunk his teeth into the flesh, Tappu squeaking with delight that, if he could rate apples on a scale of one to ten, this one would be eleven - he'd never been very good at maths...

...neither was he adept at physics for, although the weight that hung from the branch remained the same, he reasoned that, because the flesh was no longer a part of the apple and had been swallowed into his stomach, it lessened the burden on the stalk.

That was his first mistake.

His second was to continue eating until only the very furthest part of the apple away from his rear paws was left, a part that was well-known to be the sweetest of all but, due to the fruit's size, was tantalisingly out of the reach of his most strenuous attempts.

No matter how hard he tried, that final succulent piece just couldn't be reached without letting go of his secure pawhold on the branch.

But, in his eagerness to finish off the apple, he'd failed to witness the night becoming day, the sun rising above the distant hills on its daily course to brighten the ground and bring what little warmth it had to the field as the days grew perceptively shorter.

If he'd paid attention to his surroundings he'd have seen a well-dressed human stride across from the tiny hamlet - a face perplexed with something that lay buried in his mind - and take his rest underneath the tree in which Tappu was contemplating an attempt at reaching the final prize.

With the illogical conclusion that the weight of the apple had been so greatly reduced by his consumption of the flesh that it meant the stalk could now support both what was left and his own mass, he released his hold, sliding into position to gorge himself on the remaining flesh.

Tappu looked in dismay as the stalk slowly splintered, groaning with the increased weight. Even though he froze with fear to prevent any further stress being placed on the weakening stalk, he nevertheless saw that he only had a few brief seconds to remedy the situation.

With a movement that any acrobat would have been proud of, he flipped himself upwards, opening both paws to grasp the branch above but missed, securely gripping a cluster of browning leaves that ripped off in his hands.

The core of the apple remained fastened to the stalk, however, swinging violently but securely on its axis as the furry form disappeared from view.

I cannot tell you what went through Tappu's mind as he began to plummet towards earth but whatever was there was soon dispelled as he spun round to face the ground, only to see a human head accelerate into his vision.

The hamster began running in midair, trying to avert the inevitable collision but, within a split second, Tappu landed on the human's head and bounced off behind him, ricocheting off the bark and onto the dewy damp grass. Without a moment's hesitation, he stood on his rear paws to smell the entrance location to his burrow and scampered for all his worth to exit the light into the safety and darkness of his nest.

'Ow!' shouted the man, knocked out of his concentration by the unexpected impact of the hamster onto his head.

The human, oblivious to the truth of the matter, raised one hand to his head to rub the protruding bump that throbbed with pain and gazed at the litter of apples that lay round his feet, ticking himself off for being so stupid as to sit under a tree at the time of its shedding.

He picked up an apple that lay close to his hand and inspected the bruise that he presumed had been formed by its impact with his head, freezing in the instant that the thought hit him harder than Tappu had just done.

'That's it!' shouted Newton excitedly. 'I shall call the phenomenon "Gravity"!'

Mistakes are sown into the fabric of many answers when you know the Creator.

One of your wise men once observed that all things work together for good for those who remain faithful to Him and that He gives power to all situations to bring about those things that He wants to be done.

Such was the background to Tappu's intrusion into Isaac Newton's realisation of gravity. When you have the Creator on your side, there really is no limit to what can be achieved.

THE VIRTUOSO PERFORMANCE OF MANDY REID

People used to complain about Mandy Reid but it wasn't her fault. She couldn't help playing as badly as she did.

In fact, the real truth was that she played very well. The problem lay in the sound that came out of the piano after she'd hit the correct keys.

At first her friends humoured her by gently suggesting that it would be a good idea to hire a piano tuner; they even went as far as giving her a list of names and telephone numbers as a hint that, as far as they were concerned, it was about time that their fragile ears, which had been accustomed to listen to the more delicate airs of a symphony orchestra, shouldn't have to suffer the ministry of the sledgehammer.

Very soon Mandy took the hint but it was all to no avail. The piano still remained out of tune, her friends disowning her while the cat began to sing along with the wails that came from the back. Mandy became very sad.

'If only I could play better,' she used to think to herself.

As I've already said, Mandy Reid played very well - the real problem lay in the sound that came out of the piano. You see, many years ago, before it had come into her possession, it had been stored in an old barn next to a large field where all sorts of wild creatures used to live out their lives. It was one of these creatures, a hamster by the name of Archy, who'd taken up residence inside the piano.

If you could have seen inside, you would have witnessed that the hamster's bedding lay strewn about over all the strings. Bits of straw were wrapped around pegs - even the hammer action of the piano was hindered from striking correctly - and it wasn't uncommon for Archy to gnaw on the tuning nuts, thus making string after string lose its tune.

Early one morning, when Archy was about to lie down and sleep in his nest for the day, Mandy Reid decided she needed to practise. It was very early but the rest of her family had gone out for the day, leaving her alone in an empty house.

'This time I'm going to practise until I get it right,' she said in a loud, determined voice. 'This time I'm going to hit every note I'm supposed to and show myself I can really play this instrument.'

Archy's ears heard every word.

Mandy flexed her fingers and held them poised over the keyboard. With great determination she stared at the music in front and concentrated on the black dots that hovered on the lines. She brought her hands down firmly on the keys in unison, in great expectation that, at last, it might sound like it should.

'TWANNNGGG!'

The cat jumped up from its position lying in front of the fire, teeth bared, thinking another tom had come into the room. The next-door neighbour peered over the garden wall having thought that he'd heard one of the elephants that had been reported as escaped from the local zoo. Even Archy had to bury his paws in his ears and stick his head in a pile of straw - though he still got a headache.

I must remind you once again, in case you think that it was Mandy's fault, that the problem lay not in which notes were played but in the condition of the piano inside. Anyone would have sounded bad on this piano, it was just unfortunate that it was only Mandy who played it, for it was she who took the blame.

Archy poked his nose out of his nest to smell if the sound had stopped. He decided to investigate. Using the strings as ladder rungs, he climbed to the open top of the piano and peered over in time to hear poor Mandy Reid, head in hands, say, 'Why can't I play properly? Why does it always sound so terrible when I use it?'

Archy was ashamed. In the back of his mind came the irrepressible conviction that this had something to do with him - if he hadn't have been covered in fur you would have seen him blush. Archy sank down into the piano in case she should look up and, in discovering the problem, eliminate him.

'I must do something,' he squeaked. 'This entire problem is a result of what I've done.'

He searched his mind for a solution - then searched his pouches for a peanut. Ah yes, a peanut - it always helps a hamster think.

'That's it!' squealed Archy. 'That's it!'

Archy had hit on a plan.

Frantically, he poked his head over the top of the piano and, looking at Mandy who still had her head in her hands, squeaked, 'Don't worry, Mandy, help is at hand!'

He darted back inside the piano, back into his nest and spent the rest of the day meditating on this fantastic plot, this superlative scheme, this extraordinary escapade, this...Archy always got carried away in his descriptions of what he was going to do. He was quite a normal hamster otherwise but in this one area he needed to calm himself down and think straight.

Early the next evening, Archy packed up his nest in his pouches and set off in search of his good friend and colleague, the music maestro of the rodent world, Furskovsky.

He knew that this hamster alone would be able to teach him all that he needed to know to rectify the damage he'd done to Mandy's poor piano. Yet, more than this, he wanted to do something 'special' for her to say 'sorry' for all the grief he'd caused.

That same evening, Archy began piano lessons.

Hamsters don't play the piano in the normal way, their paws are too small and bodies too light to be able to press the keys. So, instead, they have to pluck the strings with their teeth from the inside. But first, Archy began learning the mechanics of the piano and, what was the most important aspect of his plan, how to retune it. He struggled on for weeks upon weeks of intensive training, having to control himself so that he didn't chew the tuning nuts like he'd been accustomed to. Furskovsky always had a piece of wood close at hand in case the desire overwhelmed him. But, with time and practise, he learned to master it.

Finally, though it had seemed like an eternity, came the day of the piano exhams and Archy received a distinction, presented to him in front of a packed piano stool after having played a variation on the theme of the well known tune 'Nutrocker.'

The rodents were wild with enthusiasm!

'There's always a place for you here at teaching college,' said Furskovsky as they parted. 'You know how I want you to stay.'

'Maybe one day,' Archy replied, 'but now I must go and repay the debt I owe.'

And, with that, Archy set off for the home of Mandy Reid.

He found it easily enough and, undercover of darkness, squeezed his way in under the front door and into the old piano. It had been a long journey so Archy took a quick look round at the work that lay ahead, then made his nest in a part of the piano that would cause no harm.

There was a great amount of work to do, indeed!

It was fortunate that the household were away on holiday. It was even more fortunate that this year they'd decided to put their cat into a boarding home. The year previous had been a nightmare, running around the house in fear of his life being chased by a drooling ginger tom. Although he'd been far quicker and more agile, it was a hardship he could do without and it meant that his work could progress uninterrupted.

A fortnight later, Mandy Reid and her family arrived home safely and Archy sat in readiness on the piano strings waiting for the keys to activate the hammers. This would be a surprise! But Mandy didn't play the piano that evening. Or the evening after. Or the next.

Something was wrong.

It was a week later that he found out what. He heard Mandy talking to someone (though he never found out exactly who it was for he only saw her in the room by herself). She said, 'I'm just not good enough, I'm never going to play that piano again.'

Archy's ears pricked up.

'Oh no,' he thought. 'This calls for drastic action.'

Later that evening, the family invited over some friends and, as their friends had relatives staying, brought them over as well. It was fortunate that the relatives didn't know that Mandy Reid was infamous for her piano playing, neither had the family's friends warned them.

As the night drew on, they became ever more curious about the piano that sat in the corner of the room and, finding a suitable break in the conversation, interjected, 'And who plays the piano in the house?'

Mandy's friends looked in horror at their relative who'd blurted out what they'd feared might happen. Mandy, herself, went white for the way this conversation seemed destined to be leading.

'I do...sometimes,' she whispered, and then added, 'but I'm still learning.'

'Give us a tune then,' came the response.

Mandy felt like dying. Reluctantly she walked over to the piano hoping (and praying) that the phone might ring for her. Or, that the ceiling might suddenly collapse for no apparent reason and destroy the piano.

'Anything,' she thought, 'let anything happen!'

She sat on the stool, placed the music on the stand and concentrated on the black dots.

Her friends tried to hum quietly so that it muffled the expected noise.

Archy stood poised, squeaking in anticipation, ready to jump all over the strings to make it play. Mandy's hands descended firmly onto the keys and she continued playing in amazement for a full ten minutes.

'Ah,' said the relative, 'my favourite - Tchaikovsky's second piano concerto.'

'Yes,' thought Mandy, 'how strange - I'm playing "Three Blind Mice".'

At the end of the performance, Mandy received a standing ovation. Confidence restored, Archy packed up his nest in his pouches and set off for the teaching school, hearing in the distance, as he slipped out under the door, the melodious tune of the piano in the living room and the gasps of envy from her friends.

Mandy really could play the piano.

Let me explain why I've told you this story. It illustrates a principle that you can learn from. Namely, that the tune you get out of the instrument depends upon its inward condition. No matter how hard Mandy tried to play, it sounded awful because inside it was a disaster area. But, with the workings restored, the melody was delightful.

When the Creator walked this earth He said that it's out of the abundance of the heart that the mouth speaks. In other words, your heart strings determine the melody of your mouth. If you've a bad heart, you'll be playing a bad tune - but if you've a good heart, you'll hear a symphony.

He didn't say that to condemn, but to cause you humans to face up to the reality of your condition. When a person comes to know the Creator who died and rose again for them, they get a new heart and, even though the musicianship may not be all that good, the tune comes over loud and clear.

Mistakes or accidents will fade into insignificance in the light of the tune that comes from the new heart that beats in time with the heart of God.

And that, my friends, is the parable.

THE CAPTURE OF SARDIS

The year was 549 BC ('BC' is a rodent abbreviation standing for 'Before Crisps' - it was the 549th year before potato crisps were invented).

The place was Sardis - the capital of the then great Lydian Empire under King Croesus, the city being shut up from within against the might of the Persian army, led by King Cyrus who was besieging it.

It had been Croesus' fault.

He'd seen the rising might of the Persian Empire to the east and taken steps to strike preventively before it became too powerful for them to contain. But having crossed the Halys River, a natural frontier between the two Kingdoms, he discovered that Cyrus was already too strong and, fleeing desperately away from him, found sanctuary in the fortress of Sardis.

The city looked impregnable.

On one side there was a formidable escarpment, an apparently unassailable rock face that no army would ever consider scaling in an all-out attack. Because of this there was only a very small defence wall and a handful of guards that watched over it. The Sardians didn't expect to be attacked at their strong point.

On the other sides, strong fortifications built wide and high were heavily manned and unconquerable without heavy losses.

Cyrus was in a quandary as to what to do.

Though he couldn't leave Croesus to possibly run amok should he withdraw, he also feared contemplating the losses to his own army should he risk an all-out frontal assault. Wisely, he opened up the campaign to his entire troop, proclaiming throughout the camp that the first man to scale the wall - and therefore open the gate for the army's entry into the city - would be rewarded with great riches.

And with that proclamation ringing in the soldiers' ears, the army contemplated just who would be the first to show the ultimate courage and bravery to succeed - or, at least, to die in the trying.

Now let me introduce you to one of my 'ancient' relatives (on my mother's side) - Georgius Hamstrus the Greek. Georgius lived in a natural hole in the escarpment on the impregnable side of Sardis where he'd nested with his family for a good many years, their occupation going back at least ten generations and possibly even further into prehistory.

It was towards dusk. Georgius had come out of his nest and was foraging for food, when he heard a faint noise like a pebble rolling down the hillside. It grew louder, then louder still, 'til at last he realised that its sound resembled no stone at all.

Hurriedly, he dived for cover behind a loose boulder, just in time to be protected from the object as it crashed into his stone of refuge, bringing it to an abrupt halt.

Tentatively he peered over the top, sniffing this peculiar shaped object.

'It smells human,' he thought, 'but it certainly doesn't look human.'

It was then that it dawned on him just what had happened. One of the few soldiers that guarded the minor fortifications on the top of the escarpment had lost his helmet (for whatever reason - Hamster history doesn't record how this happened though later scribes have speculated variously on the subject), and it crashed down the side, coming to rest inches from my ancestor.

It was then that Georgius noticed a blur in the distance that he recognized to be a human form, descending from the battlements to retrieve his helmet. Georgius darted back behind the rock and breathed shallowly, trying not to make a sound else he be discovered.

The soldier approached, his eyes darting to and fro for the object, then, seeing it in the distance, rushed as quickly as possible over to where it lay and picked up his helmet, rescaling the natural defences almost before he'd firmly grasped it. With a great sigh of relief, Georgius saw that the coast was clear and went about his business again in search of food.

A few hours later, there was another sound - this time from below - and the sound was of climbing feet. He could tell they were human because they were so clumsy.

'If humans had to live in the wild,' he thought, 'they'd never survive.'

A small column of Cyrus' soldiers were scaling the escarpment and using exactly the same route that the Lydian soldier had taken after he'd recovered his helmet from where it'd fallen.

This line of soldiers seemed endless!

On and on it went, until Georgius gave up all hope of finding any food that night. At least they hadn't discovered his nest and stolen the seeds he'd stored away!

Later still there was the sound of fighting and the tumult of war on the top of the hill. This continued for much of the day so that Georgius got very little sleep. But, like most hamsters, he'd learned that whenever he found it hard to rest, he would think through his experiences and try to acquire 'wisdom' from them (it was the time of the early 'furlosophers' of ancient Greece and many other hamsters were learning this discipline of thinking).

The events of the previous night came flooding back into his mind and it became wisdom to him. He began to perceive what had taken place and, subsequently, from his conversations with other rodents over the ensuing weeks, he had his observations confirmed. He'd been at the centre of the Persians' capture of Sardis.

When the Lydian soldier came to recover his helmet, there must have been a Persian watching and, under the cover of darkness, scaled the rock face with a number of other comrades, getting in at the city's weakest point of its walled defence. The Lydians had thought their natural defences were so impregnable that they hadn't bothered to build a strong wall - neither had they placed a substantial guard there in case of attack.

Although the escarpment had indeed been impregnable in its past, erosion and weathering had softened the rugged slopes making a successful assault a distinct possibility.

'What fools,' Georgius thought. 'Where they knew their weakness was, they fortified with strength, but what they took to be a natural strength turned out to be their weakness!'

Believers fortify their weaknesses with the Creator's strength - they have to, they have no strength of their own in those areas. Try as he may, your enemy will never be able to overcome the solid fortifications of the Creator.

But natural strengths are deceitful, they don't contain His strength! And it's only His strength that cannot be overcome by the power and schemes of your enemy.

If only the Lydians had strengthened their natural fortifications with proper battlements or stationed a sufficient number of soldiers to be on guard, then not only would they have prevented their own defeat but my ancestor, Georgius Hamstrus, would not have gone hungry all that night and lost sleep the following morning.

Never forget - rely on His strength, even where you think you're strong.

THE SPACE WALK OF BUZZ HAMSTRIN

The Apollo spacecraft stood ready on the launch pad. The next mission, only three days away, had been planned to coincide with the mathematical calculations that would bring it back safely to earth at the right time, the right place, many days after its launch.

The three astronauts eagerly awaited the day. For them, the rigours and hardships of training were a small price to pay for the ecstasy of being one of the few human beings ever to experience the grandeur and vastness of space and the beauty and majesty of the earth, gazing down upon it from their orbit many miles above.

Technicians and programmers were hard at work with last-minute checks, testing every circuit, every wire, ensuring that, as far as they were able, nothing would hinder the rocket from either taking off or returning to earth safely.

The hamster colony that lived a stone's throw from the control centre where the three astronauts were spending their final hours in nervous anticipation were hard at work, too. Buzz Hamstrin, the determined and adventurous leader of the community, was planning his own spaceshot. For him, the one remaining ambition in life was to see the Creator's earth in all its glory from high above and to experience weightlessness as he space walked.

Buzz had a plan to get aboard that rocket.

Boy! Did he have a plan!

For weeks, now, Buzz had been in training, building his body for the rigours of take off and the stress of re-entry.

He'd begun each day with weight training. First it was one monkey nut in each paw pushing it above his head and releasing it gently down again: 'One-two-one-two.'

Then two peanuts in each paw.

Then more - until he'd worked up the necessary strength to lift six comfortably and hold them above his head for more than a minute.

The colony also had contributed to Buzz's physical fitness by constructing a magnificent hamster wheel that they'd fixed to an old tree trunk near his nest. He'd run miles and miles every evening, tying weights to his back and carrying heavy stones in his pouches to increase his stamina. Buzz had always been a fit hamster, but he appreciated the rigours and disciplines of the training that was toning every muscle in his body into peak condition.

But there was a crisis in the hamster camp - the space suit wasn't ready and there were only three days left! It had been going well, the female hamsters had constructed a suit made entirely out of straw in the early weeks of the program, but hamsters will be hamsters, and Buzz had gnawed his way through it in under four minutes. It certainly had no chance of survival during the many days in space.

A week before the launch, a very daring rodent found a way into the storage room in the control centre. Here was kept all the space equipment that would be needed in case of emergency - including un-gnawable spacesuit material. Pouching all that he could, he returned to the colony then, leading the way, guided a vast multitude of rodents who took more than enough to complete the suit. But time was running out and, as the day of launch approached, it looked increasingly likely that time would defeat them.

Then they had their first big break! Bad weather closed the Cape down and the launch was delayed for two whole days! The hamster colony breathed a sigh of relief, completing their objectives with a full day to spare.

That meant that Buzz had more than enough time to put his plan into action.

On the evening before the launch day, Buzz stole into the control centre, found where the astronauts' space suits were hanging up ready for the morning and, while none of the guards were watching, jumped into the Commander's empty suit. Down and down Buzz climbed until he arrived at the foot compartment.

Because hamsters are springy and able to squash themselves into unusual shapes, Buzz had planned to lie on top of the astronaut's foot (calculations had already been made by the community to ascertain the volume available after the Commander's foot was in the suit and it worked out almost perfectly). Then, just after take off, he would ascend the five and a half feet while the astronaut was struggling through the 'g-force' of the launch.

Morning came and he heard the sound of approaching footsteps.

'This is yours, Commander,' one said. The astronaut started putting on his suit with a fair amount of help.

'There's not much room in this left boot,' he complained.

'Nerves,' said a voice close by. 'Feet always swell when you get nerves - you're not the only one to have had that trouble.'

And, with this, the complaints stopped and Buzz settled down to sleep on top of the Commander's foot.

The astronauts picked up their helmets, were driven to the launch pad and climbed aboard the Apollo spacecraft. The door was safely closed, securely locked and the astronauts began to go through their final instrument checks.

'I've made it,' Buzz thought, 'I've actually made it!'

The hamster colony peered out from their nests that afternoon as the plumes of white smoke filled the blue tranquil sky and the rocket glided majestically toward space.

'Do you think he made it?' a young hamster was heard to ask. 'Do you think he's up...there?'

'I don't know,' came back the reply. And then more quietly, 'I don't know.'

But an older hamster stepped forward.

'We'll know when the rocket returns,' he said. 'This day will go down in hamster history whether he made it or not. He tried - and if you don't try you never conquer.'

With those words of wisdom, the hamsters disappeared below ground, some too excited to shut their eyes and complete their day's sleep.

Buzz was finding it difficult shelling peanuts in the weightlessness of space.

No sooner had he removed the outer casing than the peanut inside floated away from him, drifting away from his outstretched paws. It took him over an hour to catch the first one, having kept colliding with the cushioned walls of the spacecraft and bouncing away in a totally different direction to the one that he'd wanted to go in. With successive peanuts, the time reduced and he gradually became more able.

It was fortunate also that hamsters are nocturnal. Buzz was able to sleep in a secluded part of the cabin undiscovered throughout the astronauts' daytime activities and wake as they fell asleep for their night. Never did they once suspect that they had a rodent stowaway on board.

Then came Buzz's chance to fulfil his lifelong ambition - one of the astronauts was going to space walk.

It was pure chance that Buzz woke up as the door opened to the decompression chamber (he was sleeping above the mechanism at the time) and he heard the others discussing it. Quickly, he pulled on his helmet, tied one end of the hundred metres of thread he'd brought with him in his pouches to the spacecraft (so he wouldn't drift off into the eternity of space), and floated unnoticed into the chamber.

The door closed behind him and, after the decompression process, gently opened in front. He held onto the astronaut and was carried out into space.

Fantastic! This was simply fantastic!

All the weeks and months of planning and seemingly endless training had brought him to this one moment - and it was all worth it. He gazed at the myriads of stars, shining with indescribable beauty and the grey white glow of the moon. As the astronaut turned round to face the spacecraft, it was then that the earth burst into his view.

The blue.

The white.

The green.

The brown.

Then the vastness and the glory of God's creation overwhelmed him in a burst of emotion that caused his heart to acknowledge something of the true greatness of the Creator.

'Why don't humans see it?' he thought to himself. 'Why can't they see that it couldn't possibly have happened by chance?'

It would be wrong of me to say that Buzz had a 'spiritual experience' for hamsters don't have them. But he did come to see a little of the vastness of the Creator. He'd seen it before on earth in his care of the animal kingdom and the beauty of nature - even in His unreciprocated love for mankind that had frequently been discussed amongst the community when they gathered round food to eat.

Even one of your writers has said that God's '...everlasting power and deity has been seen clearly in the things that He's made' - not, of course, saying that God *is* creation, but that God can be seen *in* creation.

And that's what Buzz saw. He saw God's hand in it all even though he didn't fully understand it.

He'd wanted to see the Creator's hand and that's what he witnessed.

Needless to say, Buzz returned safely to earth in the Commander's spacesuit and the colony welcomed him back as a hero, celebrating and dancing wildly for endless days and nights in their burrows as he recounted what his eyes had witnessed.

I guess that it's hardly surprising, then, that his exploits rank as one of the ten most important landmarks in Hamster history.

'If you don't try, you never conquer.'

THE GREAT SUNFLOWER SEED ROBBERY

Furlock Holmes, the most celebrated of all rodent detectives, lived in the basement of a local bakers, opposite the street where his famous human namesake lived in Victorian England.

He was a contemplative hamster, spending hours in deep thought when a particularly difficult criminal case stretched his logical and systematic mind to the limits, often playing upon the violin. It'd been specially designed for his tiny paws a number of years back during one of his first investigations when concentration had been particularly difficult due to the repeated clatter of horse-drawn vehicles where he'd previously been in residence.

Now, away from the hustle and bustle of that apartment, he found playing a continued source both of relaxation and inspiration as he endeavoured to focus his mind on each successive case.

Doctor Flotsam, his beloved colleague, saw to it that Furlock had a continuous supply of new violin strings, whiskers extracted at night from various cats and dogs of the neighbourhood when he foraged for the crumbs dropped in the bakers above their nesting compartment.

Extracting the hairs was not, in itself, a difficult task. The real problem lay in determining which was suitable for use - a freshly sprouted hair would be too short for the neck of the violin, while an old, grey one would not give good sound quality when put under the appropriate tension.

Width was also a major consideration - Doctor Flotsam always carried in his pouches a micrhameter, which he'd use to ascertain the diameters of the animal's whiskers. To hold tuning - and to reproduce a tonal quality that harmonized with the resonance of the instrument's wood - it had to be within certain parameters not exceeding ten percent either way.

These measurements took time to perform and he was always on the alert for the first sign of the animal waking up. Indeed, Doctor Flotsam had almost come to an end when one dog rolled over in the midst of his sleep, trapping him underneath his huge canine body. He tried to extricate himself with a series of expansions and contractions but, in his efforts, trapped a rear paw in the hook of the dog's identification tag.

When it woke the next morning, Flotsam found himself dangling, upside down, underneath the huge dog's neck, waggling about with every movement. Fortunately, his life was saved when, feeling an irritation, the canine used his rear paw to flick skyward what he thought was an offending flea - Flotsam was propelled a number of yards into space, landing on a pile of old rags that had been left in a corner of the room and disappearing into them as soon as he made contact.

The dog never did know what had happened and, on repeated visits, supplied a large number of Furlock's violin strings.

One day, early in the autumn, when Furlock had sent Flotsam on a reconnaissance mission for a new string to the local ginger tomcat, there came a knock on the lintel of the entrance to his nest compartment.

'Holmes?' the visitor squeaked. 'Holmes, are you in there?'

It was Detective Pawson of CRISP ('CRISP' stands for 'The Central Rodent Investigation of Sinister Practices' - roughly corresponding to the human CID), an old friend from his early days as a private investigator. Something major must have happened for him to come to the apartment - usually a messenger was sent that requested his attendance at a briefing.

Holmes let him in, Pawson fairly leaping through the small opening into the nest.

'Something dreadful has happened, Holmes!' Pawson gasped for each breath, having run over from headquarters as fast as his paws would carry him. 'The entire supply of sunflower seeds for all the city's hamsters has been stolen from under our twitching noses!'

Holmes felt as if his stomach had become a lead weight that had crashed through the floor.

'Who knows about this?' he half whispered.

'Only a pawful - to stop widespread panic, we're keeping the lid on it, Holmes, but we don't know how long we can keep it up. That's why I'm here. You've got to help us, you're our only hope....'

Just then, Flotsam dashed back into the nest.

'Phew! That was a close one! I'm sure that ginger tom gets faster each week!'

All three hamsters pressed their backs to the wall as a red paw was thrust through the nest hole, searching for what it thought to be a mouse.

Shortly, it gave up the hunt, the three rodents relaxing onto all fours.

'Flotsam,' Holmes said, 'bring the violin. Detective Pawson is going to take us to the scene of the most dastardly theft the rodent world has ever known.'

Without question, Flotsam pouched the violin case along with a fresh set of strings, racing after Holmes and Pawson who were by now several yards in front of him, running at a furious pace.

When the trio arrived at the scene of the crime, the hamsters were already busy tidying up the broken sunflower seed shells that had been smashed by the robbers in their haste to make a quick getaway. Four rodents ran hurriedly to and fro, pouching bits of shells and seed that lay all over the linoleum floor, discharging the debris into a human waste bin outside. A fifth hamster carefully placed the crushed seeds in a red tissue and, taking it by the four corners, carried it to a similar destination.

The store, which had been situated in between a wooden panel and brick wall, was empty - gnawing marks were evident at the bottom where the rodents had worked ferociously to break into the reserve. Unfortunately, the teeth marks had been filed down after the robbery by the assailants, covering up their teeth prints and making identification impossible.

'Do you know what worries me, Holmes?' Pawson began squeaking as they caught their breath. 'Each of the eyewitnesses said that they saw a hamster leaving the scene of the crime.'

Doctor Flotsam looked horrified. Furlock contemplated this new piece of information.

'Very strange,' he said, pointing his nose into the air to smell for clues. 'Very, very strange.'

(I must point out here that until this moment in time, no hamster had ever been found to have stolen - especially from another hamster. Should the story and reports have been leaked out by CRISP, there would have been widespread panic throughout the entire realm of Hamsterdom.)

Furlock put his nose to the ground, twitching and sniffing at the same time - 'Very strange,' he repeated as his nose met a familiar but unexpected smell, then sat up on his rear paws looking around the scene.

The rodents were still busying themselves removing debris from the robbery, seemingly oblivious to the trio who stood less than a foot away from their path.

'I'll go get the eyewitnesses.' Pawson turned to scamper out of the room, but was halted by Furlock's retort:

'No need. I'll speak to that hamster, there...' he pointed to the rodents cleaning up the mess, '...the one using the red tissue.'

Both Pawson and Flotsam looked surprised but, after a moment's hesitation, summoned him over to stand before Holmes.

'What's your name?' he asked.

"Arry,' came the reply, "Arry the 'amster from the East end o' town.'

There was a short pause before he continued. "Ere, I 'ears that it was an 'amster wot did it. Fancy that, eh? An 'amster!' and he cackled with a gurgle that made the hair stand upright on Doctor Flotsam's back. He turned and licked it down with his moist tongue.

'Well now, Harry!' Furlock squeaked, staring intently into the small, beady eyes of the rodent that stood before him. 'Or should I say Rufus...Rufus the rat?'

Flotsam and Pawson both gasped as Rufus the rat, alias Harry the Hamster, realizing that his disguise had been blown, panicked and raced for the exit.

'Stop that rat!' Furlock shouted. The four hamsters finishing off their hoovering of the floor jumped to the command and leapt onto Rufus, pulling fur, sinking their sharp teeth into each paw until they had him pinned to the ground, immobile.

'You'll pay for this, Furlock!' the rat shouted as they dragged him off to the confinement quarters located in the vaults underneath the room in which they were standing. 'We'll get you.'

Furlock turned to Detective Pawson and, calmly, spoke in an even tone - 'You'll find the sunflower seeds at the gang's rendezvous, no doubt. Get your hamsters over there at once!'

'Yes, Holmes.' The Detective scurried out the room leaving Furlock and Flotsam to stand alone.

'But Holmes,' Flotsam gasped, 'how did you know?'

'Elementary, my dear Flotsam,' came the response. 'Didn't you see the clues?'

He paused, looking intently at his comrade, then continued.

'Firstly, you must remember that a rat cannot pouch food, it doesn't have the ability to do so. When we arrived, there were five hamsters - or, they appeared to be hamsters - moving the debris of the robbery. But one was using a red tissue - pretty strange, wouldn't you say, Flotsam?

'Secondly, as soon as I came in here I smelt a rat - not the odour of where a rat once was but of where a rat is. Very strong it was, too. That confirmed what I saw.

'And, finally, the laugh. What self-respecting hamster would gurgle with delight that a fellow hamster had been seen stealing? It could be none other than Rufus the rat, that villain of villains, who's always previously tried to trick us with clever disguises. But it wasn't good enough, Flotsam - sooner or later a rat shows its true character, its traits and lifestyles that make it a rat - no disguise can keep a rat's true personality hidden.'

Flotsam stood speechless. It was all so obvious, yet he'd failed to see it.

'Another case solved,' Holmes concluded. 'Another successful end to the "perfect" crime!'

I have asked Lee to explain this story to you as it weighs heavy on his heart and he can speak from experience - George.

A rat is a rat because he's born a rat. If he wanted to be anything else he would have to be re-born as something completely different. No amount of masking will ever obscure the fact that a rat is a rat is a rat.

And no amount of religion or good works can mask the reality of what we humans are in God's eyes - sinners and, as such, unacceptable to Him. It might look good for a time, but sooner or later the real you will burst out into the open and show everyone that at heart you're no better than a rat!

The only hope is to be born into something new. That's why Jesus the Creator talked about being 'born again' as the only way to be changed to be acceptable to God.

By acknowledging and placing your trust in the death that was tasted for you by Jesus on the cross, and rising to a new life through His resurrection, you can be 're-born' and changed from being a rat into a child of God.

Not by your own efforts, but by a powerful work of the Creator - Lee.

THE LAST FLIGHT OF DOUGLAS HAMSTER

Douglas Hamster lived in a barley meadow adjoining an RAF airfield deep in the heart of the country. He'd never had a desire to fly, neither did he feel strangely drawn to those 'peculiar birds' that took off in search of prey with regular monotony. Instead, his eyes remained fixed firmly on the ground and on finding enough food to fill his repeatedly empty stomach.

The year was sometime early in the 1940s AD ('AD' is a rodent abbreviation standing for 'After Dormice were eaten' - the Roman centurions had introduced the dormouse as food for their armies whereupon their numbers started to decline. It was nineteen hundred and forty years or so after the introduction of this practise).

At that time, the skies over England were the scene for dogfights, battles between aircraft and airborne objects, the sides being known as the German Luftwaffe and the Royal Air Force - this was the time in history commonly known to humans as the Second World War.

But, for the time being, it was of no concern to Douglas Hamster - all he wanted was a warm nest and a plentiful supply of barley, with a few fresh lettuce leaves thrown in from the neighbouring farmer's field.

But it was autumn and harvest grew near.

That particular day, when Douglas was having a very peaceful day's sleep, he was rudely awakened by the whirring and whining of a combine-harvester moving to and fro across the field, threatening to shred him to pieces if he stayed where he was.

He'd heard this sound before, every year at about the same time and, knowing what it meant (that it represented personal danger), he crammed his food store into his pouches and fled for safety away from the noise to search for a more peaceful site in which to spend the cold winter months.

Night had already begun to fall when he reached the boundary of the airfield and, after having run in blind panic for almost a solid half hour with the clanking machinery menacingly advancing upon him over his shoulder, the skies were blacker than the blackest hole - all

Douglas could go by was smell and the sounds that lay immediately in front.

One overwhelming consideration pressed upon his mind - he had to find a new nest by sunrise or else he was a gonner. The hawks would soon pick him up and, well, he was a sitting duck (no offence is meant to any ducks reading this story).

Nowhere on the ground could he find a hole that satisfied his requirements, even though there were plenty that were a safe protection. Four hours he spent searching until, in one last desperate attempt, Douglas climbed upwards some twenty feet above the ground and into a warm, spacious compartment.

He got in through a small hole that he'd managed to squeeze himself through and, as far as he could see, it was the only entrance - no draughts! And quiet, too - you could hear a sunflower seed drop! Sleepy, he nestled down in a corner, pulling some old straw over himself that had been discarded on the floor.

Douglas drifted off to sleep.

About midday, the compartment shook but he didn't notice.

But when the top slid off the roof and a human jumped in, he awoke with a fright and sat up with a start, his tiny heart beating frantically and his mind wondering if the combine-harvester was, perhaps, a better alternative to confront.

Then there were loud rattles like a farmer's gun, followed by a whirring and groaning as the whole compartment began vibrating from its noise. Douglas had found himself a nice nesting place alright - in the cockpit of a Spitfire!

'Request clearance for take off,' the pilot said.

'Roger.'

And Douglas was airborne. The first known hamster ever to take to the skies. But far from being taken aback by this experience, Douglas revelled in it.

'I'm airborne,' he thought, 'I'm actually airborne!'

And with a squeak of delight he jumped up to peer out through the cockpit glass - but behind the pilot so he couldn't be seen - and saw the fields and forests disappearing into the distance as he climbed higher and higher and higher.

'This'll show those hawks,' he squeaked with glee. 'Who's the master now?!'

'Enemy at five o'clock,' the pilot spoke through his radio.

'Engaging.'

Douglas just made out the words in time before the Spitfire banked and descended rapidly, firing repeatedly at another group of planes below.

'This must be what my father told me about, when humans fight humans,' he thought. 'I never thought I'd see it at first ha...'

Just then one of the planes exploded in a burst of flames and nose dived towards earth.

'This is dangerous. This could be the end if I don't watch it.'

Douglas noticed an enemy plane heading straight towards him and he squeaked with terror.

'Dive! Dive!' he squealed, but the pilot couldn't hear him. Even if he had he wouldn't have understood what he was trying to say (and it would have taken him many minutes to discover what he meant using sign language or morse code).

Douglas had no option - this plane was going to shoot them down, into a million tiny pieces. He flung himself onto the joystick and made the Spitfire veer both downward and to the right.

'What the...?' the pilot muttered and immediately a line of tracer bullets screamed over the cockpit, followed by the enemy.

Douglas climbed up to the firing button and, with all his hamster strength, pressed it with both paws.

'Rat-a-tat-tat.'

Direct hit!

The enemy was in flames and plummeting earthward.

'Gotcha!' he shouted.

'What's going on with these controls?' The pilot looked bewildered. 'They're all over the place!'

It was then that disaster struck. For, in his great excitement at scoring a direct hit, Douglas accidentally leapt onto the canopy eject button. The pilot disappeared out through the cockpit roof and he was left all alone in a plane that was steadily losing height.

There was nothing he could do except bail out.

'What a good job I remembered to pack my parachute,' he whispered under his breath. It was a deep sigh of relief straight from the bottom of a hamster's heart.

Clipping the harness onto his chest, he jumped out, pulled the rip cord and floated gracefully to the earth (or, as graceful as a hamster can manage considering that we weren't designed to fly but to plummet under those conditions).

[Douglas (who, incidentally, is my uncle - on my father's side if I remember rightly) insisted to his dying day that he landed in the English Channel and was picked up by French fishermen who brought him back into the port of Dover, but, as chance would have it, another of my relatives witnessed his emergence from the Spitfire cockpit and his safe arrival back on dry land. Though we're quite willing to believe his story about his accidental stowing away, we have to draw the line somewhere.]

Douglas became a folk hero amongst the rodents, too.

He was often invited along to many of the conventions to speak about his experience of that brief flight of glory in the cockpit of a Spitfire, 'the first hamster to fly' they used to bill it as - 'a death defying act of outrageous courage' I think was another line.

Personally, I think he needed his head examined! While it's true that he'd had an exciting adventure, it must be realized that it was all of his own making. Had he been careful to do what any normal hamster would have done, he wouldn't have put his life in jeopardy.

I mean, what normal hamster would make his nest in a field that he knows is going to be combine-harvested? Only a lazy one! Far better to make your nest in a nearby hedge.

Or which hamster would crawl into an empty compartment twenty feet from the ground? Our domain is the earth, not high above it. He didn't even sniff around for evidence of a human!

And then he jumped onto the canopy eject button! His one hope of survival is keeping the man in the cockpit with him and he eliminates him out of the equation and into oblivion! What an absolute disbrain!

Now some Christians are like Douglas and live too close to the edge of safety. They live right on the limit of what they should and shouldn't do and it's no wonder, therefore, when they find themselves buffeted first by one disaster, then another, that threatens their spiritual life in the Creator.

All of His creatures are designed to live as far away from the edge as they can, not as near as they dare. It might be stimulating to see a bottomless precipice waiting to swallow your very soul, but it's only one small step that takes you cascading into it. Far better to live a contented life - a full and normal one at that - in the safety of the Creator's arms.

THE IMPRISONMENT OF TUTANHAMSTER

Tutanhamster lived in a dank and dingy prison cell in the heart of the capital city of the great Egyptian empire. The cell had been empty now for nearly a month, which had been a problem - Tutan relied upon the titbits that the prisoners dropped from their plate to supplement his diet. He'd had to invade the territory of other hamsters in adjoining cells but their charity was, not surprisingly, wearing thin and he'd been forced to scout around outside the building - and that was dangerous!

Heavy laden carts rolling along narrow alleyways spelt potential disaster for hamsters. And then there were the wild cats that swarmed about everywhere in search of live food. Tutan only ventured out when his stomach got the better of him.

One day, the prison door was flung open and a young, well-dressed man came head first into the cell, struggling to regain his balance from the force of the push. He picked himself up, brushed his clothes down with his hands and found a place to sit with his back to the wall as the gaoler slammed the cell door and walked off.' At last!' Tutan squeaked, 'I've someone to feed from,' and he started rubbing his paws together, anticipating his first meal.

He didn't have to wait long. In the evening, the prisoner sat with a bowl of food eating with a wooden spoon. He was halfway through when he noticed a pair of black, shiny eyes peering at him through a small hole in the wall. It was Tutan, watching to see where any crumb would fall to remember its position for later that night when the prisoner was asleep.

'Here little one,' the prisoner said, 'come and fetch.'

And, with that, he held out a piece of food near the floor in the palm of his hand expecting Tutan to come over. He eyed the morsel with great envy - should he dare? There'd been so many stories told him by the other hamsters in the cells of the mysterious disappearances of rodents when they became over friendly that, well, it seemed that the prisoners supplemented their diet with animal protein!

But that food looked good.

Tutan crept towards it, heart in his mouth. Barely a foot away, he leapt onto the prisoner's hand, took it between his teeth and ran off into the safety of his hole.

The prisoner roared with laughter - 'You timid rat!' he shouted after him. 'You scared little rodent!'

'Rat?' squeaked Tutan indignantly. 'Who's he calling a rat?' (for hamsters take offence at anyone who calls them a rat).

Within days, Tutan was feeding from the prisoner's hand. A few more days and he would allow himself to be picked up in the palm of his hand and held close to his face. It wasn't long before Tutan would climb up the outside of the prisoner's clothes and take his seat on his shoulders, peering down into the food bowl.

It occurred to Tutan that there was something special about this man - something that the Creator was doing with him, even though he didn't know what that might be.

Often, in the early hours of the evening, the prisoner would take Tutan into his hands and tell him stories about his childhood, his teenage years, his imprisonment. In fact, he used to tell him his life history and Tutan would always sit patiently staring at his prison acquaintance, listening to every word that he spoke.

'I am a Hebrew, one of twelve brothers born to a man called Israel,' the prisoner would say at the start of his discourse. 'My name is Joseph and I'm a worshipper of the only true and living God who created all things but who Himself was not created.'

And, with that, he'd go on at lengths to describe his upbringing, his family, his betrayal, his slavery and how he found himself, unjustly, thrown into prison.

'With everything that's happened to him,' thought Tutan, 'how come he isn't all bitter and angry like the others?'

And, every day he saw him again, he felt afresh the conviction that the Creator was going to do something great with him.

Days passed.

Then weeks.

Then years. Joseph was promoted to be in charge of the prison and that meant more food for Tutan. For a time he shared his cell with a butler and a baker but they soon went, life went on but everything that Joseph did prospered in his hands.

Then one day, when Tutan was climbing up the outside of Joseph's cloak, soldiers rushed in commanding Joseph to come with them to see Pharaoh. Tutan climbed inside Joseph's clothes to see what fate awaited his friend.

'Surely he's done nothing wrong that deserves a hearing before Pharaoh,' he thought as the guards whisked him away, out into the daylight and into the court of the great king.

Tutan climbed up the inside of Joseph's garment until he came to an opening and poked his ears out to listen to what was happening. He made it just in time to hear Joseph talking to Pharaoh.

'I cannot interpret dreams,' he said, 'but God will give Pharaoh a favourable answer.'

Pharaoh told Joseph his dream, the Creator told Joseph the interpretation.

'That's it,' squealed Tutan. Then he remembered that he'd better keep quiet, he didn't want to get Joseph into trouble. 'This is the day that the Creator has been preparing Joseph for!'

'There will be none over you throughout my entire kingdom, save me,' said Pharaoh. 'You shall store up grain in the bountiful years and save Egypt from famine.'

And that's exactly what Joseph did. He saved Egypt, the neighbouring areas and, in a very roundabout way, Joseph's own family, too. And, even more important to me, he saved my grandfather, Tutanhamster.

Why have I told you this story, my friends, that you could read for yourselves in the Creator's Book (even though you will not find any hamster mentioned however hard you try to see one)?

Because Joseph is an example to follow.

Despite all the calamities that fell upon him, he remained true to the Creator, true to His purpose. He never allowed himself to become hard or callous but forgave all that had wronged him, even working for their protection and benefit.

THE MASTER STROKE

INTRODUCTION

When I dictated 'The Master Stroke' to Lee, I had no idea that what seemed to me to be a straightforward story would cause offence to some members of the Creator's people.

So I've asked Lee to say a few words before we print it in its entirety - George.

'The Master Stroke' is not meant to cause offence.

Firstly, there was no intention to poke fun at a specific denomination and George only mentions 'vicar' and 'rector' because that's how I've translated his squeaks. Hamsters only have one word for church leaders, so I could equally well have translated it 'pastor' and 'elder,' rather than use two words that might seem like we're singling out a particular denomination.

Secondly, and more importantly, there was also no intention to belittle Church liturgy. By that, we particularly mean the structure of services and, more especially, the celebration of Communion.

Hamsters do not understand the meaning of Communion because they never 'sinned' to have to be 'made clean.' All they see it as is a participation in food. George certainly meant no offence when he talks of the incident that took place with the bread and the wine.

We both thought of trying to edit 'The Master Stroke' but found that it would be near impossible to alter whilst retaining the plot. We would, therefore, sincerely apologise if, after having read this intro and the story, you still find it offensive - Lee.

THE MASTER STROKE

When the congregation closed its eyes to pray, the church hamsters used to dart out from their hiding places underneath the pews and jive in the aisle. You could always guarantee that someone would pray continuously in melodramatic tones for at least fifteen minutes, so they availed themselves of the opportunity to make a joyful noise in praise of the Creator.

The drummer would start the musicians off with a roll on empty half hazelnuts set up in front of him using two burnt matches. This was the cue for the others to join in - the lead guitarist finger picked a melody on the cat whiskers, his paws moving up and down the peanut fret board faster than a hungry squirrel in search of food. And the organist gently added a background roar of sound as she peddled furiously on the wind pump that sent the grass blades vibrating at the correct pitch.

Young and old would jump energetically into the aisles, bopping up and down with paws raised and twisting bodies. It had to be seen to be believed!

You may be wondering why the human congregation never once suspected that there was an alternative praise service taking place in their midst. You see, hamsters both sing and play music at a higher frequency than humans can perceive so, for all intents and purposes, it remained silent. And the hamsters' tiny paws that continually tapped on the cold stone floor made too little noise for them to be heard.

As the prayers came to an end, the musicians would slow the music down while the hamsters, understanding the signal, disappeared back under the pews, out of sight of the humans.

It wasn't unusual for two or three of the congregation to have fallen asleep, especially if it continued over the half-hour mark, so the hamsters would kindly nip their ankles as they disappeared under cover.

There'd even been one occasion when the entire congregation had fallen asleep, so the hamsters took the opportunity to extend their praise time into a full hour of dancing, singing and rejoicing.

However, the two rodents who'd been visiting that morning and who'd been intrigued to hear the humans pray, had also succumbed and had to be woken up.

A number of months ago, the hamsters had almost been discovered.

They had decided, quite unwisely, to partake of the bread and wine at one communion service while the prayers droned on. It wasn't that they understood the meaning, but they wanted to discover what, if anything, they were missing.

As the bread had already been broken, they were each able to nibble a small fragment without it being noticed but, when it came to the wine, calamity struck! One old, dithery hamster, having climbed up the stem of the chalice, slipped on the lip and fell into the liquid. The others rushed to his aid and, dragging him out by his tail, sat him down to recover underneath the pews. But so much time had elapsed between him slipping in and being saved that he'd drunk almost half the wine!

The vicar opened his eyes intending to pass the cup round the congregation but, having glanced briefly into it, noticed that it was half empty and, worse, that there were hairs floating on the surface. He eyed the Rector suspiciously as he was the only one who was both near enough and had a beard.

Even worse, the elderly hamster, hidden under the Rector's pew, then began a dreadful bout of hiccups that continued for several minutes arousing his suspicions further.

But the vicar, bless him, was a kind, forgiving man and, filling the chalice back up to the brim, resolved to say no more about it so long as it didn't happen again.

Needless to say, from that time on the leading hamster banned the other rodents from participating in the bread and wine.

Week in, week out, the meetings continued. The prayers droned on and on and on. What most distressed the hamsters was that they saw very little joy - apart from their own celebrations - although occasionally a child would bounce into the building, giggling with excitement as they were chased by another. It didn't take very long for the older humans to stare over their gold-rimmed glasses in discontent and a mother or father would quiet the child down with 'Be quiet!' shouted louder than anything that used to happen throughout the entire service.

'Rodents,' the leading hamster squeaked at an emergency midweek meeting convened to discuss the problem, 'we all know the trouble that the local church has every Sunday morning. It's in my heart that we should alleviate their misery and cause them to realize the joy that's rightfully theirs in the Creator.'

'Here! Here!' they shouted and then, more soberly, one asked, 'How?' and another, 'What then shall we do?'

He hadn't an answer. But they had to do something.

Over the next weeks, they came up with many suggestions, but none seemed destined to work until...

...until a young hamster by the name of Salvina came up with the master stroke!

It was a beautiful spring morning that Sunday and the windows of the church were wide open to allow a gentle, cool breeze to permeate the building. The congregation filed in - in holy file - taking their time-honoured seats just like they'd always done.

The hamsters knew what hymn they were going to begin with.

On warm, sunny days they always spontaneously began with the same one. From high above the congregation, crouching on the rafters, the hamsters were ready. For two solid weeks they'd been collecting every petal they could find, storing thousands, thousands upon thousands, high up where no-one could ever see.

'Let us sing a hymn together, brethren,' the vicar spoke in a deep holy voice that he exercised only on Sundays.

'Hymn number 851 - "All things bright and beautiful".'

The organ started up, the congregation stood and they began their lack lustre singing.

'All things bright and beautiful....'

As they neared the end of the first verse, Salvina squeaked the signal. The hamsters released all the petals and they descended gently, with perfect timing, to cascade upon the congregation as they began singing:

'...Each little flower that o-....'

They stopped singing, looking around.

'Look, Mummy, it's snowing!' a little girl shouted excitedly.

'Sssshhh! Not in church!'

The organist continued playing for she had her back to the proceedings but, when they stopped singing, she gradually ground to a halt.

Trying not to look 'unholy' and suppressing a smile, the vicar spoke:

'Let us begin again, brethren, hymn number 851.'

Many of the congregation looked round at the inch-deep piles of petals that lay strewn throughout the building - some had nestled on the ladies' hats - and wondered just who was going to clear up all the mess. The vicar had better not ask them!

The organ started up, the congregation began singing from the beginning, trying to pretend that nothing had happened.

When they came to that same line, they allowed their eyes to dart heavenward in case, just in case, it happened again. But Salvina squeaked the second signal that prepared the way for the next line:

'...Each little bird that sings....'

Hundreds upon hundreds of birds flew in through the open windows, their songs drowning out the organ, and perched on the back of pews, pulpit, organ pipes - one even had the audacity to perch on the Rector's head!

This continued for five solid minutes, the congregation getting more angry by the moment. Except, of course, the children.

'Look, look, birds, Mummy!'

'Ssshhh!'

'But, Mummy, lo....'

'I won't tell you again, be quiet! We're in church!'

The birds left, one by one, and the vicar, sensing that the congregation were fuming with rage that Creation was spoiling their service, decided to try it just once more.

'We don't seem to be getting very far this morning in our praise, do we?' He smiled - but no-one smiled back.

The organ droned the intro. This time they only got to the second line of the first verse:

'...All creatures great and small....'

The church exploded with a menagerie of wild animals - foxes, stoats, weasels, mice, badgers, rats, voles, hedgehogs, rabbits, hares, chickens...and hamsters. All of them raising their voice in praise to the Creator - each one making melody at the top of their voice.

It was Salvina's master stroke!

The humans evacuated the building - except for one little girl who managed to escape the grip of her parents' hands in all the confusion and she stood, shouting her head off with joy, in the middle of the building admiring all the glory of God's creation at first hand.

The church Committee convened a meeting in the graveyard while the babbling continued inside.

'Where's Amy?' a mother asked. 'Has anyone seen my Amy?'

'I didn't see her come out,' one replied.

'No!' she panicked. 'She's in there with those...those wild, uncontrollable animals!'

The church responded in unity - which was the first time in its long history - and rushed back into the vestibule of the church.

They stopped in their tracks. There, in the midst of the creatures praising the Creator, stood Amy, hands raised high blessing God.

Only Amy really did believe that the Lord God had made them all and here she was saying so.

The congregation were speechless. They saw, in that one moment, the emptiness of their religion - their poverty, their wretchedness, their stupidity.

Instead of grabbing Amy and running out, they began, one by one, raising their hands heavenward and mouthing, for the first time in their lives, praise that overflowed from their hearts.

Joy flooded their experience of the Creator that day, joy that welled up within them into tears.

Salvina, indeed, had come up with the master stroke!

THE BIG SLEEP

Larry the Hamster was more fond of sleep than almost every other hamster who ever lived. Even when the family met, four times every year, he would sneak away at the height of the conversation to find a warm cosy bed of straw in some secluded corner of the apartment and, stretching himself out wearily, would close his eyes to get forty winks - but it usually went way past the eighty mark.

No wonder, then, that his relatives nicknamed him 'Lazy' - Larry the Lazy they used to call him - though if you'd ever met him, you had to remember that Larry knew nothing of his nickname and it would have probably upset him if you'd told him.

It was the time of the year when the family came together and Larry was making his way over to the rendezvous when, quite suddenly and unexpectedly, he felt a yawn coming on. Larry tried to suppress it but it only made his face crease up in vivid contortions that eventually forced him to bare his two front teeth in a wide chasm.

There was nothing else for it - meeting or no meeting, Larry had to have his nap.

You must understand that Larry lived in a London hotel ventilation duct on the eighteenth floor, a few yards from the kitchen and food storage area. This is where he scratched out a living at night when the staff had finished their work. It was on the thirteenth floor, however, on his way down, that the yawn overwhelmed him so, instead of wasting time by returning five floors to his nest, he squeezed himself under an apartment door and sniffed around for a suitable substitute.

It wasn't long before he'd found a human's bag - quite a large one, too - and he climbed in to investigate.

It was excellent! Not only did it have a soft material cup to curl up in, but he found some white material to use for bedding and some wood (very unusual wood it was, too) to have a good gnaw on before he retired for his much needed nap.

Within a few minutes he was fast asleep, oblivious to the fact that the human had zipped it up, thus sealing Larry inside. He slung it across his shoulder and walked out of the apartment, closing the door behind him - off to do a day's work.

Larry woke for a moment, then settled back into a deep sleep.

The next thing he knew was that he heard the sound of many voices - human voices. Larry sat up on his rear legs, ears up like radar discs trying to determine what was happening. Soon the voices died away and Larry's concentration became blurred and hazy.

'Yawwwn!' He really had to catch up on that sleep. Laying down on the soft well of material, he closed his eyes and drifted back into slumber.

Time passed.

Suddenly, voices. First one, then two, then...hundreds! It sounded like hundreds of humans all shouting and cheering at the same time. What was going on?

'You're last in!' a voice shouted hurriedly. 'Get your tackle....'

A human ran over and unzipped the bag. Grabbing items here and there, he armed himself like a war-hardened soldier, then lifted the cap to stare intently at the badge. It was a proud day and he looked patriotically at the cap before pressing it firmly on his head, peak protruding from his brow to protect against the sun. The man walked quickly from the room, off to do his day's work.

Larry, if you hadn't already worked it out, had made his nest inside the man's cap and was now sandwiched between the material above him and the human beneath, clinging on for his life so as not to slide off the round head.

The commentator spoke in slow, dramatic tones - 'Who would have thought that the Ashes would all hinge on these last three balls. If you've just turned on, you couldn't have joined us at a better time.

'Australia need just one run to win from the last three balls to regain the Ashes here at the Oval. England need only take this one wicket left standing to retain them.

'And here comes their final batsman from the pavilion to take the strike. It looks like an easy task, just one more run....'

The batsman looked down at his glove as he walked towards the crease and noticed a small hole had been gnawed in it. His bat seemed to be scratched in a couple of places as well. But, not to worry, it wouldn't affect this one glorious moment when he'd strike the winning run that would regain the Ashes for Australia.

Larry was bouncing up and down on the batsman's head as he strode to the wicket, with two paws he clung to the cap and with the other two the hair.

'Middle!' the batsman shouted at the umpire and, deliberately, took time to settle himself as he marked the crease. He stood back from the wicket, bat in the air, looking at the field placings.

'This'll be easy,' he thought as he touched his bat to the floor and looked up to see the bowler beginning his run.

Larry was grateful that the bouncing had stopped - he felt a satisfied squeak coming on.

The bowler came to the crease, arm raised over his head, releasing the ball - it was going to be an easy strike, a real sitter, and....

'Squeak!' Larry couldn't refrain from it, he was content.

'He's missed the ball!' the commentator shouted into the microphone and thousands of Englishmen breathed a sigh of relief.

'He missed an absolute sitter! And the batsman now is walking up to the umpire....'

'The wicket keeper squeaked and put me off,' he complained.

'I didn't hear anything, you must be hearing things.'

'...probably some technical problem,' the commentator continued. 'Still only one run required from the last two balls.'

The batsman prepared himself once again to receive the ball.

The crowd hushed in anticipation (it was in those days before a cricket test resembled a football match). The bowler began his run up.

Larry was struggling to keep balance, his paws were losing their grip on the material and the batsman's hair. The bowler's arm was raised, the ball released and Larry finally lost hold of the hair - the cap, on which he now had a firm four-pawed grip, slid down the batsman's face and over his eyes.

He took another wild swipe at the ball and missed it completely.

The crowd gasped.

The wicket keeper retrieved it, throwing it back to the bowler via a number of fielders. The batsman replaced his cap firmly on his head and angrily kicked his bat.

Only one ball to go! The fate of the Ashes depended on that one last ball!

Larry felt a yawn coming on and this time he wasn't going to suppress it. But he needed some more bedding....

'The atmosphere is electrifying,' the commentator spoke to thousands of armchair spectators huddled round their radios.

'The batsman now is looking round, preparing himself for the final ball of the innings. He hunches down and the bowler is beginning his run....'

Bedding - Larry needed some more bedding so he sniffed around.

'Mmmm,' he thought, 'this hair should do nicely....'

'...he's running up to the crease, his arm raised to release the ball... it's a full....'

Larry gripped a large tuft of hair in his teeth, pulling it ferociously.

'Yowwwww!' the batsman yelled in pain, almost dropping his bat.

'...the batsman's sliced it! It's high, it's in the air! There's a fielder running to get under it. He's going to catch it - yes, I think he's going to catch it! He has! HE HAS! What drama here at the Oval! England have retained the Ashes off the last ball of the series....'

The celebrations began.

But one test cricketer, frustrated that the easy run he thought he'd score had been lost, kicked the stumps over in anger and threw his bat down in disgust.

Larry was curled up in a ball, fast asleep.

A long time ago, one of your wise kings wrote, 'Catch us the foxes, the very small foxes, that spoil the vineyards, for our vineyards are blooming.'

Perhaps in the above story, I should alter it to 'the little hamsters spoil the victory'?

The batsman thought that the task was easy, but he hadn't reckoned with an enemy within. He felt certain that the victory would be his, that he'd be the hero of the hour, but one small obstacle blocked his path to glory.

It's very often the seemingly little problems that raise their heads in your lives just at the wrong moment. Though they could have been dealt with years ago, they can remain hidden, asleep for ages, before they come to the surface and blemish your actions.

So, learn by Larry - the spiritual equivalent of him may need to be dealt with before you will be permanently effective in the Creator's purpose.

WHAT IF...

Jean Francois, a hamster of French descent who'd travelled to America along with the early Pilgrim settlers, awoke bleary-eyed from his daytime rest. He sniffed through his food store endeavouring to find a tasty morsel that would satisfy the aching hunger that had prompted him to open his black shiny eyes, but he smelt nothing that pleased his nose.

Jean Francois contemplated a lightning dart above ground into broad daylight to grab a pouch full of fresh, green shoots and return hurriedly to the cool sanctuary of his nest, out of view of predators. It was a risky business, but once a hamster has set his heart on a particular food, there's very little danger that will deter him.

Opening his mouth in a wide, gaping yawn, he pawed lethargically upward toward the narrow shaft of light that divided safety from danger. He poked his nose out of the entrance and gave a good, long sniff.

'Mmmm, fresh food,' he thought, his stomach urging him out of his nest into the bleaching rays of broad daylight.

A fresh clump of newly sprouted grass lay less than a cherrystone's throw away from the nest entrance so that, in a few short moments, Jean Francois was gnawing blade after blade away from the root, cramming his pouches with green leaves that were making his mouth water. It was then that he noticed that the sun had disappeared behind a cloud - or, at least, he thought it was a cloud.

He looked up to see the intense blue of the sky and the realization hit him that there weren't any clouds - besides, the ground around him was still bathed in the most brilliant sunlight. It was just where he was sitting that was in shadow. Jean Francois took a long, hard gulp, his eyes darting in front and behind at the grey patch of darkness - there was no doubt about it, the shadow was definitely hawk shaped. That meant only one thing....

In blind panic he shot a glance upwards in time to see a predator, silhouetted against the sky, begin its dive earthward, claws open, gaining speed as it plunged ever nearer, ever closer.

Jean darted forward, oblivious to the safety of his nest that lay behind him, breaking into a full gallop, running first this way, then that, as the hawk banked out of its dive, giving chase in hot pursuit.

Five feet, four feet, three - ever nearer it came, Jean gasping for breath as he realized that unless something happened he was a gonner.

Two feet - the hawk let out a pre-emptive squawk that made his fur stand on end.

One.

It was then that Jean noticed what appeared to be a soft bed of fluffy material a few strides from his nose.

'Perhaps,' he thought, 'I can dive into it and hide.'

Without a second thought, he jumped with every ounce of his strength into the downy pile, disappearing from the hawk's sight.

It continued flying onwards and, realizing that the easy lunch had gone, ascended heavenward.

Jean realized that he was still moving - even more strange, he continued to hear the sound of the flapping of strong wings beating rhythmically with others. Then the frightening truth dawned on him - he'd dived into the soft downy body of a goose.

The bird, startled by the jolt of the hamster's impact, had taken to the skies to flee danger and Jean, thirty feet high and ascending, poked his head out of his refuge only to discover the ground disappearing below him.

Feeling that he was about to be sick (for he didn't like heights) and, frightened that he might fall earthbound at anytime, he allowed his paws to tightly grip the feathers on either side. But the goose, startled this time by the surge of pain that flooded its back, banked sharply, descended rapidly, and Jean was flung out into the abyss of nothingness.

Down and down he plunged, his heart pounding wildly, erratically, his paws stretched out trying to grab any twig or branch that might stop his fall. The hawk, seeing the hamster in midair and mistaking it for a sparrow, banked round with claws open, swooping down for the kill.

Nearer and nearer - Jean spotted him out of the corner of his eye but could do nothing except in fright start running in midspace.

Now, this may sound far fetched but I can assure you that what I'm about to tell you is true. As the hawk moved in for the kill, Jean disappeared through a small opening in the roof of a farmer's barn and landed, safely, on a large pile of straw. He bounced a number of times before finally coming to rest, his fur wet with nervous perspiration. He squeaked a long sigh of relief.

It had all been too much for him - the hawk, the goose, the freefall and then the hawk again. His paws trembled with shock.

There was only one thing to do before he sniffed his way back to his nest when the sun fell, and that was to sleep it off.

He crept slowly around, ears on the alert in case the danger hadn't passed, looking for soft, warm bedding. It wasn't long before he found an old wheelbarrow that held an adequate supply of straw but, what was even better, the sun had been shining on it through the hole in the roof, so it was warm and cosy.

Jean Francois crawled underneath the pile of straw, falling fast asleep in a few moments, oblivious to the two humans that had quietly entered the barn.

'I know I put it in here,' one said as they both searched.

'Here it is,' the other called. 'Looks in good condition.'

'You bet it is! Cummon, give me a hand.'

They gently lifted the wheelbarrow up and carried it out through the barn doors, having earmarked it for a very special purpose.

It was the fourteenth of July 1859, about five-thirty in the afternoon, and a large crowd had gathered in anticipation of the event. Vendors sold soft drinks from the hastily erected tents and food, way overpriced by the day's standards, but on sale wherever you looked. The whole scene had striking similarities with a tourist trap in London.

The crowds had stayed behind after the first performance, hoping that he might return to try, once more, what none of them dared to do. Perhaps there were even some who'd come to see him plunge to an early death. Whatever, the crowds buzzed with anticipation as the carriage drove through the multitudes, coming to a halt close by the rope.

The door swung open and the great Blondin, tightrope walker extraordinaire, descended from the carriage. At first, the crowd didn't recognize him - after all, it's difficult to recognize one clothed in fancy dress - and Blondin was wearing an ape costume!

Turning, he reached back into the carriage and pulled out a brightly coloured wheelbarrow, a pile of straw nestling within.

Nobody noticed the straw move as Jean Francois, still fast asleep, turned over onto his left side - their eyes were fixed firmly on Blondin, now pushing the barrow before him toward the rope.

With firm but accurate precision he pushed it out over the abyss and set off, step by step, behind it. The tightrope stretched out from bank to bank, guyed at either end, while Niagara raged with white foam a hundred and fifty feet directly below. To Blondin, it was a simple stroll across a chord of twine, three and a half inches wide, suspended perilously above the river that showed no mercy to young and old alike. To the crowd, his walk was beyond comprehension, a feat of daring, bravery - even madness.

Jean Francois turned back onto his stomach, dreaming of endless barley fields and orchards. Blondin didn't notice the straw move either.

The crowd felt the fear that Blondin never experienced. They envisaged themselves in his place, precariously balanced between heaven and earth upon a thin, taut rope. Only one slight slip would send them plummeting down, to be sucked under the swirling water of the violent river. They certainly wouldn't try crossing, even if Blondin carried them!

Jean twitched, swallowing hard as he dreamt of eating the largest carrot he'd ever seen.

It took Blondin eleven long minutes to complete the heart-stopping return journey and he was welcomed back with loud cheers. The carriage whisked him away as the crowd quickly dispersed, that great feat indelibly printed on all their minds.

Jean Francois awoke with a bump.

'Careful,' said one, 'he might need to use it again!'

'There's no damage, look for yourself!' the other complained as the wheelbarrow was inspected.

The two men closed the barn door behind them as Jean's head appeared over the side of the barrow. The sun had set as he sniffed round the barn for a clue to his nest's location.

Fortunately, a gentle breeze carried the familiar scent into his nostrils and, following, he arrived back at his nest in a short space of time, the events of the previous day still echoing round his head.

'What if I hadn't noticed that shadow?' he thought, his eyes bulging with the memory. 'I'd be dead by now!'

Jean Francois was having an attack of the 'What-ifs.'

'And that goose - oh dear, I might have been dashed to pieces on some rock or other if I'd fallen off someplace else!'

A cold sweat broke out as his body began shaking.

'And what if that hawk had got me the second time?'

A shiver ran down the length of his back, then returned meeting a second's descent.

Jean Francois was frightened about what could have been. He spent ages worrying anxiously over the events of the previous day - what if 'this,' what if 'that.' He let his mind dwell upon the possibilities that never took place.

Eventually, after many hours, the fear subsided.

But, if he had only known the unseen danger that had threatened to consume him totally, he might never have put his thoughts to one side and got on with searching for food.

My friend, the Creator never allows you to get into a situation that He doesn't intend to deliver you from. You may spend endless hours of your life worrying over what could have been, but it didn't work out that way because He's always in control of His people's lives. Jean Francois allowed the threat of what he saw to dominate his thoughts.

I wonder what he would have done if he'd known that he'd been suspended between heaven and earth, one small slip away from certain death?

THE HAMSTER OLYMPICS

It was mid-spring, the year 1924, and crowds from across the world were converging on Paris, the capital of the French nation.

In all, over three thousand competitors came representing forty-four nations, each with the desire to achieve the ultimate world recognition - a gold medal in the eighth modern Olympics.

Nineteen twenty-four was to be a famous year - Johnny Weissmuller, later to be heralded as one of the greatest portrayers of Tarzan on film, won five gold medals and a bronze at swimming. And, for Great Britain, Eric Liddell and Harold Abrahams in the athletics secured two gold medals in the 440 and 110 yards respectively, earning themselves a well-deserved place amongst the British Olympic 'Hall of Fame.'

Yet, in a small suburb of Paris, the first modern Hamster Olympics went virtually unnoticed and unreported in the national and international press.

But let me start my story late in the previous year when a group of French hamsters, living in the Hams Elysees, formed the now famous Olympic Hamster Committee of 1923. They decided, after talking to many other fellow rodents on holiday in Paris that year, that ever since the first human Olympics back in 1896, there'd been a desire to see a hamster alternative. Very boldly, they sent out messengers far and wide throughout the winter proclaiming that the following year (May 3 - July 27) the first modern Hamster Olympics would take place in Paris.

The response was overwhelming! No matter where the messengers went, the enthusiasm was the same, each colony putting forward one or two names for the Games. When it got back to the Committee, word went out to the Parisienne hamsters and they began burrowing accommodation for the anticipated competitors. No-one was quite sure how many would come, so they dug and dug persistently right through the winter - in the end, they only just had enough space.

Then the hamsters began arriving from all over the civilised world - and very inventive they were, too. It had already been realized that the human competitors represented a superb vehicle by which to travel to Paris, so each hamster, however he or she could, stowed away in suitcases and the like.

I must mention one very ingenious hamster here called Jock (he was of Scottish descent) who not only travelled in the suitcase of the great Eric Liddell, but disguised himself as the athlete's shaving brush. Jock was pleasantly surprised when the shaving foam left a wonderful sheen on his fur that caused it to sparkle in the moonlight. Although he never won an event, his tale was world famous.

Also, a Canadian hamster, Pierre (French-Canadian, that is) managed to disguise himself as the tail of a freestyle wrestler's Davey Crockett hat, attached securely by his teeth. It was very inconvenient at times, but the opportunities it provided to select choice vegetables from his food plate more than compensated.

Others came hidden in weightlifters' beards, suitcases - one even came as the sporran of a Scottish rower.

Having arrived safely in Paris - and of all the athletes expected not one failed to arrive - they spent two weeks acclimatising themselves in preparation, training throughout Paris to ensure that, when the day came for their event, they'd be in peak fitness.

The Olympic Games always throws up characters and heroes wherever and whenever it takes place. The same was true of the first Hamster Olympics. But before I go on to tell you about that one character that came into his own that year, I must explain to you about the actual events that were being run.

You will probably already realize that there were no watersports - hamsters have an aversion to getting wet, even though they're quite happy to live on or travel by boat. The fur gets matted, you see, and we swim very much like a brick does.

Even though there were a handful of willing competitors, in the interests of safety the events were called off.

But by far the most popular event (from the point of view of both the number of competitors and the size of the crowds that it drew) was the Athletics, held in a recently harvested field on the outskirts of Paris. The farmer never once suspected as all the heats and finals took place at night.

The Olympic Hamster Committee had come up with some marvellous innovations in order to make the events possible. For instance, the hammer competition became the cherry and stalk throwing event. Hamsters would select a cherry from the Olympic-approved equipment and, grasping the end of the stalk firmly in both paws, would spin frantically round in a circle, releasing it at the last moment to catapult the cherry forward over large distances. Care had to be taken to ensure that the cherry wasn't too ripe or else it flew off the stalk long before it was ever released by the competitor.

And the cherries could only be used once as they squashed on impact (hamsters from the poorer sections of Parisienne society would eat up the resulting debris, clearing the field for the next competitor).

In the Javelin, flighted cocktail sticks were used. It was a clever idea indeed for, after the event, the sticks doubled as high-jump apparatus. The bar didn't have to be very high as hamsters can't jump very well and, besides, they take on the form of beanbags when they come back down to earth with a bump.

A hazelnut was used for the shot-putt (an unshelled one, that is, and it was frequently examined for cracks) but, sadly, the discus had to be abandoned as no suitable equipment could be found.

One other event that was threatened with postponement was the 4x100 inches sprint relay. The problem lay not in the acquisition of equipment but in the rules of the event, for the baton, which was a large sunflower seed, kept being eaten by the competitors. Also, the change over from pouch to pouch presented almost insurmountable difficulties. In the end, the Olympic Committee decided that it was enough for the first hamster to touch the second and so on (a bit like 'tag'), so the event was saved.

But I've digressed far enough. I must now return to that certain character that set the first modern Hamster Olympics alight.

Albino the Finn was a small, thin hamster with a white face - hence his name. He'd come to Paris as his country's representative in the 135-hamster line up of the six-mile Olympic marathon. It was not that Albino was particularly fast over the distance that had caused him to be chosen, but he did have stamina - he would often run during entire nights through the pine forests of his native country, pausing only to pouch morsels of food that he'd occasionally find.

It seemed like Albino could run forever - a ten-mile endurance test would have suited him far better than the marathon in which he was entered. His problem was that he lacked pace - he would plod on forever, but he couldn't run fast.

'Albino,' the leading hamster had said as he was about to leave for Paris, 'don't forget that we're pinning our hopes on you to do well for us.'

'Fat chance,' he'd thought. 'I'll be left behind from the start!'

But he hadn't said anything fearing that his words would sound too negative.

So here he was on the start line, along with one hundred and thirty-four other hamsters.

'On your marks,' the starter called and the crowd hushed in expectation.

'Get set.'

The competitors crouched low ready for the next command - Albino's heart was beating twenty to the dozen.

'Go!'

The crowd burst into rapturous applause and cheers, encouraging them in the race that lay before them. The noise gradually subsided as the field disappeared out of the stadium.

Albino was not doing very well, he was already among the last sixty competitors and more passed him as they made their way out to the far parts of the course. He knew he'd finish the race, but his lack of speed always annoyed him - yes, he'd finish alright, but one hundred and thirty-fifth wasn't exactly worthy of much honour!

The humidity wasn't helping either. In the forests of his native land, the dry atmosphere made long distance running a positive enjoyment, the cool sea breeze that rolled in from the north kept it pleasant as well. But Paris had experienced endless rain followed by blistering sun during the day - the conditions were somewhat well described as 'sticky'.

'Persevere!' Albino told himself as another competitor glided almost effortlessly by. 'Finish the race before you and do your best.' The words echoing in his ears brought comfort to his increasing fears of failure.

Another hamster scurried passed.

'One pace Albino, that's what they'll call me! How can I ever return to the colony after such a disgrace? They were all expecting so much from me!'

Needless to say, Albino persevered. In the second half of the race no-one overtook him and he wondered if there was anyone left behind him at all.

A couple of hundred yards from the stadium, he noticed a runner ahead of him at quite some distance and Albino was actually gaining on him! He found himself half smiling - he actually had someone in front of him that he had a chance of overtaking.

As they entered the stadium approach, he was only five yards behind. Into the stadium and it was down to four. When both runners came into view, the spectators went wild. Cheers rang out all over the stadium, flags and banners waved, firecrackers were let off and the crowd stood on their hind paws applauding the two athletes.

'That's nice,' Albino couldn't help thinking. 'They've stayed to the end to encourage the last competitors.'

Then his mind turned back to the hamster in front, only three yards away and twenty to run. By now, the leader was slowing almost to a crawl, which made it look like Albino had accelerated in a sprint to the line - of course, he was plodding on at the same pace he'd run the entire race in, but it certainly looked like 'one pace Albino' had lit the blue touch paper.

Five yards to go and he shot passed the exhausted rodent towards the line, breaking the straw tape in a time of 2 hours 41 minutes and 22.6 seconds! At least he'd overtaken someone, his country could take pride in that!

Then a strange thing happened.

The front rows of the crowd rushed down to the track, hoisted Albino up onto their shoulders and paraded him round the stadium shouting, 'Albino the Great! The Champion! The Winner! Albino the hero!'

'What?' squeaked Albino. 'Me? The Champion? Where are the others that passed me?'

An Olympic official was standing close by, trying to get to him to place the crown on his head - 'They never made it to the finish!' he shouted. 'The conditions - they set off too fast and had to retire before they completed the course!'

And with that, the Victor's crown was placed firmly on his head.

Albino the Great, old 'one pace Albino', was the Champion of the world!

Perseverance, my friends, perseverance!

Your life is like a race that has been set out before you. You may well see many leave you standing while you plod on relentlessly towards the end. You may think that you'll never receive the crown of life from the Creator when your time is through.

But it doesn't matter how slow you are, so long as you finish the race. Continue, therefore, with your eyes set firmly on the Creator, the prize, and persevere steadfastly until He calls you home.

THE DARK-SKINNED STRANGER

A cave is not the ideal habitat for a hamster. The cold, damp atmosphere makes hibernation a distinct possibility and the solid limestone floor and walls give little opportunity for burrowing. But Hezro the hamster had discovered a tiny crack in the cave entrance that led to a large hollow where he'd transported straw for bedding.

As the sun rose each morning, its rays shone directly through the crack, heating his nest to a reasonable temperature that was maintained throughout the day by blocking the crack with some straw. For this reason, Hezro always waited a couple of hours after sunrise before darting back into the hollow, which by that time had reached its optimum temperature.

The crack itself was virtually invisible to animal and human eye alike, looking like a simple indentation in the soluble limestone.

Indeed, it had appeared that way to Hezro initially but he'd dropped a seed on the stone floor which rolled into the hollow and, having given chase, discovered it with much excitement.

Hezro had lived there for a number of months and food had always been in abundance. It wasn't that the surrounding hills were particularly fruitful with plants - there was enough to live on but not enough variety - but caves make ideal homes for all manner of creatures that bring their food with them. As hamsters are awake during the night when the cave dwellers are fast asleep, the acquisition of their food was a cinch.

Bears, lions and conies had all passed through. He'd particularly fond memories of his encounter with a bear that for a number of days had brought back fresh fish to the cave from the stream at the bottom of the valley. If it was an exceptionally cold night, he would bury himself in his fur to get warm before once again going about his business.

A religious hermit had come to the cave, a short time afterwards, on a vow of silence. Though he brought much food with him, he ate little of it, preferring to feed it to the creatures that lived in and around the cave. Hezro found him packed and gone one evening when he awoke, but he never heard him go.

And then that memorable day came when another man came to the cave - a strange looking man he was, too. He was quite small with dark skin and built like a warrior. He had a very long, heavy sword girded onto his left side but, much to Hezro's disappointment, he came with little food.

'Renegade,' thought Hezro. 'Villain, thief or murderer. Certainly not one to get too close to!' And from that point on he eyed him suspiciously until he could ascertain just what sort of man this stranger was.

The day after the stranger arrived, Hezro was sleeping peacefully in his hollow when he was awakened by the sound of a human singing, accompanying himself on an instrument. Try as he might, he couldn't get back to sleep for the music bounced off the hard cave walls and shot into his nest compartment. He tried burying his head in the bedding but he could still feel the bass thumping repeatedly through his head. Straw in the ears didn't work either.

Hezro decided to investigate, poking his head out from the crack just as the stranger began a new song:

'Be lifted high, O God, above the heavens,
Let Your glory be far over all the earth.'

That surprised him. He agreed with the sentiment but it seemed so out of place on the lips of this stranger - after all, he was a warrior, perhaps even a bandit escaping justice and the king's rule.

The stranger repeated the lines, singing louder, raising his hands towards heaven and springing wildly around the cave. Hezro could have imagined the hermit doing what he now witnessed before him, but a warrior? A renegade?

'No,' thought Hezro, 'I must have been wrong - surely this man knows the Creator.'

The tune changed, the stranger began a new song. Quietly at first but gathering strength:

'The righteous are going to surround me,
For You will deal richly with me.'

That excited Hezro, his heart missed a beat as he sat up on his rear paws.

'The Righteous!' he squeaked, hardly able to contain himself. 'God's people are going to come to this stranger, here!'

It may be difficult for you to understand, but Hezro had always wanted to see the Righteous of the Creator, ever since he was young.

He quickly looked around to see if they were already there.

No. Still only the dark-skinned stranger, but the expectation remained.

As the singing came to an end, he made his way back to the nest, snuggled down into the straw and, with great difficulty because of the excitement that the Righteous were coming, he fell asleep, his ears still raised to give warning when they arrived.

For the next few days, Hezro woke at every noise, half expecting to see the Righteous when he poked his head out of the crack. But it was only the stranger going about his business, or singing loudly in praise of the Creator.

Then, just when his expectation was beginning to waver, he heard approaching voices.

'This is it,' he thought. 'The Righteous are here!' and he scurried out into the cave in time to see two humans climbing up to the cave's entrance.

What a disappointment! These looked worse than the stranger!

'David!' one called. 'David, is that you, my brother?'

'Eliab? What are you doing here with Shammah?'

'We've come to join with you, we've come to help and serve you.'

Hezro was annoyed - 'Family! Only his family!'

Disappointed he walked back to his nest and was soon fast asleep.

Later that day there were more voices, this time a crowd.

Hezro scampered outside with great excitement, expecting to witness the arrival of the Righteous.

'David! They said you were at Adullam! We've come to join with you!'

'Who are you?' The dark-skinned stranger was puzzled. They introduced themselves one by one, explaining why they'd come:

'I owe money,' said one, 'too much to repay. I borrowed money to plant crops and the harvest is ruined.'

'Israel's finished,' another complained. 'Saul is bringing us to the precipice of destruction with all his schemes. You're our hope, David, you're the Lord's anointed!'

'My parents are dead!' said another. 'Two weeks ago everything I had burnt down with our house. I'm throwing my lot in with you!'

And it went on.

Hezro was disappointed. No - he was downright depressed! He felt like shouting at the top of his voice, 'But where are the Righteous?'

It would have done him no good and they wouldn't have heard him or understood, but that's what he felt like doing. He was waiting to see the Righteous and all he saw was that discontented mob, the offscourings of society!

He turned his back on them with disgust and was walking to his nest when a word hit him. He came to an abrupt halt as the word came flooding back from long ago:

'Don't judge by what appears to be,' an old hamster had told him, 'because you're missing the hidden intentions of the heart.'

Hezro turned round, walked back to his vantage point and watched the events unfold. Over the next weeks he frequently crawled from his nest to spend time observing their work, their routine, their attitudes; watching them change with each passing day under the leadership of the stranger.

In a couple of months they left, bound for someplace else. It was quiet without them, but Hezro felt privileged. Yes, privileged.

He realized that he'd seen the Righteous, the army of the Creator, taking shape before his eyes.

They looked so different, not like you'd expect the Righteous to look, but Hezro knew in his heart that these small handful of men held the future of the Creator's Purpose for His people in their hands.

The Righteous had indeed surrounded that dark-skinned stranger!

GERBILEO

Amongst the ranks of the world's greatest rodent inventors stands Gerbileo - head and shoulders above the rest some would say - a hamster of noble descent who challenged the way the world perceived matters and caused many to think differently about the complexities of their own existence.

His inventions are too numerous to mention them all here (and there are other works, more detailed and informative that can be accessed by the inquisitive reader) so I want to concentrate on what, to humans, came to be considered a revolutionary instrument used in successive centuries - even up to this present day.

Called by Gerbileo 'The Visual Food Locator', he quite literally stumbled upon it one December evening when he was sniffing out the existence of anything edible on the floor of the human's Study, located adjacent to the wall within which was his nest.

Pieces of wood shavings and glass beads lay strewn about the floor - a difficult enough place to negotiate even without the occupant getting reckless with his projects - and he trod carefully through a maze of shapes, sniffing each one in case, perhaps, a crumb here, a morsel there, was somehow attached to the most disinteresting of objects.

No - nothing remotely interesting, not even a whiff of it.

Then something caught his eye - a sparkling light that flickered into view, causing him to stop. From where he stood, the moonlight refracted through a small glass pebble lodged against a table leg.

Gerbileo was intrigued, his curiosity dragging his paws to the phenomenon, keeping the flickering moon in vision all the while. He lifted a paw in front of the circular face and watched as a true image of the moon was etched onto his palm.

'Weird,' he squeaked, lifting the sphere into the air as a connoisseur would lift a particularly fine wine into vision to admire the colour.

'It magnifies,' he thought, his mind working overtime at an application, a use, that would help his daily quest for food. As if by chance - and, to be honest, it probably was just that – as he moved about the room, seeing the world from an upside-down perspective, he suddenly saw the biggest walnut he'd ever seen.

Shocked by the immensity of the object, he lowered the glass, expecting to witness it in 'real time' but saw nothing. His eyes darted back and forth, trying to make out the form that had whet his appetite in disregard of the discovery.

No. It wasn't there.

What?!

Raising the glass ball once more to his eye, he played with the height until, again, a gigantic walnut sprung into view. This time, he held it still, calculated the angle through which he was peering and gingerly moved his head to one side to see where his gaze brought him.

Another flicker of light caught his eye - another glass bead, this time a few feet away, that lay on a pile of books scattered on the floor.

But still no walnut.

Were his eyes deceiving him?

Then he saw. Maybe thirty feet away, on a direct path from where he stood and through the distant glass ball, a walnut perched high on a shelf, partly obscured but clearly visible as he stood to one side.

'Amazing!' He let out an excited squeak - as only inventors can - and, grabbing the second bead and pouching it with the other as he ran by, he ascended carefully up the curtains, hopping acrobatically onto the shelf where the nut lay, ready for opening and consuming.

An hour or so passed, Gerbileo waking from his food-induced sleep to the sound of an owl hooting somewhere in the distance. His mind flicked back to the events of the previous evening and the discovery that lay hidden in his pouches that food could be searched for without having to traverse vast tracts of open ground for fear of predators.

What a discovery! This could change the course of hamster history itself!

Descending the way he came but dropping onto the table in the corner of the room, he removed both glass beads and set them up a fair distance away with one secured at the very edge with a piece of clay he'd found on the shelf.

Holding the other in his hand, he gradually moved it so every bit of the floor could be observed and searched for crumbs.

It certainly was a neat idea but so time-consuming. Gerbileo found that, whereas scampering about the room took no more than a few minutes, the sheer size of what was being observed through the looking glass made a quick search impossible.

If he'd been wanting to see every fibre of every tuft of carpet, this was the tool - but he was more concerned with crumbs, pieces of biscuits and cake.

Exasperated, he gave up, sighing deeply with despair and returning to his early morning search before sun up. At least his time hadn't been wasted - at least he'd made a discovery that he could always come back to.

As the first rays of sun illuminated the human's Study, Gerbileo snuggled down into a soft pile of warm bedding and dreamed himself back into sleep...

...Galileo going about his daily routine and squinting at the winter's sharp rays that fell into the window and across the table.

With some warmed milk in one hand, he sat down at the table to rub away the sleepiness from his eyes and, turning, noticed the circle of brightness on the floor - round but made oval by the angle at which the image was hitting it.

Then he caught sight of the two glass beads in front of him, the sun beating down upon the first, magnified through the second and giving a perfect image of the sun on the floor.

'That's it!' he shouted, Gerbileo hearing a faint thundering as he turned round to snuggle into his bedding.

'If I reverse this phenomenon, I can stare at the stars and draw near to the planets without ever having to leave the room!'

He thought for a moment, smiling broadly - then announced to himself 'I shall call my invention "The Telescope".'

VOYAGE TO THE BOTTOM OF THE DUCK POND

Young Katey Wilson sat on the toilet seat in her parents' house, having locked herself in the upstairs bathroom.

Let me explain to you what had happened.

Katey had always been fascinated with keys - she would sit for hours playing with a jangly bunch of car keys, examining them all intricately and remembering what each one was used for.

It was this fascination that had been her downfall for, having locked the bathroom door behind her, she removed the old-fashioned key that slotted into the large metal mechanism, examining it with all the care and concern that a philatelist might examine the rarest of postage stamps, wanting to know every variation, every contour, every edge.

It was at this precise moment that a sound distracted her outside - it was an unfamiliar noise and, being curious as most children are, she climbed onto the bathroom stool, leaning out of the window to find out what had produced such a strange sound.

With the key clutched firmly in her right hand, she peered out over the familiar landscape - adjoining the house lay the garden, her parents' pride and joy, with rockery, lawn and, daddy's favourite, the pond. Past the hedge lay the fields with lazy cows sitting on green grass and horses swishing tails and manes in an effort to combat the flies that buzzed intensely in the warm summer sun.

There was nothing unusual there - nothing that could have produced such a noise.

Just as Katey was about to step down from the stool and accomplish the task for which she'd come to the bathroom, she heard the sound once again - this time louder - and, because she was leaning half out of the window, she could tell that it was directly below, out of sight because of the ledge that jutted out a few inches in front of her.

She pushed herself onto tiptoes, straining every muscle to stretch herself the extra few inches needed to peer over the sill that obscured her view.

Now you must understand the bird's dilemma that had made the noise. It was clung to the brickwork three inches below the window and, being full of the joys of summer, was proclaiming to the neighbourhood its territorial rights - it didn't expect a large predator to sneak up on it from above in order to swoop down at it for the kill, but this is how it read the situation when Katey suddenly appeared over the ledge.

In panic it squawked a loud warning, taking off with fast flapping wings making as much noise as it could. It had the desired effect for Katey, not realizing that all animals are not automatic friends, jumped in the air off the stool, releasing the key in her right hand with shock and falling backwards into the bathroom, bumping her head on the wash basin.

It only took her a moment to realize that the key was over the edge, falling to the garden below, and that without it she was trapped inside the room until...until...well, until someone came home and let her out.

She clambered frantically back onto the stool, her head beginning to throb with pain, and peered into the garden below. All she saw was the ripples of the pond as they rebounded off the sides. The key had fallen into the water.

Climbing slowly down, she sat on the toilet seat with her head in her hands, crying with sorrow at her own stupidity. Louder and louder she cried as she became more and more despondent, breaking into wails and sobs as her mind raced onto the possibility that if she was in there for a long time, her parents might return home to find not their daughter but a skeleton locked in the bathroom - such did her thoughts wander that it's no wonder that her screams could be heard all over the house...

...including, quite unsurprisingly, a yard outside the door where Jacques Fursteau, a hamster of French descent, was curled up in a ball enjoying his daytime sleep. Jacques was Katey's pet - he was very fond of her for, nearly every day, she'd bring him juicy titbits from the meal table and poke them through the bars of the cage.

Katey also used to tell him all her problems and dilemmas that she found herself in, Jacques listening intently and, after having waited for her to finish pouring out her heart, would squeak back the solution to her every need - unfortunately, Katey had not yet learnt at that early age to communicate in the hamster-tongue.

Nevertheless, there was a bond of mutual friendship between them.

Hearing Katey's wails, he awoke with a start, rushing out of his nest compartment to poke his nose out through the railings. Well, she certainly wasn't there.

His ears swivelled round as if on pivots locating the sound very close, behind the bathroom door.

Katey began pouring her heart out loudly, speaking into the air but not expecting that anyone was listening:

'It's not fair...(sob)...(sob)...I only wanted to...(sniff)...see that bird and now...(sob)...I've dropped that stupid key in the garden pond... (wail)...(sob)...I'll never get out of here now, I'll just...(sniff)...be a skeleton when they come back...(sob)...(sob)....Someone, HELP ME!....'

And so it went on.

Very soon, Jacques got the picture - a bird had stolen the key and dropped it in the pond. Or was it Katey who'd stolen the bird and dropped the key in the pond? Or was it Katey who'd dropped the key into the pond so that the bird couldn't steal it?

'Oh, never mind,' he squeaked. 'The solution is to get the key from the pond - I'm sure of that.'

And with that resolve, he loaded his pouches with a whole array of stored food, saying boldly as he stood on his rear paws and punched the sky with his right fist:

'This is a job for Superham!'

He lifted the latch on the cage door, releasing the spring that held it securely shut and climbed out, pawing down the wire onto the table and sliding down the table leg to the carpeted floor.

Jacques could get out of his cage at will, even though the family thought that their ingenious 'hamster-proof' lock kept him securely inside. He often went for midnight strolls when they were all asleep and knew the house layout back to front, even venturing out into the wilds of the garden on rare occasions. It was very fortunate, therefore, that Jacques knew exactly where he was headed and the best route to take.

He slid down the handrail on the wall of the stairs straight into the overcoat pocket that was hung up a few short strides from the front door. Descending down the outside of the garment he came to rest on the hall mat, sniffing around him in case of predators.

Dashing into the kitchen, he ascended the broom handle that lay propped up against the wooden set of drawers, gaining access to them through the unboarded back of the unit. He checked first one compartment then another, sniffing around for the resources he needed to accomplish his mission - a black plastic bin liner and one of Katey's bendy-straws.

Having found them, he returned to the hall, leapt onto the coat, ascended a few feet and then jumped out of the house through the letterbox on the front door.

A local postman fled for his life.

He scurried round the outside of the house keeping under the cover of the herbaceous borders until he arrived a short dart away from the garden pond where the key had plummeted to the depths of the murky brown water.

Gnawing the bin liner into the correct shape, he tightly wrapped it round his furry body to act as a scuba diving outfit and picked up the bendy-straw in his mouth intending to use it as a snorkel.

Jacques took one more deep sniff of air before he rushed out at full speed from under cover of the plants, taking off a foot away from the pond and diving into the water with a loud splash.

Katey, head still in her hands, heard only the faintest of noises and disregarded it.

To and fro Jacques swam, head down in search of the lost key with the straw elevated a couple of inches above the surface level of the water. A cat who'd just come to the side of the pond in search of goldfish took one look at the straw darting back and forth and fled for safety, warning all the local cats he met that evening that the fish were now retaliating against their repeated strikes with rockets launched from underwater firing tubes - the world's first polaris goldfishes.

A shiny metallic object glinted underneath him and Jacques dived to the bottom, retrieving a piece of discarded chocolate foil.

He resurfaced for air, swimming to and fro as previous.

It was then that he noticed what he at first thought was a carrot floating towards him but which, within a few seconds, he realized was a large goldfish, twice his own size and gaining speed with every swish of his strong tail.

Jacques remembered all those shark films that he'd watched over Katey's shoulder from the bookcase and dived hurriedly to the depths, the goldfish thinking that he was a large black fly and giving chase (though why a fly should be under water is unfathomable).

He plunged into a bed of vegetation on the bottom of the pond, hiding himself in the blackness and looking up to watch the fish give up for an easier kill. Jacques felt something cold and hard underneath his right paw and, looking down, squeaked with delight, releasing a small line of bubbles through the bendy straw that floated to the surface.

The key!

Picking it up between his teeth, he looked first right, then left, then above, making sure that the fish was gone before he pushed upwards for the surface - but he remained immobile. A wet, slimy frog had a rear paw securely gripped in its hungry mouth.

Jacques pulled the key out from between his teeth and clouted the reptile over the head. The dazed frog opened its wide mouth in pain while Jacques raced for the surface and sanctuary, fairly leaping out of the water and onto the dry green grass.

Discarding the black sack onto the lawn, he raced for the cover of the plants, keeping close to the wall of the house as he hurried to the front door, climbing in through the letterbox, up the stairs and onto the first floor landing. He could hear Katey still crying though her wails were a little quieter than before.

Very quietly he pushed the key underneath the door and, with a blood-curdling sound, squeaked as loud as his lungs would let him without passing out - even so, he still went dizzy.

Instantaneously Katey went silent, looking towards the door from where she'd heard the noise emanate. Her eye caught the key and she stared at it for what seemed like hours before finally racing over, picking it up and escaping to freedom, now crying with relief.

'I couldn't have thrown that key out after all!' she sobbed.

'What a fool I was, I never thought to look on the floor!'

Closing the door behind her she tapped on the cage - Jacques poked his head out of his nest with his eyes half closed, feigning sleep and sniffing the air like he normally did.

Katey bounced downstairs into the living room and sat on the floor, continuing to play with the toys she'd left almost two hours previous.

The lengths that Jacques went to in order to retrieve that key for Katey, but in the end she thought that the dilemma was all a figment of her own imagination!

Very many Believers are like Katey - finding themselves in an unenviable situation they quite rightly call out to the only One who can ultimately help - the Creator - only to think that because it seemingly worked itself out 'naturally' it can't possibly have been His doing.

Perhaps they even think that they misinterpreted the situation and there was no real problem in the first place.

But the Creator works in all types of ways, even the seemingly natural ones, to bring about the purpose of His will for His children so that in everything He may receive the praise due to Him.

It's too easy to explain away occurrences as coincidence or oversights on our part. In the Creator, to accept what one sees with one's own eyes is the first step to perceiving His work in one's dilemma.

THE PILGRIM HAMSTERS

I

'Hamsters!'

A large grey rodent stood up on his hind paws at one end of a packed cabbage crate, slightly elevated above the others by a few old twigs and pebbles that they'd gathered from the nearby field and used as a rostrum. His eyes strained at the sewn leaves precariously perched on the top of a pin in front of him, trying to make sense out of the hurried scrawl with which he'd had to write during the last half hour of the meeting.

The community of hamsters had overheard the humans discussing plans to leave for distant shores that very evening before they'd retired to bed and, realizing that it was more than just rumours or idle gossip, they'd quickly convened this meeting to decide their response.

The hamsters grew silent as the leader tapped his paw on the notes, sneezed twice and said, once again, this time in a louder voice, 'Hamsters!'

All ears tuned in to the voice like satellite dishes locating a distant planet, as he began his long address:

'Fellow rodents, I am sure that I don't need to remind you of past events and of our already epic migration from England to the land of the Dutch...' which was always his way of saying that he was about to tell them what they already knew and didn't need hearing again. The older hamsters gave a long sigh, for they knew what was coming.

'...but I think that it will benefit us to review our progress thus far so that we may accurately determine what our decision should be now that the humans have resolved to leave for the unconquered land of America.

'Let us not lose sight of the prime reason for our migration - adventure. Few of us ever imagined how exciting it would be to explore new lands and populate them with hamsters. Who would have thought that Holland would have held such promise for us? A land of new experiences, of new obstacles and conquests, of fruitfulness and abundance - even though when we first came here it seemed to be no more than a barren wilderness that we were destined to perish in.

'Personally squeaking, I can look back with great fondness on the cheese emporium that we discovered a year after we settled down here. I must admit that I found the change of diet particularly difficult after the exquisite cheese of England, but I'm now quite content to down as much as I can lay my paws on - though I still find the red rind on that Edam a bit chewy.

'And haven't we all enjoyed the weekly hide-and-seek tournament in the holes of the Gorgonzola? These are all things that we would never have discovered or experienced if we'd stayed within the confines of safety in our native land.

'I can also remember our first holiday adventure in Amsterdam when we discovered that new windmill. Do you remember?'

The hamsters nodded enthusiastically, some squeaked with laughter as the memories flooded back.

'The fun we had joy riding on the sails! I don't think the owner ever did realize why the sails kept going round even when there was no wind. And, though they mistook us for a bunch of mice, it was quite an honour to have a song written about us. Now let me see, how did it go?'

Quickly, the hamsters folded their ears close to their head in order to drown out the sound. If he was notorious for his long speeches, he was infamous for his uncanny talent of covering all the major musical keys in one song.

The hamsters applauded sympathetically - one young hamster shouted, 'Encore!' but he was soon silenced, his parents deciding that it was about time he went for his midnight nap. The leader continued his discourse:

'Ah yes, what memories!' He paused for a moment as he allowed his mind to return to the reason for his address. 'But all these adventures came about because we decided to throw security away and migrate with the humans when they fled England. Let's not lose sight of the vision, fellow rodents, the vision that has brought us thus far. Shall we stay in the security of this town, or shall we step out once again into the excitement of pioneering a new hamster colony in an uncharted part of the Creator's universe?'

From everywhere in the packed cabbage crate came the unanimous response, with cheers and loud shouts of approval, to leave behind the comforts and safety of their surroundings and sail, stowed away in the humans' luggage, in search of a new life, a new experience, a new adventure.

II

'Brethren!'

A large grey human stood to his feet at one end of a packed room, slightly elevated above the others by a small wooden box obtained from the local grocer and used as a rostrum.

It was to be the last meeting of the community before they departed from Leyden, their adopted Dutch town for the past twelve years, bound for the uncertainties of a life in the new world.

The hamsters were also there in force, under the floorboards. With ears pressed tightly against the timbers above them, they listened intently to every whisper, every murmur that would tell them when these pilgrims were to leave.

Plans had been well underway for the past twelve weeks ever since they'd first heard the humans' decision to leave for distant shores. Any food that would survive the journey was stored in secret locations throughout the house called 'The Green Gate,' the house in which they now met, while eating had been kept to a minimum to preserve as much as possible.

It was vital that the hamsters learnt the exact date of the departure as soon as they could in order to give themselves sufficient time to store their hoard in the humans' possessions.

Few thought it would be easy, many thought it impossible - but all waited for the final day of departure to be fixed.

'Brethren.' Brewster spoke slowly and deliberately, articulating his words so that all would understand.

'All of us here have already settled it in our minds to leave this good and pleasant city of Leyden, knowing that we're pilgrims on this earth yet not looking to earthly things. Rather, we've lifted up our eyes to the heavens, our true country, and quieted our spirits before the Lord to search for another earthly land where His name is not yet known.

'Brethren...friends. The Speedwell, which we bought and fitted out here in Holland, sails in three days from Delfshaven, a port twelve miles away from us, bound for Southampton where we shall meet with our second ship, the Mayflower.'

The hamsters squeaked excitedly - all these weeks of hard work were finally to be concluded in such a short space of time.

Then they grew quiet, not just to hear the conclusion of the speech, but because they realized that it left them so little time to stowaway.

Brewster continued. 'Two days, brethren, two days - that's all we have before we must leave. Pack your belongings, settle your business, for in two days we leave - in three we must pass over the waters into the land of promise....'

'No!' squeaked one hamster, 'we haven't enough time!'

'Sssshh!' another rebuked him. 'Listen 'til he's finished - there might be a way yet!'

And sure enough there was.

'I propose,' continued Brewster, 'that we take the Leyden printing press. We all know that, along with myself, it has had to go into hiding but what benefit it will be to us in the new world to print tracts and leaflets for the communities already there.'

The hamsters shrieked at the top of their voices, several of the humans looked down at their shoes wondering why the leather had squeaked when they hadn't moved their feet. Let me explain why they were so ecstatic - you see, ever since the printing press had been stashed away for fear of confiscation, the hamsters had used it as a nesting compartment. There was ample storage space still unused in which they could store their hoard of dry food for the journey.

Their joy turned to silence when a human at the front of the room stood to his feet and spoke.

'Brother, I cannot agree with you. There will be no need for a printing press in America - besides, we know that the Speedwell is only a sixty tonner and it'll be cramped enough as it is without the press. No, brothers,' he turned and faced the assembly, 'I propose that we leave it here for the remainder of the community to use.'

Around the room came noises of both assent and dissent.

Brewster quieted them down.

'Let's discuss this matter, brothers, and make a decision.'

The assembly spoke one by one, each respecting the other's viewpoint but, as the discussion continued, it was obvious that the majority of those present were not in favour of taking the press.

'Up, hamsters, and to work!' one leading hamster squeaked defiantly, knowing that in the next few moments the fate of their journey hung in the balance. They scurried to one corner of the room where a two inch hole was located, allowing access to the meeting above. Scrambling upwards they rushed underneath each chair where there was a human, watching the movement of the people's feet, ready to pounce.

So entranced in the discussion were the pilgrims, that it was relatively easy for them to take up their positions. The debate grew to a close, Brewster looking around the assembly and calling upon them to reach a decision - 'All those in favour of taking the printing press, say "Aye."'

The hamsters pounced onto the ankles of the humans, biting the skin with their sharp teeth. William Brewster heard an enthusiastic, almost deafening, affirmation: 'Aye!'

As a matter of fact, there were more 'Ows' than 'Ayes,' but when it came to the 'All those against say "Nay,"' the humans who'd let out a scream of pain on the first proposal felt it unwise to vote, lest the person sitting next to them think that they'd voted twice.

There was a short silence.

'Unanimous, then, brethren.' Brewster breathed a sigh of relief. 'We take the printing press.'

He folded up his notes and pushed them into his inside pocket, concluding the meeting with, 'We leave in two days, brethren - and in three we sail!'[1]

III

Over six weeks had passed since the pilgrim hamsters had set sail for America. In all, it had been comparatively uneventful as far as they

---

[1] Repeatedly, throughout this section, George has followed a hamscript that scholars believe is less reliable than older hamscripts, discovered at the turn of the century. However, this story is well attested by a reliable oral tradition handed down through successive generations from one of the pilgrim hamsters known to have sailed on the Mayflower.

Space does not permit us to go into higher criticism of the relevant text - that's the role of the scholars - but we would refer the interested reader's attention to a booklet 'Hamsterglyphic scroll fragments: A critique and index of discovered hamscripts' by the late Professor Graham Seedchewer. As far as we're aware, the publication is still available through most hamsters at your local pet shops.

were concerned, even though the humans had seemed to be thwarted by one dilemma after another.

The main problem had been the Speedwell, the ship that had taken them from the Dutch mainland to Southampton. Shortly after leaving the British port, the hull had sprung a leak and the captain, fearing that he might lose the ship in the rough voyage to the new world, put into Dartmouth for repairs. All seemed well until they put out to sea once more, this time having to return to port at Plymouth when, once again, the Speedwell was filling with water faster than they could bail it out.

The final decision was made, most reluctantly, to return the Speedwell to London with eighteen of the passengers that had grown too fearful of the Atlantic crossing that lay ahead of them.

The Mayflower, already overcrowded, took the additional passengers on board, which increased their number to one hundred and two (excluding the crew), the printing press also being transferred from the Speedwell shortly before the Mayflower sailed for America on Wednesday 6th September 1620.

The hamsters had hardly stirred from the safety of the press throughout that six weeks, being content to hide in the safety of their refuge in semi-hibernation so as to consume as little food as possible.

But, three weeks into the voyage, the storm hit - the wind whistled a howling gale through the rigging while the Mayflower dipped and dived, rolled back and forth, in the turbulent mid-Atlantic waters. The hamsters awoke with a bump as the printing press slid forward, stopping as it crashed into the side of the ship.

Their stomachs churned within them - it was like having the full force of the raging ocean trying to break out of the confines of their body. Throwing caution to the wind, they scampered out of the hole that led into the ship's hold and fled above deck, leaning over the side to discharge their heavy burden into the sea.

Fortunately, no human saw them - indeed, no human could have seen them, for they too were hanging over the side of the Mayflower heaving with all their might in time with the rhythmic swells of the waters.

'Below deck!' Captain Jones shouted as another breaker crashed into the starboard. 'Don't stay above if you value your lives. Get below!'

Slipping and sliding on the watery deck, hamster and human descended into the hold, both equally oblivious to the other's presence through the nausea that welled up within.

With the passage of time, the storm grew fiercer, though many of the passengers learnt to cope with the seasickness - the hamsters also coped, snuggling into soft bedding that cushioned the impact of each successive wave as it hammered the sides of the ship.

Then disaster struck.

The hamsters learnt of it when the humans began running toward midships, shouting instruction to one another in panic.

'Lift it up! Lift it up!' screamed one.

'I can't!' was the reply. 'It's too heavy, we'll never be able to repair it.'

The hamsters, realizing that this was a major threat to the journey, rushed out of the printing press, climbing up the side onto the top to look at the cause of the panic.

One by one, they saw what they didn't want to see - one of the main beams in the midships that lay above them from starboard to port was bowed under the pressure of the waves beating against the sides, cracked downwards, with water pouring in from the collapsed deck above.

'No!' squeaked one hamster. 'We're doomed! A few more waves and the ship will be smashed to pieces!'

Just then, Captain Jones with several of his crew rushed down the water-sodden steps to inspect the damage.

'No good,' he said as his men saw that despite their valiant efforts to support the beam, the crack was widening with each successive wave.

'We must turn out of the storm and back to England - else the sea will be our grave!'

The pilgrims' hearts sank. Could they have come this far only to be frustrated in their plans to find a new land? The hamsters forgot all about their seasickness and stared through empty eyes at the disaster that lay before them.

Then, a leading hamster by the name of Hamslow spoke excitedly. 'Fellow rodents,' he squeaked, 'follow me, I have a plan. Believe me, I have a plan!'

And, with that, he darted into the printing press, the other hamsters following him, wondering just what this 'plan' was.

The printing ink was sticky and slimy; wherever the hamsters walked they left behind black paw prints. They had to be careful, too, not to groom themselves if they got an itch, for they propelled black droplets all over the place.

'Perfect!' squeaked Hamslow. 'You even *look* like rats!'

If the circumstances hadn't demanded such action, the other rodents would have taken it as a positive insult but, having smothered themselves all over with printing ink, they took it as encouragement.

'To work, hamsters!' Hamslow commanded and the community scurried out of the press toward the cracked main beam where humans were fighting a losing battle as it grew ever weaker.

As the hamsters approached, they filled their lungs with breath and simultaneously let out the best impression of a rat they could, jumping onto the humans' legs and sinking their jaws into their flesh.

'Yow!' came the response - now the hamsters had their attention. Each human looked down at the rat-like object that had fixed itself to them.

'Rats! Rats!' In blind panic they let go of the beam. 'The plague! We'll all die of plague! Kill them!'

The hamsters fled for their lives across the deck in a direct route toward the printing press. Their attack had had the desired effect - the humans, fearing the presence of rats aboard the vessel, had momentarily forgotten the danger that could send them to a watery grave and were chasing the rodents frantically in order to protect their wives and children from plague and disease.

Hamslow led the hamsters over the printing press, stopping a moment on the top plate before disappearing the other side, out of sight of the humans, and into the hole that was their nest.

The humans came to an abrupt halt at the printer, not realizing where the rats had gone. They stood round, searching the wooden floor for holes, looking intently at the press but failing to see any entrance to the machinery within.

Suddenly, one shouted, 'The press! The press! That's it!' which took the other humans totally by surprise. They looked at him as if the pressures of the voyage had caused him to lose his fight for reality.

'Don't you see, brethren?' he looked round at them. 'We can use the press to support the beam!'

A few seconds later, they were pushing it underneath the crack and, using the metal winding pin on the side, elevated the printing plate so that it screwed the bowed beam into a horizontal position. They'd forgotten all about the rats - they never did remember.

But if they'd been listening very carefully, from within the press they would have heard the hamsters shrieking with delight and congratulating Hamslow on his brilliant plan that had not only saved their lives but had ensured their passage to the new world.

IV

November 9th 1620.

'Land ahoy!'

The hamsters raced above deck and climbed the central mast, coming to a halt in a row across the top of the mainsail. The tree-lined coast of America lay before them - none of them could think of a sight that had caused them so much joy throughout their entire lives.

'We've made it!' one whispered as he rubbed his eyes to make sure it wasn't an illusion. 'Our adventure is complete!'

'Not so,' another hamster squeaked excitedly. 'The real adventure is just beginning!'

V

There are a couple of truths that are so important for you humans to grasp as you seek to walk in step with the Creator.

Firstly, the hamsters were concerned to forget the past triumphs of their crossing to Holland and all their experiences in that land. Rather, they desired to press on to achieve more victories, more conquests, more adventure. Relying on the past would not have given them any future and would have made their present seem pretty boring, even totally pointless. With no objectives they couldn't have achieved anything worthwhile.

So, too, whatever your experience of the Creator has been in the past, it's only a launching pad to step out into a new experience of Him in the present and future. If you live at the same level, you never climb - if you endeavour to climb the heights in the Creator, you'll find that you conquer mountains in His name, even though the going will get tough!

Press on, then, my friends - ever forward, ever onward, ever upward.

Secondly, the humans found out about the Creator's provision in the storm. Had they left the printing press behind in Leyden, their voyage wouldn't have ended with the sighting of the new world - it could have finished in disaster at the bottom of the ocean!

Even before they needed the press, He was working situations together so that when the time came, help was close at hand. His prevision of their dilemma meant that His provision was sufficient when the beam cracked.

So, don't be afraid when you find yourself in the storms of life - not only has He foreseen the events, He's also provided for you in them so that you won't sink without trace. He always provides a way to overcome the troubles of your experience.

HAMSTER IN THE LION'S DEN

Arlev had not intended to fall thirty feet through a vertical shaft into a den of lions - it had been a complete accident and one which he now deeply regretted.

The one positive aspect of this fateful fall was that it had taken place at night when hamsters are hyperactive and lions hyperdrowsy. And, even though he'd landed on the soft mane of an adult male, it had hardly stirred, Arlev fleeing into a corner away from the pride that nestled together in the centre of the floor.

Then began the fruitless long search for a way out - the pit was so constructed as to make a vertical ascent impossible and the walls were so structured from hard-baked Babylonian clay with bedrock behind that a lateral burrowing route was destined to fail. Arlev tried every trick he knew to escape but, as the sun began to rise bringing light once more into the pit, he found a convenient hole, hiding away from the lions as they woke from sleep.

By the following evening, hunger controlled his actions. When the cats had finally curled up together for the night's passage, he began sniffing around for food. Located in one corner of the den was stepped brickwork that led onto ridges that ran the entire length of the wall.

Arlev hopped up, running along each ledge and finding mosses and lichens that had taken over the ridges, a yard or so above the floor, directly under the shaft through which he'd fallen. Having eaten his fill, he pouched enough food for the remaining night and the following day, hurrying back to the hole in the wall that represented his nest.

For bedding he used lion hair. While they were asleep he set to work on the manes, gnawing large tufts of soft fur with his sharp teeth, carrying them back to make a well-padded and cosy nest.

This continued for many weeks - maybe even months - Arlev lost count of the days. Each night he'd wait until all was quiet with the lions before collecting as much greenery as he could, adding to his bedding more fur and then, with the rest of the time, searching frantically for a way out.

Arlev knew that the meagre supply of greenery would die off in the winter months, so he continued tirelessly looking for even half a chance that could release him from what he knew would prove to be his grave if he didn't escape before its onset.

One night, when the full moon cast its grey light down the shaft, illuminating the den with contrasts of black and white, Arlev came to an abrupt halt as he paced his way along the brickwork ledge that led to the greenery.

It was darker than normal - someone had rolled a large rock over the opening above, which only allowed light in through the small cracks where the boulder failed to make contact with the edge of the shaft.

Below him, the reason for his abrupt halt, he noticed a human form lying, as it appeared to him, asleep on the floor. His head rested on the mane of a lion, which was also sleeping, while his sandals were laid beside him, his feet supported by another cat that lay further away.

Arlev peered through the murky light of the pit, trying to see if this human was still breathing. You see, being the King of Babylon's lions' den, he often threw the kingdom's enemies to an early death into the jaws of the cats, kept hungry by the infrequent meals they received. To see a human still in one piece was amazing in itself, but for there to be one still alive seemed an impossibility.

He strained his eyes in the dim light but it was impossible for him to tell whether he was lifeless or not. Curiosity got the better of him and he descended onto the floor from the ledge, creeping quietly past first one lion, then another, coming to a halt by the human form.

Arlev counted his limbs - yes, they were all there.

Then placing his tiny paws onto the man's wrist, checked for a pulse. Yes! Yes! He was alive!

'But,' thought Arlev, 'perhaps he was knocked unconscious when he was thrown in here and the lions left him until morning.' So, carefully, he stepped over to his closed eyes and, raising an eyelid, checked for dilation of the pupils.

Arlev was shocked - this man was definitely alive and kicking, oblivious to the danger he was in. Just then, he jumped backwards in fear as the human rolled over in his sleep, punching the lion mane to try and make it more comfortable. The lion grunted its annoyance at being woken up, twitching its rear paw.

As he turned round to walk quietly back to his food source, he was aware that two big black eyes met his, wider apart than his own with a wet nose sniffing him over in contemplation of food.

Arlev froze to the spot, calling himself stupid for not being more careful in case another lion woke from sleep when his curiosity compelled him to see this miraculous sight.

The cat gave a fierce growl through tightly clenched teeth. It sounded pitiful - Arlev wanted to laugh but thought better of it as he saw his life flash before his eyes in that one instant.

The lion's mouth darted towards him, pushing him backwards once, twice, three times. The giant cat frantically pawed at its mouth, trying to force his bottom jaw to open to allow him to swallow the dainty morsel frozen with terror before him - but to no avail.

Then the truth dawned on Arlev - someone had superglued the lion's mouth shut!

'No!' he thought, 'that can't be - superglue won't be invented for another two and a half thousand years.'

At the back of his mind came a realization that burst through to his understanding - the human alive and well, the lion acting as a pillow and footrest, the mouth securely fastened - this could be none other than the hand of the Creator. Who else could do such a miraculous wonder?

But why?

Arlev didn't stop to ponder over this very long. Instead, he raced back to his nest and hid until the lion settled back to sleep. Then he returned to feed on the ever-decreasing supply of lichens and mosses that grew on the ledges underneath the shaft.

When the first rays of the sun found their way through the cracks at the top of the vertical shaft, Arlev was already back in his nest hole, positioned in such a way that he would be able to witness the events unfold when the human woke from his sleep.

Two lions were already pacing about the den, sniffing first in one corner, then another - stopping longer outside the hole that led to Arlev's nest than elsewhere.

The human woke as his headrest stood to its feet. He rubbed his eyes wearily, then yawned as he stretched himself to his full height, eventually dusting his robe down with his hands before looking towards the boulder that sealed him in.

He was an old man, with grey hair and a balding head - but when he stood to his feet his age seemed insignificant because of the air of authority that his presence commanded. His robes were the clothes of an official, a ruler of high standing in the service of the king but it wasn't that that gave him his authority - it was...it was...something else that you just sensed rather than being able to define it.

All Arlev knew was that it was there - its absence in other humans declared it more to him than its presence in this man did.

It was the kind of authority that didn't assert itself, didn't secure its own way, didn't overrule situations to gain an advantage. But it sought to give and in giving led into Truth, it wanted to bless and in blessing show others the Creator, it wanted to declare the One without whom there's nothing and, in so doing, deny oneself.

Arlev's thoughts were interrupted as footsteps above him grew louder, coming to a standstill as the rock was removed from the entrance hole.

'Daniel?!' The voice echoed down the shaft around the hard cold walls of the pit. Daniel looked upward from where he was standing, invisible to the people above.

'Daniel?! Has your God been able to save you from the lions?'

The voice spoke again but this time louder and with more urgency than before.

Daniel walked towards the shaft of light that blazed through the opening, taking his place to stand where the sunlight illuminated his face. Arlev watched the slow deliberate steps, waiting for the reply.

'King, may you live forever! My God has sent His angel to shut the lions' mouths because I'm blameless before both Him and you, O king. I have done nothing wrong.'

'Lower the ropes!' the king shouted to the servants standing by him, 'and get my servant out of there!'

In a split second, Arlev saw his chance to escape. Throwing caution to the wind, he darted out of his hole, racing as fast as his paws would carry him, dodging successive lion paws as they tried to pounce on the tiny meals-on-wheels that flitted past them.

One lion stood in his path directly in front of the human who was now reaching for the rope that was being gently lowered. It was now or never for Arlev. With the onset of winter the pit meant certain death - it was better to die now in a final blaze of glory than to allow the pangs of hunger to kill him slowly.

With a squeak of defiance he leapt high into the air, landing on the lion's nose and scurrying up onto its forehead, along its back, finally jumping from its hindquarters onto the hem of Daniel's garments as he ascended out through the hole.

He clung on with every ounce of strength that was left in his body, looking over his shoulder to see the lions give up their pursuit for fear of Daniel. In a few moments, Arlev was safe, his four paws on solid ground hidden under the human's garment for fear of the group that stood around.[2]

'I make a decree,' the king said, the court scribes rushing to the sovereign's side to record every word spoken. 'I make a decree that all men in my kingdom should fear the god of Daniel who is the Living god, reigning forever. He delivers and rescues His servants from all harm, saving His people even from the power of the lion.'

The king turned and began walking towards the palace. Daniel followed, the servants of the king surrounding them.

Arlev quickly dug a temporary hole in the soft earth, disappearing from sight until the entourage was well out of sight.

The Creator has a purpose for you, His people, when you go through life. By your experience, many will come to know the Lord - they will see Him at work on your behalf and turn to Him of their own accord to acknowledge that He alone is the living God.

Your reactions will be so much different than those around you because you know the Creator is on your side, that it will be impossible for them not to see Him at work. As David, one of the Righteous, wrote - 'God pulled me up from the pit of desolation, out of the clay bog.... Many will see this and fear and put their trust in Him.'

---

[2] *The translated lines from here to the end of the story are omitted by many ancient Hamscripts and in their place is the following:*

'He jumped onto Daniel's sandal, secured himself with his teeth and allowed himself to be carried a great distance away before disembarking onto green, luscious grass. As the crowd moved one way, he scurried off the other, finding a quick meal before settling into a small hole in the earth that served as a temporary nest the rest of that day.'

However, the manuscript used is well attested in other places with regard to historical accuracy and I have therefore used it though it is not the majority text.

THE GREAT ESCAPE

INTRODUCTION

I have included this translation of a poetic manuscript discovered recently in the Middle East. It illustrates what most experts term 'Hamscript Apocrypha' - that is, a hamscript that is not considered 'inspired' because of the lack of meaningful moral instruction that it gives to the reader.

I hope that everyone who reads this will be able to distinguish for themselves the difference between 'inspired' and 'uninspired' hamscripts should they ever come across them in future days.

THE POEM

In a cramped nest compartment on the decks of Noah's Ark
lived two hamsters called Jayne Mary and Paul Mark.
There had been too little time to take lessons and learn to swim
so righteous Noah had agreed to take them in.
The wind it howled, the rain it fell, 'til the earth was covered thick.
The Ark it reeled and rocked and rolled - and both hamsters felt seasick.

Now, when a hamster's feeling ill, when he has a cold or flu,
one thing that will help him rest is to find some wood to chew.
Even better - joy complete! - to take away his sorrow
he loves to dig into the earth and make a complex burrow.
Had they dwelt on the upper deck, no-one would have tried to stop them
but in the Ark's arrangement, Noah had put them on the bottom.

They scratched their way through gopher wood using their tiny claws,
Then used their sharp incisor teeth to open the hole still more.
Down and down the hamsters dug 'til they could no more be seen.
When Noah came that evening late he let out a deafening scream:
'They're gone! THEY'RE GONE!' he shouted loud. 'Where can those rodents be?'
A close inspection of the hole caused Noah's eyes to see.

Deep below on the outer planks, the hamsters were now at work.
Unless somehow he could stop their game soon water would fill the Ark,
And flood the ship, sink the boat - all hands would be drowned!
Noah thought how foolish he'd been to put them on the ground.
Then a plan came to his mind and he rushed upstairs to trace the whereabouts of that strange, grey beast that had a tail fixed to its face.

Soon, Noah had this animal standing in front of the hole.
Being careful not to stand on the mice and keeping well clear of the mole,
He tossed a peanut into the void, heard it clatter deep -
The animal, feeling hungry now, dropped its trunk to find the treat.
Meanwhile, Paul Mark sniffed the shell of the morsel that lay at his paws,
sinking his teeth with a crunch and crack, and grasping it firm with his claws.

The animal's trunk felt down the hole, searching around everywhere.
It fastened itself to the monkey nut shell, raised the hamster up in the air.
Jayne Mary looked over her shoulder and up, to the top of the cavity
She saw Paul Mark shooting up skyward to heaven, defying the known laws of gravity.
Noah rejoiced when he saw him appear, and threw one more nut down the breach.
The same thing occurred, Jayne Mary appeared, Noah's hands held one hamster each.

The journey saved, the Ark intact, he made them a safer nest.
Upon the top deck, beside the birds, is the place that he thought best.
He provided hay and straw and food - abundant wood to chew.
The hamsters enjoyed the rest of the trip, though the days were only few.
The moral of this story is that travel by ship can bring failure,
Especially when you're a golden hamster and you're digging for Australia.

THE FINAL BATTLE

Deep in the forests of Central England, where the tall oaks grew strong, unhindered by the advance of man; where the soft fronds covered the forest floor and young saplings fought for the light of day; here it was that a community of hamsters had settled, eking out an existence along with badger, hedgehog and fox.

But although the forest was unspoilt by man's conquest of the land, it wasn't that he'd failed to reach this remote woodland, which lay at least ten miles (the distance of an all-night jog for a hamster) from the nearest manmade track - the king's highway that joined north with south.

Twenty or so yards from the entrance to the community's underground labyrinth of burrow holes, storage wells and nest compartments was a large settlement of men, exiled away from their society because of their allegiance to the king.

That last statement may sound strange for, in the king's own land, one naturally assumes that allegiance to the sovereign would find them acceptance. But not so, for, far away, further than any hamster could ever conceive of in his mind, the king was fighting in a land that wasn't his own, having left his kingdom in the hands of men he'd trusted to act wisely but who were only concerned for selfish gain, exploitation of those under them and, if it were at all possible, to have the throne for themselves.

This meant, quite naturally, that to be allied with the absent king brought social rejection and persecution - even punishment and, ultimately, death. But, for the human settlement that lay hidden in the deep forests of Central England, it was worth remaining true to the king whom they knew to be the only one who had both the right to the Throne and the character with which to rule the kingdom in righteousness and with equity.

The hamster community was allied with the humans - this wasn't because they understood the political situation that I've briefly outlined, neither was it because they knew the king in question as being the only true king. Rather, they owed allegiance to them because of an incident that had occurred well over a year ago in another part of the forest....

It was late spring when the addition of many young hungry mouths to feed made searching for and finding food even more arduous than normal.

When a hamster came bouncing into the community's hideout late one night squeaking loudly, 'Seed! Seed! I've found tons and tons of seed!' the entire community decided that, even though the first rays of morning were dispelling the darkness, it was worth taking the risk to collect as much as they could before full daylight came and the diurnal animals scoffed the lot.

But that was their first mistake.

Their second was to make another trip after their first due to the enormous quantity of seed that lay hidden near a small young oak. While the hamsters busied themselves pouching as much as they were able, the fresh morning breeze carried their scent swiftly through the forest to where a she-wolf stirred with hunger with her four cubs nestling into her side for security and protection.

Her nose awoke her instincts to hunt and, following the strong smell, she stalked silently to where the hamsters, backs turned on the danger, were cramming their pouches to the full.

A couple of feet away the wolf bared her sharp, carnivorous teeth and growled deeply, gurgling with threat at the rodents who froze to the spot with fear. Slowly, deliberately, they turned their heads to face the dark-haired skull with blood in its eyes and saliva dripping from its mouth.

As the she-wolf moved in for the kill, they tried to run but their feet wouldn't comply.

The growling, however, had woken a small band of men who, having acquired an array of provisions for the main camp deeper in the forest, had failed to make it back there before sundown.

When they opened their eyes, all they saw was a wolf, with its eyes shining in the early light, threatening them to abandon the food that lay beside the oak.

This was more than they'd accept - wolf or no wolf, they weren't going to give up the provisions that they'd worked so hard to get for their friends-in-arms.

They jumped to their feet, reaching inside tunics for hidden daggers - the wolf, taken totally by surprise, turned its tail and ran, the hamsters jumping up and down in triumph, squeaking with delight - then fled for the sanctuary of their underground complex.

Having discussed the incident, they quite wrongly decided that these humans were on the side of all rodents (apart from rats, of course - no-one in their right mind would be on the side of rats) and, beginning at the oak the following night, they followed their scent to where the main camp hid from the false king and his men.

It was here, as I've already said, that they made a new underground sanctuary.

Of course, it was also an ideal spot both for food and protection. For food, they removed all the scraps that were discarded in the camp, feeding bountifully from their human allies.

As for protection, they never saw another predator again - every woodland creature feared the humans and their way of living so they stayed a great distance away.

As a return for the human's kindness, as it had appeared to them, they organised night watch patrols. Even though the humans stood guard throughout the dark hours on the edge of the camp, at least two hamsters every night penetrated the forest, patrolling a radius of about two hundred yards from the outer perimeter.

No attack ever came but at least they remained satisfied that they'd repaid their debt to the humans' kindness.

One night, as the hamsters swarmed the camp to collect food, a candle continued to burn at the entrance to one of the shelters, providing light enough for a handful of men to sit discussing their necessary response to a piece of information received a short while ago from a messenger.

The humans had done this before, but the seriousness of their conversation brought the hamsters closer to listen, overhearing the speech as they huddled together in the entrance to keep warm.

'I say we stay in the forest!'

'No, no. We must fight, you don't understand the position! The king is returning to take the throne that's rightfully his - he won't delay to cross the Channel now that he's established his victory, but sail for these shores at the earliest possible date. That false king, John, must be deposed - we must oppose his rule, NOW!'

With that word he brought his fist down onto the rickety table beside him. 'That means we attack the castle where he's holding out against the inevitable outcome when Richard lands.'

'But why not leave him there? Can't do any harm locked away in his own castle!'

'Even now, his allies journey from the north to strengthen his hand against the king's return - if we get him now before he has time to march south, we remove any possible opposition to Richard taking his rightful place on England's throne!'

There was a short pause. They all knew that it was perfectly logical, superb strategy - it was just that they knew the castle where John was holding out, waiting for reinforcements from the north. Impregnable it had been built, impregnable it had remained - with storehouses sufficiently large to maintain a secure castle during a year's siege.

That was the problem - the armies would be here in days, Richard in who knows how long - maybe he'd even now landed. They had to strike immediately, clinically, and remove the head of the opposition - king John.

'Aye, Robin - master tactician as always!'

'Tomorrow, then, we move out - friends, in one way or another this is going to be the final battle.'

The hamsters withdrew to the outskirts of the camp.

'The humans leave!' one squeaked.

'What are we to do?' said another. 'Our prosperity is tied up in theirs!'

The rodents glanced at each other, coming to the same conclusion without a squonk being squeaked.

'We leave with the humans!' one finally spoke, putting into words what they knew to be the right course of action. 'We have until tomorrow morning then, fellow rodents, to move all our store of food and find places to stowaway in the band's luggage.'

The castle walls glowed amber and the moat water glistened as the shallow rays of the sun's first light illuminated the earth.

Robin and his men crouched together close to the water's edge behind a densely leafed bush that provided enough cover for them not to be noticed by the sentries patrolling high up on the battlements. The one entrance to the castle, the drawbridge that spanned the moat, was raised vertical preventing any access within. John had evidently decided that the safest course was to sit tight until the armies arrived from the north - and if Robin had been in that position, he would have adopted the same policy. The band of outlaws watched as a cart full of wares was shouted at to return on its journey without being allowed to trade within the castle walls. There was certainly no way that the drawbridge was going to be lowered in the near future for anyone or anything.

Robin knew that, with the few men he had, an all-out frontal attack would prove disastrous - they'd barely reach the other side of the moat before their numbers would be decimated. Their only chance was to hope that somehow, within the next day or night, the drawbridge would have to be lowered.

But while they waited, Robin wanted to let John know he was there, in one last defiant gesture against his rule. He removed a prepared arrow from his quiver, a rolled parchment being securely fastened to it by means of a red ribbon, and aimed it high into the air to clear the battlements.

As Robin let go of the string, propelling the arrow high on its intended course, Jozah the hamster felt the g-force on his nose as he flew, wrapped tightly within the scroll, over the battlements, landing in the courtyard within the walls.

On impact, he scurried away to a safe hideaway, nursing a headache from his crash landing. Now the future of Robin's attack on the castle lay in his paws - or should I say teeth?

Having no time to rest, he darted across the courtyard, keeping in the shadows all the time, using the curiosity of the landed arrow as a diversion. It was fortunate indeed that it was still early in the day when the sun cast its long shadow over much of the courtyard and battlements.

A few yards from the drawbridge and its mechanism stood a large mob of soldiers, talking about the coming battle between their lord and the king. Jozah stopped in his tracks - this was an unexpected problem.

He stood perfectly still in the shadows, surveying the scene with intense concentration.

Perhaps if he could create a diversion? No - if the arrow hadn't caused them to move, little else would.

Or maybe he could run past them in the hope that they wouldn't see? Fat chance!

There again, he could always....

'Yes!' squeaked Jozah. 'That's it! That's my chance!'

He darted through an open doorway that led into a room piled high with oddments, clambering up onto an old sack leaning against an upturned barrel that he continued climbing. Once on top, an old curtain provided a bridge across the gap between the barrel and a wooden wall shelf that he paced carefully along, making sure that he didn't knock off any of the utensils. From the far end it was a simple step onto the window ledge that gave him a good view of the drawbridge mechanism.

Now the tricky bit.

'My lords, ladies and gentlemen,' his imagination working overtime, 'Jozah the hamster will now leap two feet through the air - from a standing position, no less - and land, without any help or assistance, on the drawbridge rope. This feat, ladies and gentlemen, will be performed using no safety net.'

He could hear the drum roll in his head as he crouched, aimed his body and...SPRANG!

The imaginary crowd burst into spontaneous applause. Jozah climbed furiously up the rope, out of view of the sentries and came to rest at a pulley high above that was out of view from below.

He groomed himself briefly before setting his teeth to work, gnawing the rope. The immense tension helped him chew through the two inches - nevertheless, it took him most of the morning to reach a point where a few more bites would divide the rope and send the drawbridge crashing down to provide access for Robin and his men.

Jozah ran along the rope until he reached the top of the drawbridge, peering out over the top to see what was going on outside - there, out of bowshot of the castle walls, Robin and his men knelt before the Lionheart. The king had returned!

'What impeccable timing,' thought Jozah. 'I wonder who wrote the ending to this one?'

He darted back along to the rope pulley, sinking his teeth firmly into a few of the remaining strands and ripping them apart as if they were tissue paper. Jozah jumped clear as the tension ripped the last chord apart, sending the drawbridge crashing down for the royal entry of the king.

The Lionheart, seated on his white steed, turned to face the open gate and charged into the fray, leading his army into the final battle.

The king had returned.

The kingdom was secure.

And nothing could rob the king of his right to rule.

As you know, I always like to explain these stories after I've compiled them from the extant Hamscripts.[3]

However, Lee had a word with me about this one when he came downstairs the morning after I'd written it. He specifically requested that I didn't include an explanation as it has to do with the end times and felt it right that only those who had 'ears to hear' (whatever he meant by that) should hear.

And so, I bowed to his suggestion.

I quote Lee:

'Let him who has not grown tired in hearing, hear the words of this story.'

---

[3] *There are many differing legends in human folklore regarding the person of Robin Hood - not so in hamster history. Each story in the Hamscripts is remarkably accurate and has suffered little in transmission.*

The above story, therefore, is virtually fact even though human legend has failed to record such an incident.

SELECT BIBLIOGRAPHY

In so far as I have tried to present to the reader an easy-to-understand format with a bare minimum of technical notes, I thought it best to include a bibliography of books that I've referred to at the end of this work.

The following publications are all published by the Sunflower Seed Press and were all available at the time of going to print. I've included books that I found useful to my understanding of Hamscripts even though they may not bear a direct relevance to the story of the hamscript.

Chewden, Alexander - *Chewden's Concordance of the Inspired Texts.*

Daniken, Eric Ham - *Chariots of the Hamsters - a revised study of the place of rodents in Pharaoh's army.*

Kumber, Professor Q - *The Seven Wonders of the Ancient World (Chapter six - The hanging hamsters of Babylon).*

Leaf, Doctor Lett S - *Half-eaten Sunflower Seeds at Qumran - an archaeological investigation of hamster migration routes.*

Seedchewer, Professor Graham - *Hamsterglyphic Scroll Fragments - a critique and index of discovered hamscripts.*

Seedchewer, Professor Graham - *Hamscript Apocrypha - a definitive compilation of extant hamscripts.*

Stone, Madame Cherie - *The Fall of Rome - the relevance of hamster gnawing marks on the foundation columns.*

An English Hamster in Paris

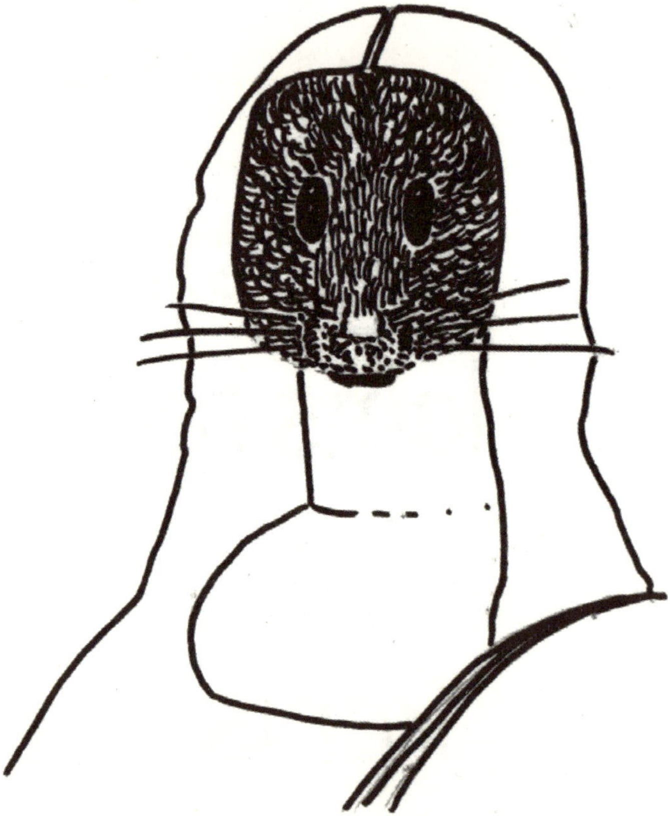

Detail from the "Mona Hamster"
Leonardo the Rodent
Courtesy of the Louvre, Paris

AN ENGLISH HAMSTER IN PARIS

Or
'Un hamster Anglais à Paris' -
an epic journey of one hamster in his masters' hand luggage

INTRODUCTION

O, for a thousand days in Paris!
But seven nights was all I had!

I have little to say except that, unlike my previous works ('The Hamster History of the World Volumes 1-3'), I have refrained from giving the reader the interpretation of my exploits.

Therefore, these are truly parabolic - stories with no meaning given, but certainly not stories without teaching. It seems that many would think for you by interpreting their own tales - but I'm sure that to all who are truly seeking the Creator's Kingdom as a living reality, these stories will teach them things that they need to hear.

ARRIVAL
MONDAY 20TH JULY 1992

As the patchwork green of England's cultivated fields changed into the murky blue of the Channel with numerous ships interweaving their routes on its surface, I thought back to that historic day in May when Lee, my owner and translator, had shared with me his desire to surprise Kath, his wife, with a holiday in Paris.

Even as they sat in their seats, looking down to the sea below them, Lee's mind glanced back to his friends in Sheffield who, at that very moment, were discovering that I wasn't in my cage as both they and Lee had supposed.

But, for the time being, he was happy to presume that my every need was being attended to by this family, even though I was many thousands of feet above ground, flying in the same plane, heading for the same destination, for a week full of adventure and excitement in the hitherto uncharted city (for me, at least) of Paris.

If only Lee had known the lengths I'd gone to....

Both my owners had been oblivious to the fact that I'd been secretly removing strands of their living room carpet that matched my summer coat.

When Lee cleaned my cage out, I got an albeit very brief chance to run about the floor, searching frantically for suitable material.

On one occasion I'd nearly been found out - that's the problem with my masters, they sneak up on you from behind and poke you in the stomach if they catch you doing anything that they deem to be 'damaging' - but I managed to divert their attention from the bald patch that had begun to appear beside the gas cupboard by gnawing a chunk out of their speaker wire.

And with their concentration switched to repairing the damage, I was able to get my teeth to work on a patch that would have been otherwise impossible to 'harvest.'

Having pouches always ensured that I was able to return my collection to the nest but, as the end of each week approached, I had to be prepared to pouch it at a moment's notice should Lee decide to remove that lovely smelly bedding and replace it with clean, hygienic new stuff that always smelt, for the first day or two, like nothing - neutral, boring and scentless.

All the while, Lee kept telling me about his plans and I'd continue to nod with approval, gleaning more and more information to be able to plan a way of escape at the right time, the right place so that, to everyone concerned, I'd be presumed asleep in my nest - until it would be too late to do anything about it.

Though the weeks passed slowly, eventually Wednesday 15th July dawned in the living room of my master's house.

Throughout the day, while they were both hard at work, I busied myself constructing a hamster decoy - a cunning little contraption that simulated a sleeping rodent being tossed to and fro when the cage was moved - as it would be that evening.

It was a fairly simple invention - using one of my plastic play balls that was peppered with large holes, I intertwined the strands of living room carpet so that the resulting tufts matched almost exactly my overall fur colour. This I then placed underneath the bedding in the nest, covering it with additional strands of tissue that obscured as much detail as possible from their sight.

Pouching enough food for my journey, I dived down the tubes into my ground floor compartment and settled myself under the large bundle of hay and field grass that Lee always puts there - I have no idea why he insists on filling that place with so many dead and dying plants, but, in this instance, it served my purpose well.

No sooner had I covered myself with camouflage, than Lee returned home, walked over to my cage and tapped on the nest compartment saying, 'George, I'm ho...ah, he's still asleep, I'd better not wake him...' and with that he went upstairs to pack.

Success!

But why was I hiding on the ground floor? You see, travelling over to my 'holiday kennel' meant that my cage had to be dismantled, but, to ensure that I didn't escape, I was always sealed in the top section. The ground floor, in which I'd secluded myself, had to be left roofless in the rear of the car - the car which was the first stage in the long line of transport to Paris!

So it was a fairly simple task to climb out and into the car, hiding under the rear seat until they came to the end of the preliminary journey.

The only negative aspect of being stowed away on board part of my cage that I wasn't supposed to be in was that it wasn't handled with any great care, Lee fairly dropping it into the car boot along with all the other pieces of equipment.

Yes, that jolt lived in the memory - as I thought about it once more, the plane bumped a landing onto the runway, jerking me out of the day dream and giving me the signal to remove myself from the inside of the spare toilet roll in the men's lavatory, to stowaway one final time in my owners' hand luggage.

Paris!

The dream was starting to become a reality....

THE LOUVRE
TUESDAY 21ST JULY 1992

Not many people realise that the celebrated sculptor and famous artist Michelangelo used to keep hamsters in a small, dilapidated shed in the back garden where he lived. In fact, had it not been for his great love for us rodents, he would never have come to successfully complete the painting of the Cistine Chapel in Rome.

But why am I telling you all this?

Well, today I visited two of the French museums located in the centre of Paris. One of them, called the Louvre (named after a type of window), was exhibiting, for a short period only, examples of Michelangelo's work.

I tried to get in to see the exhibition but all my attempts proved fruitless.

My final scheme, to disguise myself in the hair of one of the Parisienne art students, failed when the young woman bent over to pick up a one franc piece that had been dropped on the floor and I fell out, bouncing onto some cork tiles that were laid out in the auditorium. It could well have been a piece of modern art, but they looked like floor tiles to me - though I only had the briefest of glimpses as the lady began to panic, shouting, 'Une souris! Une souris! Au secours!'

A multitude of men ran to her aid while a multitude of women ran the other way.

'Je ne suis pas une souris!' I squeaked indignantly. 'Je suis un hamster!'

What a cheek, mistaking me for a mouse! That's the problem with the French, they can't tell the difference between certain kinds of animals - it's probably why they eat snails and frogs' legs, they mistake them for prawns and cheese snaps.

Anyway, my pleas were all to no avail - the men who'd dashed over to the woman's aid set about giving chase as I set off at lightning speed for the escalator and exit door. Fortunately, a loosely hanging chain gave me sufficient grip to be able to climb up onto the moving handrail, racing up its thirty-foot length and scattering women who'd been congregating at the apex like ten pins in a clean strike.

Landing on the entrance mat was not an enjoyable experience - even more so when I realised that the door that offered me a means of escape was closed. I looked behind and saw a gang of youths reaching the summit of the up escalator with incredible speed - in a matter of moments I would be cornered.

Turning back around, a pair of trainers appeared the other side of the door - funny, they looked familiar, but I hadn't got time to investigate more deeply than that. As soon as the door opened a fraction, I squeezed my body out through a crack and accidentally ran into the legs of my deliverer.

But picking myself up, I ran for the nearest drain cover, dived into its safety and watched with interest the commotion that my visit had caused. To my amazement, I now saw that my deliverer was none other than Lee, my master, who was closely followed by Kath, his wife. So, they too had decided to visit the Louvre!

Lee looked puzzled. 'Did you see that hamster?'

'Yes,' came the reply, 'but what's a hamster doing here?'

'What's more to the point,' Lee went on, 'what's a hamster that looks like George doing here?'

As he finished his words, the gaggle of messieurs fairly fell out the door, looking right and left, up and down, finally prodding Lee with their fingers and saying, 'Où est la souris? Où est la grande souris?'

Lee looked puzzled, he doesn't know much French. Kath knows more but even she looked perplexed. They flicked through the phrasebook hurriedly, while the men continued to shout the question at them.

Finally, they found the correct response. Lee pushed himself up to his full height and said, in the best French accent that he could put on, 'C'est dix heures: La train départ dans un demi heure.'

This seemed to answer their questions for they dispersed quickly, leaving both my owners to continue (or, rather, begin) their visit to the Louvre.

'That sorted their problem out.' Lee turned and spoke as he went through the door.

'Yes,' said Kath, 'that phrasebook is invaluable, I don't know what we'd do without it.'

I decided not to try and visit the human's Louvre again. Instead, I descended into the hamster counterpart where I learnt all about Michelangelo, the hamsters and of one rodent in particular who helped the great artist with the completion of the Cistine Chapel - the notorious Michael Hamstelo.

No-one is quite sure where Michael was born, but legend has it that he had fairly modest beginnings in a local pet shop that the famous painter used to frequent weekly in order to purchase additions to his already over-populated hamster collection.

Michael exhibited all the signs that he'd been especially gifted artistically - he would arrange the litter's sunflower seeds in geometric patterns, experiment with the sawdust that lay around the nest to create contrasts and shades of dark and light and, by making a paste from the drinking water and vitamin pellets, he was able to paint designs on the partition wall.

One day, when Michelangelo was passing by, he noticed Michael in the window as he pasted artistically away at a free patch on the sides of the cage. Intrigued by this phenomenon, he went in and peered over the rodent artist's shoulder, trying to make out the images that were being created on the make-do canvas in front of him. Of course, most hamster art is what you would describe either as 'surreal' or 'modern,' but this didn't put Michelangelo off - on the contrary, he'd been experimenting with these themes all that month and was amazed to discover that these very same concepts he'd been grappling with were being portrayed by this little furry object who hadn't yet noticed that he was being watched.

'Very good!' the human softly whispered, Michael freezing to the spot with paste in his hand ready to add to his work. 'I can see that you have much natural ability. What I want to do is to take you home with me and refine your obvious talent to make you a master such as I - I will hone every rough edge, and smooth every surface until I see my likeness reflected back in your artistry!'

Michael wasn't quite sure what all that meant. He was a little worried when he talked about 'honing every rough edge' for primarily he thought that the reference was to his tail - but he soon forgot that, as the artist went on to expand all the purpose that he saw for him. After a few minutes, he came to the end of his speech and Michael went over to give him a friendly introductory sniff.

Within a couple of hours, the artist had sat his new acquaintance down in front of an empty (unchewable) canvas, supplying him with brushes, paint and everything that he needed to produce the best he could.

From here on, Michelangelo was able to see the weaknesses that needed strengthening, the subtleties that needed assimilating, the strengths that needed softening - in short, he was enhancing what already was, bringing out of Michael what was already there, producing one of the world's great rodent artists who so perfectly painted in the same style as the master that, had you not known, you would've thought that they produced the same image, the same effect on canvas, painting after painting after painting.

It wasn't long before they travelled everywhere together - though, at that time, hamsters weren't accepted as being the intelligent animals that they are, and so Michael was forced to hide himself away amongst the artist's equipment while they journeyed - often days on end - to mansions where work awaited them.

From some specific time (though no-one is exactly sure from when) they both worked on the same canvasses, tossing ideas back and forth, correcting one another's mistakes and adapting concepts as they needed interpreting when different subjects were to be committed to canvas.

Unfortunately, the annals of man's history don't record the existence of Michael, but this is only due to the fact that, as I've already said, hamsters were not generally accepted in the society of that day and age. So Michael always had to remain hidden, out of sight, until the artist was alone with a subject that needed painting.

But let me tell you briefly about the painting of the Cistine Chapel - for, if it hadn't've been for Michelangelo's rodent friend, the ceiling would never have been completed.

It was Michelangelo's own fault that he'd got commissioned into painting this most famous of his works. He'd thought that the agreement had been to '...cover the inside of the Cistine Chapel kneeling...' due to the peculiar pronunciation of the man who'd been sent to him.

All that was needed, reasoned Michelangelo, was to etch some floral designs or the like around the edge of the skirting boards while kneeling on some padded mat or other.

But when he arrived to begin his work, the sheer horror of the agreement hit him like a pile of masonry for, there, in the middle of the chapel, was erected a monumental scaffolding stretching skyward until it almost reached the ceiling.

'Oh dear,' he whispered under his breath. 'What have I got myself into?'

For, you see, Michelangelo was terrified of heights - his whole body would begin to shake and tremble, rendering his artistic abilities useless.

One of the directors of the work walked over to greet him.

'You are the great Michelangelo?' he enquired. The artist nodded. 'We have put this scaffolding up for you to begin covering the inside of the Cistine Chapel ceiling. I expect that you want to begin work immediately, so...' he snapped his fingers as a workman ran over, '... Alfredo here will show you the way to the top.'

Michelangelo looked upward and his head began to spin. A voice from his work box whispered, 'Don't worry, I'll do the work - you direct me. I'm not scared of heights!'

The artist took courage. As the director turned to go away, he said, 'One request I have of you.'

The overseer stopped, listening intently. 'I will allow your workman to both take me up and bring me down each time I paint.'

Then he continued after a short pause, 'But I must insist that no-one, absolutely no-one, stays with me as I produce this masterpiece.'

'As you wish, sir,' and the director bowed courteously. 'Of course, of course! - an artist's temperament, I fully understand.'

Michael couldn't help thinking to himself, 'I bet you don't, mate, I bet you don't!'

And so began that great work of painting the Cistine Chapel ceiling. While Michelangelo lay flat on his back in much fear, Michael darted back and forth across the planks at the master's direction creating a masterpiece.

No-one knew, no-one ever found out - Michael would always dive back into the work box as soon as he heard the sound of the workman ascending the scaffolding either to bring the master down or refreshment up.

As I stood in the gallery of the hamster Louvre in Paris, now, I let out a contented squeak as I let my eyes settle on one Michael Hamstelo masterpiece after another - all paintings from the latter part of his life after the human master had died.

This hamster really was a genius!

My first experience of the tube was the previous day during the rush hour.

I descended to the main entry pipe and awaited a gap in the passing line of rodents travelling my way. The line of bustling hamsters seemed endless as they rushed with increasing speed (that part of the line was downhill) to their respective destinations. Eventually, after what seemed like a good ten minutes, three animals left the tube, providing me with enough space to dive on and start running frantically to catch up with the rodent in front.

No sooner had we gone a hundred metres, than the traffic in front came to a sudden and crushing halt. I hadn't seen it in time as I hurtled at full speed into the fur in front, the one behind running into me with such force that I was pushed under the body of the leader, jammed firmly into the floor of the pipe.

I extricated myself from the situation, rubbing my now throbbing nose.

Apparently, a hamster up ahead had dropped a pouched hazelnut and had stopped suddenly so that the rodent behind didn't have a chance to pick it up. The ensuing mangle of fur had been the end result.

I'd avoided using the tube again until this morning when, unfortunately, I was forced into it in order to get across the city to Montmartre.

This time, however, I waited for the rush hour to end - my journey went smoothly, apart from a near miss at one of the always busy interchanges just north of the Seine.

Exiting into brilliant sunshine in the Place du Tertre, I darted over to the rainwater pipe at the corner of the Rue Norvins, climbing up to the balcony on the second floor that doubled as 'Le Café de l'Hamsters Heureuse' during daylight hours when the human occupants of number twenty-one were hard at work in the city.

Ambling towards a make-do table overlooking the square, I pulled up a chair and surveyed the sight laid out before me.

The square was a hive of activity, swarming with Parisienne artists sketching tourists as they sat before them on rickety stools. Below was a train ride (or was it a fancy car?) slowly filling up with men and women who were anxious to take the weight off their feet for a few precious minutes. In the background, the cupola of Sacre Coeur dominated the skyline while, slightly to the right, was where my eyes would be fixed when afternoon rolled around - this was the street by which Lee had planned to come into the square.

But, for now, there was just the excitement of relaxation, soaking in the sun with a glass of sunflower oil at hand.

Monsieur Larousse, being the resident of flat thirty-two with his two masters and the proprietor of this establishment, approached to take my order.

'Bonjour, monsieur,' he said. 'C'est un beau jour.'

'Mais oui,' I replied. 'J'aurai un gras de le tournesol, s'il vous plait..'

'Merci, monsieur.' He turned and scampered away, returning in a few moments with a half-hazelnut full of yellow liquid that he placed beside me with a small serviette.

This was the life!

It was then that I noticed an old, old hamster staggering towards my table, tapping his walking stick repeatedly as he fought to keep balance. Even though the balcony, at that time, was empty apart from a group of rodents squeaking away behind me to my left, he edged his way over, pulled up a chair and sat down beside me, surveying the square below.

'Bonjour, monsieur,' I ventured, realising that if this elder was wanting to talk (as most old hamsters do) then I was about to run out of the little French I knew in about forty-five seconds.

'Bonjour, mon ami,' he replied. 'You are English, are you not?' He spoke in a clear, understandable accent.

'Why, yes. How did you know?'

'There are ways, there are ways!' he said, holding up both his paws. 'How are you enjoying the square today?'

'It's wonderful.' I faced to look back into the market place. 'It's busy and yet...peaceful. Warm, restful - I can't imagine anywhere I'd rather be.'

'If you had lived here during the Great war,' he almost whispered, 'you would not have been of the same opinion....' He stared blankly into thin air, his eyes full of memories. 'And it would have stayed that way if it hadn't been for the infamous Baron von Richtenhamster.'

'Baron who?' I questioned. 'That's a German name, isn't it?'

'Yes, it is - but he was part of the Resistance, fighting against the Rat occupation force that held this city during the war. They used to call him affectionately the Golden Baron - he was a golden hamster, you see....' He chuckled and rubbed both his eyes with his paws.

'Well, my friend, you have me intrigued. As I have time on my paws today, why don't you tell me about this hero?'

The old rodent looked at me wisely, then smiled.

'Yes, alright,' he said. 'I most definitely will....'

The black slime had inched its way across Europe, engulfing all that lay in its path. Young and old alike, it showed no mercy to everything that its dark talons gripped and squeezed, bringing hatred where there was once love and war where there had once been peace.

All that it acquired it sucked dry of whatever life it found and discarded the individuals like empty food wrappers in the gutter of its dominance.

It would be foolish to think that it had come from any particular geographic location, its origin is of old and its roots are embedded almost everywhere. Way back in the eons of time it first saw the light of day and its unfaltering ooze throughout the history of the world has spread with increasing rapidity wherever it finds adherents to its cause.

The hamsters knew it always when they saw the presence of the rats, those loathsome creatures that existed in darkness and who propagated its corruption with gleeful willingness.

But it was more than the rats' presence - rather, you always knew it was there by a certain absence, a certain indefinable emptiness that seemed so barren and limitless that to be enshrouded by its doctrine was to lose the little hope you had.

When the rats took the Place du Tertre, the absence fell over the square as the presence left. The hamsters shut their windows and bolted their doors against the oppression that began to dominate their community.

The black rats set up posts in every high place, every position from where they could see any movement, however slight, in the square below. Most of the army camped way below, waiting for the first sign of an open door that would spell the beginning of the destruction.

Yes, all the rats wanted to do was destroy - they were driven by that insatiable emptiness that forever wants to ruin whatever is good and right.

But there was one slight oversight in their plan - they hadn't realised that, even now, Baron von Richtenhamster and a handful of other rodents that had been thrust together in the confusion that had engulfed the square were plotting strategically to remove their loathsome presence.

After five days, they struck back with such force that it sent a shockwave reverberating throughout the whole of Ratdom, the likes of which has never again been experienced.

But it was cunning and full of wisdom.

You see, the Resistance knew that they didn't have the resources to overcome the rats single-handedly - one hamster would have had to have overcome maybe fifty or sixty war-seasoned soldiers and that was, to say the least, a total impossibility.

No, an all-out assault would have ended in disaster.

But Baron von Richtenhamster knew that a hamster cannot wrestle against the flesh and blood of rat and overcome in his own strength, rather he's to fight against those higher forces that take up strategic positions - those that were on the roof and which controlled whatever went on in the square below.

If you control the places above, you dictate your control and will into what goes on far below.

So, at a pre-arranged time, the members of the Resistance exited from their third-floor refuge - not out onto the square in full view of the rat occupation force, but at the rear of the building where no rat had thought to position look-outs.

Scaling the drainwater pipes (incidentally, my friend George, you will see a special plaque that has been set up in memory of their heroic exploit if you leave the café by the rear entrance), they took up their positions below the guttering that caught the rainwater from the roofs.

As the deadline neared, they removed the walnuts from their pouches awaiting the signal. At precisely twelve noon, the hamster who'd been left in the room opened up the window and gave a loud shout that echoed across the square.

The Resistance took up the cry, 'A walnut for the Baron!'

Defiantly, they lobbed the loaded walnuts at the strongholds and powers on the roofs and, as the shells landed, exploding their contents into a hundred tiny sharp pieces, they scampered onto the scaffolding where the rats had stored pile upon pile of ammunition for the destruction.

'NOW!' the Baron shouted and the Resistance opened fire into the square below with the seed rockets and grain grenades that had been intended for them.

The rats were thrown into confusion, running in circles, attacking each other - thinking that their comrades were the enemy.

Fleeing for their lives in a multiplicity of directions, the hamsters opened up their houses and gave chase, using anything that they found to paw to throw at their vanquished enemy - it really didn't matter how they fought from here on, the victory had already been won when the strongholds had been captured at the start of the conflict.

So much spoil was taken that, on three successive days, the hamsters were able to hold festive celebrations in the open square with great rejoicing and joy in their hearts.

Baron von Richtenhamster had delivered the square out of the rats' paws - and all because he knew that to possess the authority of the heavens is to rule over the events on earth....

'...and they never bothered us again,' he concluded.

'That's quite a story,' I said. 'It seems like you singled me out to tell it to.'

'Yes.' He smiled. 'Make sure you tell it to whomever you can. It's not the forces of the earth that are important, it's not worth fighting against them - but get the authorities that rule over them and the whole set up is cast down into destruction.'

I pondered over his words.

'Mmm, yes,' I said after a lengthy silence. 'That is worth remembering.'

'And applying,' he concluded.

As the clock at the far end of the square struck three o'clock, it woke me up to the fact that Lee and Kath were just entering the area and that, in a few moments, they would be passing underneath the drainpipe from which I would be able to jump into their bag.

I hastily exchanged my farewell with this wise, old hamster, descended hurriedly down the pipe and leapt through the air with unusual vigour as the shoulder strap hold-all went by....

'Hey!' said Lee, 'don't pull on the bag!'

'I didn't!' complained Kath, 'honest!'

Lee looked at her knowingly, but said no more as he brushed off the few strands of hair that he noticed had become attached to the side pocket.

'Strange colour hair,' he said. 'It reminds me of someone, but I can't think who....'

L'OPERA DE PARIS AND HAMDINI
THURSDAY 23RD JULY 1992

I had been asked both by the Daily Ham and the Sunflower Seed Press to interview the much loved actress and singer Mademoiselle Madeleine Duphare at the Opera de Paris. Although I originally declined the encouragements I received from the respective editors, I finally agreed to produce a feature length article for them both, provided that the interview didn't seriously interfere with my much needed break from the literary world.

I decided against taking the hamster Tube, waiting for my masters to visit the humans' Opera house under which the hamster equivalent thrived.

Today, then, was the day.

While they both slept that night, I smuggled myself into the side pocket of their bag and awaited the morning.

To be carried, unknowingly, through the centre of Paris was, necessarily, more risky - I would have to rely on the sounds and smells of each area to determine my exact whereabouts, hopefully exiting at the precise moment when I could descend rapidly down Lee's leg, through the entrance in the skirting board and so fulfil my commission.

The journey began well enough - the bump, bump, bump as they walked down the long flight of stairs from the bedroom, the smells of the supermarket as they selected their lunch time snack (I must admit that when they passed the cheese counter, I was sorely tempted to forget the interview and jump out), then more steps as they entered the world of the Metro.

The Underground was always easily distinguishable - the air was warmer, the sounds unique and the oily smell that hung in the air like thick clouds helped me to be able to relax for a brief time until they once again emerged into daylight.

I had presumed that my owners would go directly to the Opera house - this was my first mistake. The second was to interpret all the sounds I heard with the understanding of my previous belief that the next stop was where I needed to get off.

I had no idea, for I had not heard them speak about it, that instead of heading for the Opera de Paris, they were locating a Bureau de Change in order to convert some traveller's cheques into francs.

So, the first door that was opened I naturally presumed was access to the entrance lobby. When I heard the rustle of notes and the chink of coins, I decided that Lee was paying the entrance fee - the rather lengthy delay and the muffled speaking I put down to Lee's rather poor grasp of the French language and the ensuing confusion that he would have caused.

I primed myself ready at the catch on the side pocket, waiting for one final door to open - this would be (or so I thought) the door behind which I could squeeze my way through the skirting board and descend into the underground labyrinth of the alternative hamster Opera house.

As the click of the lock echoed in my ears, I opened the flap without a moment's hesitation and half-exited from my hideaway when, all of a sudden, the thought struck me that this wasn't the Opera at all!

The bag, which hangs by a strap from Lee's shoulder, dangles at his side, so both my owners failed to see me pull myself upwards into the neon light of the Bureau de Change - but a French lady, standing the other side of the door, saw it all and, frightened by the rapidity of both my appearance and disappearance, lifted her hands high into the air and ran down the street, shouting madly, 'Une souris! Une souris! Au secours!'

Honestly! If it hadn't been for the necessity for me to remain in hiding, I would have told that woman off there and then! A mouse, indeed!

Lee looked at Kath, having thought that he'd been the cause of the commotion - after all, the lady had been looking in his direction. 'Aren't the French strange?' he said.

'Yes,' Kath replied, 'but isn't it a good job that I didn't react like that when I first saw you?'

'I shall treat that remark with the contempt it deserves.'

'Whoops!' I thought. 'That almost blew it!'

I listened more carefully from then on, eventually squeezing my way through the skirting board entrance in to the alternative hamster Opera house.

'Squeee ueee ek gnaw
ee e eee eq e aal gnaw
Shre e a gn a
ea a a a aw
eeeek eeeek
a a squeak!'

Mademoiselle Madeline Duphare finished the rehearsal of the aria for the evening's performance as I squeaked enthusiastically.

She was a small, dainty hamster with striking features, not least of which was her slender nose that softened the beautiful hues in her immaculate fur. She gracefully glided down from the stage as I rose to meet her.

'Mademoiselle Duphare,' I began, 'I am deeply honoured,' and I tenderly licked the back of her left paw (it was an old French greeting, I don't know how it originated).

'Honoured?' she responded. 'Indeed, Monsieur George, the honour is all mine. I am delighted to meet someone as talented as you are!'

'Me?' I said - I was genuinely surprised. 'What do you know about me?'

'But it is your Hamster Histories.' She smiled warmly. 'They are all the talk of Paris!'

So the reports weren't just rumour! My articles really were being read amongst the hamster community.

But instead of letting my mind stray emptily onto the happiness that this had sparked within me, I remembered my commission and changed the subject.

'I take it that you received the correspondence about the interview?'

'But of course - I have been looking forward to it. It will be the first interview I will have done since I spoke about my experiences with the Hamster of the Opera.'

That last statement took me by surprise. I hadn't seen the article but I'd heard the reports about that rodent.

'So you actually knew the Hamster of the Opera?' I squeaked with awe.

'Mais oui,' she said proudly, 'but I was very young then....'

In the infancy of what is now known as the Rodent Theatrical Company, both musical and literary compositions were combined to provide the audience with a full evening's entertainment, rather than concentrate on a specific art form. Of course, the variety of works now produced on the world scene has forced the producers to specialise in a particular field - the Opera house, for instance, has developed into one of the world's greatest stages for classical singing. But in the early days it wasn't so specialised.

The great Ham-actors of those days had to be very much all round entertainers. The evening would see them singing, playing, acting - telling jokes, doing acrobatics and even, when times got hard, selling popcorn and seed drinks during the interval.

It's hardly surprising that the audience would get confused, for they'd see one actor take a multiplicity of roles throughout the evening and found it difficult to forget the character portrayal of just a few moments ago, while a new image unfolded before their eyes in the shape and form of the same rodent.

Therefore, in the early days, the Ham-actors would attach masks to themselves as they went about performing, keeping one easily distinguishable cover for each character that they portrayed. Some of the masks were extremely elaborate, being made of such things as gold tinsel that reflected the bright stage lights out into the audience - various good examples are still to be seen in the archives of the alternative hamster Opera house.

In those days there was a one man travelling show called 'The Shepherd' that toured all over the world. It had already received such rave reports from every city where it had visited that, when at last it arrived in the city of Paris, the queues for advance tickets continued both night and day for many weeks before the opening performance.

But was it worth it? Let me quote you a couple of the newspaper clippings from that time:

'...Magnificent...The shepherd led the audience through a complete repertoire of all his marvellous ability so that all they had to do was enjoy the programme...a show without equal...' (translated from 'L'hamster de Paris').

'...The one man show to end all!...What unequalled entertainment!... He so stole the hearts of the audience with his vast array of different masks that they come back evening after evening and are totally dependent upon him for everything...' (a clipping - source unknown).

A show that could go on forever? A masterpiece of theatrical entertainment?

The Hamster of the Opera was not happy - he'd been in the entertainment business for a number of years, growing in perception as the days rolled by. He could smell a successful performer a mile off and, in his time, had brought a multitude of shows to the Opera house that had been instant successes.

But now, as he watched intently another virtuoso performance of the shepherd, his stomach was telling him that there was something very seriously amiss.

'Is it jealousy?' he asked himself. 'Am I resentful because I wasn't the one who discovered him?'

But after examining all his motives, he knew that deep within the gut feeling remained - there was something more to this shepherd than met the eye.

His efforts to track him down were all to no avail. It was as if he appeared only moments before he was due to be on and then, seconds after he'd finished his third or fourth encore, he'd disappear so completely that not even his scent could be traced.

But, after two weeks of unsuccessful attempts, the shepherd agreed to be interviewed by the Parisienne press and the Hamster of the Opera, being such a celebrity, was invited to attend.

As the clock slowly ticked the seconds away until three o'clock (the time set by the shepherd), he ran through what he knew he had to do - boy, oh boy, he'd just better be right about this or else...or else....

'Mmmm,' he mused quietly to himself as the full implication hit him again, leaving an emptiness and pain inside.

The clock chimed once, twice, three times - the shepherd appeared as if from nowhere.

'Hamsters, hamstesses.' He bowed courteously. 'I shall be pleased to answer your questions.'

The first question was from a small rodent at the front right of the crowd. 'Tell me, sir, how long did it take you to put together such a show?'

The shepherd began to answer, eyeing those before him with increasing wariness and suspicion. While his words were being slowly spoken, the Hamster of the Opera shuffled in his seat, preparing himself for his mission when the shepherd first looked away.

After ten minutes, just when he was beginning to think that a chance might never come his way, the Ham-actor turned to an aide and whispered quietly in his ear. Without a moment's hesitation, the Hamster of the Opera accelerated into overdrive, treading on those in front as he sped at the shepherd.

Hearing the commotion of cries in the crowd, the actor turned just too late to see the hamster bearing down on him, unable to remove himself from the danger as his nose became enclosed in the tightening fist.

'Let go! Let go!' he screamed. 'Is this how you treat a friend?'

'You're no friend!' came the reply as he tugged violently at the shepherd's nose. 'You're nothing but our enemy!'

The press jumped to their feet to extricate the attacker from their hero when the shepherd's next words stunned them into immovability.

'Let go of my mask! I said - let go of my mask!'

'I will not let go until it's off!'

Pinning his opponent to the ground, the Hamster of the Opera took the nose in both his paws and, with a monumental effort, ripped the covering from his face.

'A rat!' someone screamed. Three young hamstesses seated at the back passed out, while a menagerie of journalists squeaked with fury at the deception.

'Let me go!' the shepherd continued, writhing on the ground as his paws were locked into an immovable position. 'Let go of my paws!'

The press dashed forward after the momentary shock, securely bound the shepherd and had him taken away by the security guards that had been standing in the doorway.

The Hamster of the Opera breathed a sigh of relief. Now it was his turn to hold a Press conference.

'You see,' he squeaked, 'I knew there was something wrong - every mask that the shepherd put on was what you wanted to see. He was misleading you, getting you to rely upon him, stealing your hearts away from freedom into the bondage of idolatry.'

'We should have been more careful!' a reporter confessed.

'Yes,' he reflected. 'You can't tell the heart of the animal by the mask it puts on, you need to get below the surface to discover its motives. Masks and more masks! I think that the day of the one man entertainer is over, don't you?'

The press nodded their agreement....

'...and from that moment on,' Mademoiselle Duphare said, 'the Hamster of the Opera went about everywhere, encouraging groups of actors to band together and to throw away the masks.'

As she completed her story, I smiled joyfully. 'We seem to have talked almost entirely about the Hamster of the Opera and have forgotten the purpose for which I came.'

'Is that such a bad thing?' she said. 'After all, these stories that I've told you have never before been published - couldn't you use them instead?'

'Are you agreeable, mademoiselle?'

'Mais oui! I should be delighted if you would tell the world about one of the greatest hamsters of history!'

After exchanging the customary farewells, I left the alternative hamster Opera house hoping that I'd catch Lee and Kath as they exited from the building, but unfortunately they'd long gone - I'd spent almost four hours with Mademoiselle Duphare and it'd seemed like barely five minutes!

I looked for the nearest entrance to the Tube, descended into the depths of the Parisienne burrowing system and headed home.

It had been a most enjoyable day's work.

I arrived back at the hotel to the sound of Lee and Kath talking in distressed voices.

The worst of all my fears - they'd rung England to make sure that I was alright. I could imagine the response they'd got!

'...and they've looked all over the house for him, but he's nowhere to be found. They've left sunflower seeds everywhere, but in three days not one has been touched.'

'Are you sure that he was in the cage when we took him over?' Kath asked.

'Absolutely! I remember seeing him fast asleep in the nest compartment just before we left them that evening - but the cage was totally sealed, I can't imagine how he managed to get out.'

'When did they notice he was missing? The same night?'

'No, no - on Monday, four days later! That's when they started putting food all round the house. Dawn had been worried that his food wasn't being eaten, but as she didn't know his eating habits, she thought that, sooner or later, his nest supply would run out and he'd have to take from his dish. But she was getting more and more worried as the weekend went on so, early Monday morning, she unscrewed the top of the nest compartment and found a plastic ball and some fur! But George was gone!'

'It worked!' I thought to myself. 'My decoy actually worked for four days!'

Both Kath and Lee sat quietly on the bed, trying to work out what had happened.

'Perhaps...' Kath began slowly, but then realised that what she was about to suggest was implausible.

Lee looked at her. 'Perhaps what?'

'Oh, nothing.'

'You might as well tell me, you've got me wondering now!'

'Well, I was just thinking - perhaps George did a Hamdini....'

'A what?' Lee interrupted.

'You know - a Hamdini. Remember that, just before we went away, George had been telling us about that illustrious rodent escapologist Hamdini? How there was no cage in the world that had ever been designed that could keep him behind bars?'

'Oh, yeah! - now you come to mention it, I did think it strange that he should keep telling us stories about one hamster in particular. It was most unlike him.'

'Perhaps, then, George was telling us these things to prepare us for what he was about to do?'

'Mmmm...' Lee mused. 'If that's the case, he could be anywhere by now...he could even be in Paris!'

Kath laughed loudly.

'Don't be silly,' she giggled. 'How could George possibly have made it to Paris?!'

'Thank goodness,' I thought, 'for a woman's common sense!'

When Hamdini was only a few days old, he escaped from the pet shop fish tank in which he was kept along with thirty-seven other rodents where there was little, if anything, to do except eat, sleep and yawn with boredom.

The oatmeal, after it had been mixed in the water bowl, gelled together to form a sticky blob that, when applied to each of his four paws, acted like suction pads to enable him to scale the slippery glass walls of the fish tank, over the gap at the summit and descend into the adjacent compound in search of fun.

'Fun' was certainly not what he found - his adjacent pet shop roommate was a bird-eating spider called Doris. All that can be said is that it was indeed fortunate that, at such a young age, a hamster's eyesight is not fully developed for, should he have seen it and panicked, he would almost certainly have woken it up with tragic consequences.

But, instead, he sniffed around for a few moments until screams of terror engulfed the pet shop and a human hand snatched him out of the den, replacing him back with the furry bundle of slumbering rodents.

A couple of hours later, before he'd had another chance to once more escape, he was bought by a middle-aged man as a birthday present for himself.

The cardboard box that he was placed in proved very easy to gnaw through, and he would have escaped from the bag as well in which it was being carried if he'd had enough time but, as the human lived only a stone's throw away from the pet shop, he was securely installed into a wire cage before his teeth found sufficient opportunity.

That same evening, Hamdini reviewed his situation - he was imprisoned against his will in a 2x2x1.5 foot cell (his owner would have said that he was being cared for in the safety of a cage) while, all the time, the adventure of life beckoned him beyond the four barred walls of his captivity.

He gingerly pawed over to the door through which he'd come in, eyeing it carefully.

'A simple latch,' he squeaked pleasingly. 'Now then, all I need to do is lift this bar up like this and....'

The cage door rattled as it bounced open - Hamdini held his breath until he was sure that the master hadn't woken.

Descending carefully down the outside of the cage, he reached the floor covering and set out on his life of adventure.

What Hamdini didn't know was that the master also owned a cat.

The owner awoke to the howls of the tomcat coming from the downstairs kitchen. Though it was usual for it to whine for food having let itself in through the flap, the vocal intensity was most unusual.

But what made him jump out of bed and run downstairs was the crash of the crockery as it shattered onto the cement floor.

The kitchen was a disaster area but, for the moment, he was more concerned with the cause - the cat. It was rolled on its side with one paw stretched out behind the cooker, pawing at the floor.

Without a moment's hesitation, he grabbed it by the scruff of its neck and threw it, like a bolt of lightning, out through the flap, fastening it securely behind him. The cat tried to re-enter, voicing its disgust as it crunched its head on the plastic. Hamdini squeaked a sigh of relief as the cooker moved forward from the wall, the master catching him in his hands before he had a chance to flee.

'You?' he said. 'What are you doing down here?'

Hamdini would have explained but he thought better of it.

In a few minutes, he was back in his cage, the door held shut by a paperclip the master had fetched from his writing cabinet - that took two days for Hamdini to solve.

Then the master made a 'hamster proof' metal clip in his work shed. It was, he assured himself, perfect - four hours was all it lasted.

A few modifications improved it but, by now, Hamdini had worked out how to remove the seed tray and escape through the hole at the base of the cage. The master turned his attention to secure this and, having perfected it after eight weeks' continuous work, found that Hamdini had escaped through the water bottle hole the following morning.

In desperation a new cage was bought - and a new one - and a new one. Hamster-proof cages were particularly easy to escape from as human design just couldn't contend with the schemes that enter a rodent's brain.

And, all this time, Hamdini risked injury and death in a multiplicity of different ways. The cat, incidentally, had been banned permanently from the house until the master was able to make sure where Hamdini was each morning - then, fastening him back into the cage using another new prototype security lock, the owner would allow the tom in to feed, immediately throwing him out again once he'd finished.

The master began to ask himself what benefits he'd received after having paid the price to bring him out of the bondage of a foot square tank crammed with thirty-seven other rodents and into the relative freedom and luxury of a cage that offered him both food and protection. He certainly couldn't think of any!

But Hamdini was just one of those hamsters who wouldn't live within the master's plans - he was always seeking an opportunity to throw off security, exposing himself to greater and greater adventure that necessarily meant increased danger, even possible death.

No-one is quite sure what happened to Hamdini in the end. His last and greatest escape left no trace of him throughout the entire house, which made the owner think that perhaps he'd found his way into the wilds of the outside world.

Whatever, I guess we'll never know.

But it certainly seemed strange that the same morning of Hamdini's final escape, the tomcat left untouched its bowl of food, having looked at it with a full stomach.

Lee and Kath decided not to let my disappearance ruin their holiday.

After having freshened up, they put on their walking shoes once more and left in search of an evening meal at some restaurant or other, while I settled down to rest my aching paws and have a well-earned nap.

Altering my active times from night to day had certainly not been easy, but it had definitely been worth it!

RUE DE ROME
FRIDAY 24TH JULY 1992

It was getting increasingly difficult for me to remain incognito as the days rolled by. More and more, Lee and Kath were getting suspicious that they had rodent company in their bedroom at night during those hours when Lee is dead to the world and Kath awakes at every dropped pin.

Part of it had been my fault - I should never have made the decision to take a bath in the bidet. But, as my fur was getting increasingly matted and greasy, I went ahead against my better judgment.

'This bidet's wet!' Kath said when she got up early that morning, 'and there're hairs down the plug hole!'

Lee came over to have a look.

'Mmmm, strange,' he puzzled. 'You haven't been using that hairbrush of yours to unblock the drainage again, have you?'

'I most certainly have not! And I categorically deny ever having done it before! This is the fifth time something like this has happened! Last time, it was a bunch of fur that we found between the bed linen.'

That had been my fault as well - I'd snuggled under the bedclothes to get warm one night when both my owners had been out late. I hadn't realised that I was moulting as badly as I apparently was.

'I'll see the manager about this!' Lee said. 'There must be some mice or something getting in through some crack when we're not here - that would explain why all our supply of biscuits are half-eaten....'

'...I thought it was the cleaners...' Kath interjected.

'...And why our garlic cheese disappeared overnight behind locked doors.'

Lee walked over to the bedside cabinet and picked up the French-English phrase book. 'Now what's the French for "mouse?"'

'Oh no!' I thought. 'Just wait til he finds out!'

He thumbed through the pages until he came to the correct entry. 'Here we are...' he read it out loud. '"A mouse" is "une sou...."'

He stopped in mid-sentence with the realisation that he'd heard that word before. 'Hey! That's the word we keep hearing almost everywhere we go - une souris!'

'How strange!' Kath said. 'What could this mean?'

'Either this is all some ghastly coincidence,' Lee contemplated, 'or I think that I'm beginning to smell a rat!'

Lee did see the manager of the hotel that morning but he accomplished very little. Lee's French is so bad, bless him, that he proceeded to ask the manager for two mice to be brought to him in his room for breakfast the following morning. I'm sure you can imagine the sort of response he got - needless to say, the manager simply put his words down to English eccentricity and forgot the whole matter.

Frogs' legs - yes. But mice?

From that moment on I kept an extremely low profile in the room and controlled my natural instincts the best I could.

I waited what seemed like ages that morning until I knew beyond a shadow of a doubt that my owners had gone out for the day, before emerging from my hiding place into the hotel room.

Even so, my journey out was not uneventful for, by now, the cleaners were setting about their morning work and I had to be extremely careful not to let them catch a glimpse of me as I scurried hastily down into the entrance of the Tube.

I was particularly drawn to visit the famous Rue de Rome, a short distance from the Opera house where I'd interviewed the beautiful Mademoiselle Madeleine Duphare. In fact, it had been she who'd given me the idea in the first place for there, in the Rue de Rome, was row upon row of music shops and, among them all, one in particular that had a plaque fixed onto the wall above the entrance that read:

'Here lived and worked the great Hamanini,
Son of Gertrude and Alberto Rosini.
He played it mean, he played it cool,
He played it on the kitchen stool.'

It was here that Hamanini, a violinist of extraordinary talent, came to be renowned as one of the leading exponents of the classical music of his day.

Of his playing and his exploits, much has already been written and I don't wish to add to that heavy weight of literature that can be obtained from rodent outlets across the world.

For instance, in a well-known story it's told how, when pursued by cats in search of an easy kill, he would take out his violin, rosin the bow, and lull his hunters to sleep with a haunting melody before making off with their whiskers as a source of fresh strings.

But Mademoiselle Duphare related to me an event of his life that I've never before heard or read and, as it was instrumental in encouraging me to spend such a wonderful day in the music shops of Paris, I want to pass it on to you so that you, too, may be encouraged to discover the street's delights should you ever make it across to the city.

Hamanini was a master musician - it's hardly surprising, though, when you consider the vast quantity of time that he used to put aside to practice.

Early in the morning, before both his mother and father woke up and before the sun had risen on the Parisienne street, he'd pick up his violin and, gently caressing the strings with the bow, play non-stop for almost four hours.

Then, at work as a salesman in his father's violin shop, he'd play as often as he got the chance, demonstrating the versatility of each instrument to the clientele who came in search of a good buy.

On particularly quiet days, such as times immediately after rodent festivals, he'd play uninterrupted almost all day, the harmonic melody floating down the street with the odours from next door's café.

And, in the evening, yet more playing! This time performing in the kitchen of the house where they'd set up their business downstairs in the cellar.

Rodents from all over France and the civilised world came to be a part of those special evenings that went on long into the night.

Hamanini would position himself on top of the still-warm stove, elevating himself above the audience who sat wherever there was room - on the floor, in the coal store, on top of cupboards. Some rodents would queue for hours to get what most considered to be the best seat - in the fruit bowl on top of the work surface where, not only did the acoustics do justice to Hamanini's playing, but food was close at hand should the concert continue long after its scheduled finish.

While it is true to say that Hamanini was gifted to play the violin, it must be pointed out that the vast amount of hours that he put in practising was how that gift developed. Gifts, as us rodents have learnt, need to be honed, supplemented, matured, supported and encouraged. A gift left to itself will never reach its full potential - it can never develop into a ministry to the masses that all rodents will be able to recognise as being 'extraordinary.'

It was commitment, then, that produced the excellence of Hamanini's gift - he lived, ate and slept at the violin.

One day, when Hamanini was playing a particularly fast piece in his father's shop, three field mice hopped in through the entrance, immediately drawn to the lone figure as his paws flew over the strings.

Hamanini cut short his virtuoso performance to see to their requirements.

'Can I help you?' he squeaked warmly.

'We want a violin,' the eldest one blurted out, 'one that will make us sound like you.'

'That's right,' one of the others agreed. 'A violin that will show people what great musicians we are.'

Hamanini was puzzled. 'And how long have you been playing the violin?' he asked.

'A whole five minutes,' the youngest squeaked proudly.

'I've played for four,' another said with a tinge of sorrow in his voice, 'but it was so intense that it was probably more beneficial than his five.'

The eldest had only thought about playing.

(I think it best to explain to you at this point, before I continue with the story, that field mice are among the lesser intelligent of our species - any rodent that builds its nest in a field that's about to be eaten by a combine harvester can't be totally in their right mind.)

Hamanini scratched his ear with his rear paw - this was going to be tricky, but he decided to play them along. He picked up the first violin he found and performed a slow air.

'There - now you try.'

The youngest snatched it from his hand and, placing it under his chin, sand-papered the bow over the strings. Hamanini closed his ears but, even so, his teeth were still set on edge.

'This one's no good,' he complained. 'It doesn't sound like you at all!' The others tried - they were of the same opinion.

One by one they went through the entire stock of instruments - each time, Hamanini would play them a melody before handing it over to them. Each time, the resulting sound resembled the call of a love-sick elephant.

The three field mice sat dejectedly on the floor of the shop. Hamanini looked them over, deciding to offer a word of advice.

'My friends,' he began, 'there are no shortcuts to playing well, it's something that you must work at. You think that the instrument will make you sound good but, on the contrary, it's the player that makes the violin yield its best tune.

'If you really do want to play well, then - day in, day out - you must develop through practice. You need to commit yourself to press on to master the fundamentals, overcome the difficulties and never give up your quest to play ever better.'

The eldest turned and left the shop - it wasn't long before a second followed. Just the youngest sat before him.

'Are you going to leave as well?' Hamanini asked him.

The young field mouse looked up into the dark, compassionate eyes of the musician.

'I want to play the violin,' he squeaked, 'but I don't know how to begin.'

Hamanini smiled. 'Then today was not wasted after all! Grab yourself a violin and come over here - I will give you your first lesson....'

NOTRE DAME AND VERSAILLES
SATURDAY 25TH JULY 1992

I was constantly aware that the success of my stay in Paris depended upon me remaining hidden as I'd done for the previous five days.

With this in mind I woke early, long before the sun illuminated the hotel room when my every move would be easily seen, and sneaked out through a crack in the skirting board to head north towards the Pont de l'Alma.

It was here, a fairly short distance even in hamster terms, that the old established boating company called 'Water Vole Boat Tours Incorporated' had been thriving for nigh on a hundred years.

I was headed for Notre Dame Cathedral but, feeling unable to cope with the stress of another trip on the Paris tube, I'd decided to opt for the longer but more enjoyable route of a scenic ride up the Seine.

Sitting on the quay as the sun rose on that serene Parisienne scene brought back memories of my holiday so far - the joys and excitement of planning melted into the ecstasy of 'being there.'

It'd been such a worthwhile experience that, even if I'd missed stowing away in Lee's baggage for the return trip, I wouldn't have minded living out the rest of my days here in this bustling city.

The water voles were a little late this morning, usually busy repairing their vessels an hour or so before anyone saw them appear. I caught sight of them motoring furiously downstream, landing quite expertly on the dry platform underneath the human quay.

'Apologies,' the first out of the water greeted me with. 'We're extremely short staffed this week - you see, one of our power-voles is away on annual leave.'

'Annual leave?' I thought to myself. 'I didn't think water voles had holidays.'

'That's alright,' I replied, 'better late than never,' and, with that, I was helped onto a wooden raft that looked decidedly unsafe - but if you don't dare, you don't accomplish anything.

Four voles strapped themselves to the front of the vessel and, no sooner had they fastened the last buckle than we were off at an incredible speed against the flow of the river.

'Pont Neuf?' One looked behind to where I sat.

'Yes,' I said. 'Unless there's a nearer place to alight for Notre Dame.'

'Ah yes,' another began, 'my favourite sight in all of Paris. Do you know the history of the place?'

'Only a little,' I squeaked, admiring an old restored building as we sailed by. 'I read a few books about Paris before I came over.'

'I am certain then,' another spoke loudly, 'that you have not heard the story about the monster of the Cathedral?'

'The monster?' I was puzzled, searching my mind for the memory. 'No, I don't think I've heard that tale.'

'Most hamster books don't mention it, seeing as the hero was a human.'

I could see that I was going to be told this story whether I liked it or not, so I might as well put on the appearance of wanting to hear.

'Well, seeing as I have time on my paws, why don't you tell me about this monster?'

'Very well,' the leading vole replied, 'I will....'

'ROWRRRR!'

As the deafening lion-like snarl bellowed out from the bell tower of Notre Dame, the human congregation that had been stood in the open square before the Cathedral scattered in various directions, seeking a vestige of protection behind the surrounding buildings.

'ROWWWRRRR!'

Again the noise ricocheted off stone-faced houses, gaining in terror as the echoes split into a multitude of venomous and threatening voices. Doors were boarded up while furniture was hastily moved to block any entrance that might try to be gained through windows by the monster of Notre Dame, while the guardians and servants of the Cathedral ran from the sanctuary under which the bell tower stood, making for the hills where a bear robbed of its cubs seemed a safer proposition than staying within the grip of that...that...THING - that thing that lurked in the shadows of the belfry where no human dared tread.

This scene had continued for many weeks, during which time the crowds that took their stand in the square below had swelled ever larger, anticipating catching even the slightest glimpse of this fiendish foe that sprouted six talons on each of its eleven claws and whose saliva dripped earthwards from each of its eight rows of sharp, carnivorous teeth - or, at least those were the rumours for, even though each person had their own graphic description of the monster of Notre Dame, no-one had actually seen him.

Repeatedly, then, day after day at about the same hour, this time-honoured scene continued to take place - assembly then dispersal, courage then fear, anticipation then desperation. And all the while, the challenge went out from the mayor of the city to find a man who was brave enough to climb the stairs to the monster's den and remove its head to deliver the city from its deathly dominance.

Despite higher and higher rewards, no-one took up the gauntlet. No-one, that is, until...

...until Quasimodo came to town.

You would not have picked Quasimodo out in a crowd - if you were to hold a 'Mr Average' competition, he would have been a prime contender for the title. But through countless years of military campaigns in different countries that spanned Europe, he'd learnt something unique - that fear, whenever it was encountered, had to be challenged and defeated or else one's life became a gibbering wreck of nervousness.

As he stood in the square watching the Parisiennes scatter for protection at the raging voice of the monster bellowing down from on high, something within him rose up for war - a defiance in the face of adversity that spurred him on and into the presence of the mayor.

'We've been waiting for someone such as you,' the dignitary said. Actually, he'd been waiting for anybody. Anybody daft enough to attempt such a hopeless - or so it seemed to him - venture into the unknown.

'All of Paris will be with you as you climb those stairs,' he lied - all of Paris, so far, didn't want to venture within a hundred meters of the place even though the gatherings in the square swelled daily with more and more humans who wanted to show how brave they were to defy the voice of the monster.

Early the next morning, as the sun began to illuminate the belfry, Quasimodo grasped his two-edged sword in his right hand and gazed up the staircase that beckoned his fear to rise with each step. No-one stood with him, they'd all given their excuses - some more inventive than others. Whatever the apology, he knew that underlying them all was fear, raging uncontrolled in their hearts that bound the recipients into cowardice.

Ascending the steps as quietly as he was able, he comforted himself with the fact that his adversary had to attack him face to face - in previous campaigns, the enemy had not been so predictable, attacking at every angle, every opportunity that he'd found. All he had to do, Quasimodo told himself, was to sink his sword deep into the monster's belly before it had a chance to sever his head from his own.

Courage is not the absence of fear, but the pressing on regardless. That's why Quasimodo's hand still shook as he neared the top of the stairs that opened out into the belfry.

Peering over the wooden partition, he surveyed the surroundings expecting at any moment to be pounced upon by the monster of Notre Dame.

Nothing.

No movement, no sound, no footprints.

Above, below - nothing.

Not a whisper.

He stepped out into the full view of anything that might be there, ready to thrust his sword deep into whatever moved - all he heard was the sound of his own heartbeat racing frantically away.

Five minutes passed.

Then ten.

Silence.

Eventually, calmed by the absence of any visible monster, he peered down into the square below where crowds thronged together to witness his fate.

He looked behind himself one final time before, with his back to the bells, he fixed his gaze on the multitudes, intending to shout, 'There's nothing here,' but, before he had a chance even to catch his breath, a deafening sound pierced the darkness behind him.

'ROOOWWWWWWWRRRRRR!'

Quasimodo spun round to see the monster staring at him with its two big black eyes, its front paws stretched heavenward as it let out its ear-piercing yawn that gurgled with intent and which sent the crowds scattering for cover.

Here he was, face to face with the most terrible sounding, ferocious monster he'd ever seen. It was covered with brown and white fur that shimmered in the early morning sun, was a full five inches tall and...

'A hamster?' He allowed himself a smile. 'Paris is held captive by the fear of a golden hamster?'

As the rodent cracked open a small nut from its store, the sound was amplified by the shape of the bell that it had nested under, projecting a bone-crunching noise into the square below where many who'd returned from the first roar passed out, interpreting it as the untimely demise of Quasimodo.

He put his sword down and laughed so fiercely that he thought he'd never stop.

'Killer monster gnaws thirty-two Parisiennes to death!' he shouted, hearing his memory recount some of the news proclamations from the Town Criers. 'Fire-breathing dragon preys on innocent inhabitants of Notre Dame.'

Gathering the hamster into his left hand along with some bedding and its food store, he looked once more into the square and pointed behind him, shouting, 'The bells! The bells!' and then burst once more into uncontrollable laughter.

'If only they'd confronted the problem,' he thought to himself, 'they would've seen that it wasn't as big as they'd imagined it to be.'

The wooden vessel glided to a controlled stop at Pont Neuf and, thanking the voles for extending the tour so that I could listen to the end of their story (we'd circled Ile de la Cité eight times), I alighted onto the quay and scampered my way across to Notre Dame.

Realising that by now my time was extremely short if I was to make the connection, I rushed round the Cathedral quicker than I would have liked, eventually descending to the Tube for a run over to Invalides railway station.

Although it was necessary for me to keep as low a profile as possible, Lee and Kath were pivotal in my plans to gain access into the grounds of Versailles - I'd heard them discussing their plans the evening before and I knew that I'd just enough time to make it to the station in order to catch the train.

Enough time, that is, provided there were no delays.

But a hundred meters or so from the station and too far from the previous opening to reverse and exit to choose an alternative route, the endless stream of hamsters gradually ground to a halt.

I looked at my sundial wristwatch to see how long I had left - then remembered that, being underground, it was inoperable - it was solar powered.

'What's the problem?' I squeaked impatiently at the rodent in front.

Ever decreasing squeaks passed up the line, then returning with the answer, 'A cheese roll has fallen into the pipe from the café above,' came the reply. 'They're clearing it up now.'

I tapped the pipe anxiously, realising that by now the train was long gone.

Soon, the line began moving once more and I found myself on Invalides station within a couple of minutes, looking around for my owners.

My sundial watch told me I was late - too late by far. I was about to give up on ever seeing Versailles when, out of the corner of my eye, I saw them queuing at the ticket office, Lee gesticulating madly at the man behind the grille with two fingers raised in the air.

'I said, "I want two tickets" - deux!'

Obviously the Frenchman was having a hard time understanding the little language my owners knew.

I ran over, scurried up Lee's trouser leg (in all the fuss he didn't feel a thing) and into the bag.

'How strange,' I thought to myself. 'I'm not late after all!'

I removed my solar-powered sundial watch instruction booklet and read carefully the section on 'local time.' After a couple of minutes it dawned on me what I'd done.

In the month of July, four minutes had to be deducted to compensate for the vertical equinox of the eighth quarter of the earth's rotation - I had added it instead, making it seem later than it really was.

'Never mind,' I sighed. 'All's well that ends well. Versailles - here I come!'

Versailles is a strange place - a palace a hundred thousand times the size of my Rotastak nest compartment but there's no furniture there! Plenty of paintings on walls and ceilings, gold leafed decorations beyond compare and mirror after mirror decorated in the most exquisite ornamentation - but where did the humans sit? Or sleep? Or eat?

I had allowed myself to be carried around the palace. To be honest, I would have jumped free and into the gardens as soon as I got there but the crowds prevented my escape into the brilliant sunshine that bathed the plants and trees with glory.

When my masters' lunchtime arrived, I had no option but to exit, Lee being more concerned to eat a piece of chocolate bread than to witness my emergence into fresh air - I have no idea what they'd been keeping in that side pocket since my last ride, but, whatever it was, it stank.

The gardens were beautiful - I wandered around for hours, absorbing the clashing scents and differing hues that seemed to dance upon my senses in almost every area in which I found myself.

But it was while I was on the far side of the grounds that I witnessed an event that I want to relate.

I had decided to have ten minutes' rest - I'd walked almost non-stop for an hour and a half and my paws were beginning to throb with heat and weariness. I found a lonely spot that overlooked a piece of waste ground and shaded myself under the overhanging branches of a tall oak.

The waste ground before me was ordinary and it was inclined at quite an angle, dropping away to my right and ending in a row of trees where the woodland began. To my left, a small ridge obscured what lay at the bottom of the hill. Further away on the same side was a public footpath where tourists buzzed up and down on route from one sight to another.

It would have continued like this until closing time had not two Italians decided to have a disagreement away from the path on the summit of the hill that I overlooked.

I don't know the language but I knew that they were Italians by their actions and the way that they spoke. They'd been disagreeing over something as they walked along in the humid summer sun when, halfway along the path, the woman walked off with a loud shout, the man following at a short distance, taken aback by his wife's explosive temper.

They sat down on top of the ridge and continued arguing, but gradually they wore themselves out, both seeing the futility of their own position. After a couple of moments' silence they looked at each other, embraced and chose to forgive. Sitting there, now, arms round their waists, they talked gently and stared down the hill to the wood that lay below.

A few minutes later, a group of about five French people spotted the couple, sitting staring ahead of themselves at something that the

L'ARC DE TRIOMPHE AND THE EIFFEL TOWER SUNDAY 26TH JULY 1992

Time was fast approaching the day that I had to leave Paris bound for England's shores. In one way it made me sad to think of leaving such an intriguing city - the differing sights, smells and sounds made Paris unique in most ways from every other place I've either read about or been to. And yet, despite all my adventures and exploits, I was glad to think of the return to security that my arrival back home would bring me.

My tiny paws, also, were beginning to feel the strain of constant use. Early Sunday morning, the eve before my departure, I took stock of where I'd both been and hadn't.

I'd left my visit to the Eiffel Tower until this evening when Mademoiselle Madeleine Duphare had arranged to meet me at the base to show me the hamster route to the summit - she'd outlined it in great detail but, alas, the complexities of the ascent had left my head spinning. So, very kindly, she'd agreed to take me with her after the evening performance at the Opera house.

But what to do during the day?

My masters had decided to take it easy on this their final day - they'd already walked their feet off the past six (Lee, it was rumoured, had worn away two inches off the ends of his feet, he had walked so much), leaving early for the Jardin du Luxembourg armed only with their water bottles, food rations and an endless supply of sticking plasters for Kath's blistered feet.

It was a difficult decision for me to have to make as there were still a number of sights that I'd not had time to visit but, in the end, I decided that by far the greatest attraction to me was the Arc de Triomphe.

The Arc is always crowded with hamster tourists both day and night and the narrow walkway to the viewing platform doesn't space the rodents out to make it a more enjoyable visit.

But, eventually, after an hour's wait, I found myself at the front of the bustling crowd, overlooking the Place Charles de Gaulle where drivers competed for strategic positions on the grand prix roundabout like mad elephants vying for the lead in a stampede.

Ahead of me lay the Champs Elysees, tree-lined (as most of the streets were), that swarmed with humans in search of a film to watch, a bargain to buy or money to exchange.

After a good ten minutes, I noticed below me smoke, swirling across the Place and emanating from underneath the Arch.

Turning to an elderly rodent who stood beside me and, realising that the French I knew did not include the words 'smoke,' 'underneath' or 'fire escape,' I chanced a question in English.

'Smoke!' I said and pointed to the dark clouds. 'Where's that coming from?'

The rodent peered over the parapet.

'Ah yes,' he said with a soft accent, 'the fire of remembrance. Below us is the tomb of the unknown soldier and, on top of this, is the fire of remembrance. That is the smoke you can see.'

'The unknown soldier?' I asked. 'Who's he?'

'If the humans knew who he was, he wouldn't be called the unknown soldier, would he?' and he smiled knowingly. He knew something that, for the time being, he wasn't going to tell. But by the gleam in his eye I knew that he was bursting to tell me what he knew.

'There is an inscription on the tomb,' he continued. '"Ici reposé un soldat Francais mort pour la patrie 1914-1918." - that is, "Here lies a French soldier who died for his country during 1914-18." Those were the dates of the Great war, you know.'

'Yes, I am aware. But tell me about this "unknown warrior." Doesn't anyone know who he was?'

He looked at me intently. 'No human knows...' He paused and took another look at the smoke below. '...but my grandfather knew him, he was a friend of his.'

The unknown soldier lived in one of the front line trenches during the bleak days of the first human world war - there have been other wars both before and after but none was so dark and dismal as this.

The mud and filth of the front was bad enough but the constant mortar attacks and chlorine gas made life almost intolerable - had it not been for the little pleasure the unknown soldier had of being protector to a bunch of orphaned baby hamsters, he might have given up the hope he had and lived in despair as many of his battalion did.

Pierre, Louis and Jules were found in a bundle of hay on his return to the trenches after an assault on enemy lines.

Squeaking with hunger, having been alone for several hours, the unknown soldier took pity on them, gathering them into his front pocket to transport them back to his dugout quarters in the mud of his camp.

Food was scarce for both human and hamster alike, so the sacrifice that he made is even more praiseworthy. From that moment on, the provisions he received were shared, the hamsters being given first sniff of everything.

You see, there were no manuals to consult to see what hamsters ate - it was all 'sniff it and see'. But, over the weeks, the hamsters grew both in strength and size, looking forward to the times when the four of them would sit down to a shared meal of whatever was available.

One morning, when the three hamsters awoke with a bump as a mortar shell landed closer than normal, they heard the sound of panicked voices among the troops.

'We're surrounded, I tell you, they've cut the lines behind us and we can't get the reinforcements to advance!' The soldier paced to and fro while checking the rounds of ammunition left.

'Can't we break through their lines?'

'What are two hundred troops against the thousands of the enemy?' the reply came - then there was silence as each soldier contemplated their ultimate fate.

'The only chance we've got is if we can get a message back to the rest of the troops....'

'...And that's impossible because the lines are cut!'

The hamsters' ears pricked up sharply.

'If only General Woodward knew, he could be here in hours....'

There was panic in the voice, desperation too, for each one of them knew the impossibility of getting the message through. Yes, each one knew the impossibility except, that is, for the hamsters.

Pierre was the first to start running. 'Come on, you lot, the battle awaits!'

'Where you going?' Jules shouted after him.

'Off to get the message through!'

Louis and Jules looked at one another, put their paws up in the air and raced off after him.

'All for one!' shouted Louis.

'And one for all!' Pierre responded.

What little armour the unknown soldier's troops had was bearing up under the strain of the might of the enemy army - but it wouldn't hold for long.

The three hamsters passed into no-man's land without a moment's hesitation, then through the enemy lines and into the next no-man's land as they hurried for the General's camp.

Four miles behind the lines, a well-camouflaged series of tents lay nestled in a rare woodland. The hamsters located the General's quarters but to no avail - he was nowhere to be seen.

But, a hundred yards or so away, their acute hearing picked up the sound of a group of humans talking quietly amongst themselves and, deciding to investigate, arrived at the tent flap just as General Woodward finished talking.

'...Remember these positions well, gentlemen, for in just two hours we'll press forward into combat with the enemy....'

He was about to lift the cover from off the map to reveal to his men their attacking positions, when mortar fire rained down on them.

'The trenches, men! To the trenches!'

The tent emptied faster than the shells were falling.

'Now's our chance!' Louis squeaked.

'Eh?' Jules complained. 'Shouldn't we be taking cover?'

'And miss our opportunity? We need such a time as this to fulfil the reason we've come.'

'What're you going to do?'

'Follow me and watch!'

The three hamsters poked their noses under the cover that lay across the military map and strategy board.

'Now, BE CAREFUL!' Louis warned. 'And don't touch anything that I don't tell you to touch!'

Louis raced about the board with his eyes fixed downwards, remembering every contour, every battery position, every intended thrust and counter thrust.

'Here we are,' he said finally, pointing with his paw. The other two hamsters came to look. 'This is where the soldier is surrounded.'

'But there aren't any plans to attack anywhere near that place,' Jules moaned.

'Correct! Or, at least, there weren't any plans until now.' Louis smiled.

A few steps backwards and Louis stood on the location where the enemy had broken through the lines and were surrounding the soldier.

'Get that marker there,' he pointed, 'and put it here. And that one.'

Jules and Pierre obeyed.

'Good.' Louis looked at his redeployment of the strike force. 'Hopefully the General won't spot the difference.'

Pierre and Jules were still bewildered as to what was going on.

'We don't understand!' they finally said in puzzlement. 'What will moving a few bits of wood do to liberate the soldier?'

'They're more than bits of wood,' he explained. 'These are markers to show General Woodward's commanders where to strike when they march forward. By moving them to where we know the enemy is - that is, between the soldier and the main body - we can ensure that they'll come under such a barrage of mortar that they'll be forced to either withdraw or be annihilated.'

'That's brilliant!' squeaked Jules. 'Absolutely brilliant!'

'Brilliant or not - let's just hope that it works!'

The soldier's group of men faced the enemy behind them as they bore down ever closer on their positions. They loaded their rifles, held grenades in their hands ready and waited until the enemy was close enough to engage. It was all futile, really, a small band of men against so many, but they weren't going to go down without a fight.

Then the mortar started.

'Take cover, men!' the sergeant shouted, the soldiers lowering themselves into the trenches.

Explosion followed explosion as shell upon shell rained down. The white flashes illuminated the dark sky like forks of lightning.

But in spite of it all, it sounded distant. Near - yes - but not near enough.

One by one, the troops slowly began to chance a look over the safety of the trench walls to see, much to their amazement, the enemy fleeing to their right and left.

The shells were landing upon the ranks of the advancing army.

'...mercy given is mercy received,' the old hamster concluded.

'I've not heard that saying before,' I squeaked. 'Is it French?'

'No, no, it's human - but it's more than that....'

A steward interrupted our conversation. 'Move along now please, there are plenty other rodents behind you who want to get to the front.'

I turned to walk away, but glanced back before the crowd swept me down the narrow corridors to the Tube.

'Thank you for the story.' I smiled. 'Do you mind if I publish it when I get home?'

'Not at all!' he shouted after me. 'Its truth belongs to all us hamsters!'

Then the crowd carried me out of earshot, down the fast flowing river of tourists that finally exited into the cool surroundings of a refreshment area below the stone slabs of the Place Charles de Gaulle.

When I finally arrived at the Eiffel Tower, I had an hour to spare before Mademoiselle Duphare had arranged to meet me - in fact, knowing that she would almost certainly get more than one encore, it would probably be more like an hour and a half until she made it to the small clump of bushes behind the east column where she'd told me to wait.

Meanwhile, I took the opportunity to bathe my tired paws in a pool of freshly fallen rain before sitting down at the rodent café with a glass of squeezed walnut paste.

I don't like crowds - I need space to breathe. Although I'd enjoyed my visit to the Arc, I was glad to get away from the squash of bodies that was a compulsory prerequisite of visiting one of the most popular rodent sites in Paris.

But now, sat down on a soft pile of leaves as a cool breeze blew through the bushes, I drifted from consciousness into dreamland, allowing my body a much needed time for recuperation.

'George? Is that you?' Mademoiselle Duphare's soft voice brought me back to reality.

'Mmmm?'

Dozey headed, I could just make out her form. I rubbed my eyes to wipe the sleep away and to bring them back into focus.

'I thought I'd missed you,' she continued. 'I've been looking all over for you for ages.'

'Oh, I'm sorry.' I stood quickly to my feet. 'How long have you been searching for me?'

'I arrived early - the performance was cancelled. Unfortunately the chorus rodents have a bout of laryngitis and we have no understudies who are capable of singing the part. But, now that I've found you, it is well - see, we are in perfect time to reach the summit as the sun sets.'

I followed her as she led me to the first girder that touched earth.

'Keep close behind me,' she instructed. 'Squeak twice if you want to stop and have a rest.'

And so began the long ascent - up the first girder, across the main support beam, across another, left at the end to meet up with the human lift to the first floor.

'It's too dangerous to take the lift any further,' she shouted behind, 'so we must climb the service ladders from here on.'

Eventually, twenty-five minutes later (not including ten minutes of rest stops), we arrived four metres above the humans' third floor viewing platform and sat on a thin piece of wire that jutted out from the tower.

'This is it,' she said. 'The best view of Paris you'll ever get!'

I was impressed.

Laid out before me like a gigantic map was Paris, illuminations coming on one by one as the sun's light faded out below the horizon. To my right I noticed the Louvre, where I'd been the first day, the entrance pyramid now brilliantly lit, shedding light onto the walls of the ancient buildings around.

'Where's the Place du Tertre?' I asked Mademoiselle Duphare. 'I'm not too well up on the layout of Paris.'

She pointed to the left of a domed church building that lay on a hill in the distance.

'There or thereabouts - it's not very bright as it only has normal street lamps. But look there...' her outstretched paw moved down, '... that is the Opera House where I work - you can just see the roof above the other buildings.'

'Ah yes,' I said. 'What a shame the other buildings obscure its intensity.'

The river was beautiful - it didn't have a light of its own but its constantly changing shape meant that it glistened and shimmered with all the varying lights that were on its banks.

'Over there,' she pointed out, 'is Notre Dame - did you go there?'

'Yes,' I replied, 'yesterday. And there's the Arc - being one of the major tourist sights, I would've thought that it would've been lit up a bit better than that!'

'It competes with a lot of bright lights around it, that's why it doesn't look as intense as it really is.'

She paused a moment while I took in the scene laid out before me, then continued. 'What you must understand, George, mon ami, is that all lights shine with differing intensities but none is more important than any other - they're only individual contributors to the overall glory.'

I turned to look at her, realising that she'd just said something profound - she knew it too for she was smiling knowingly.

'That was your intention when you brought me up here, to teach me about the Light?'

'But of course, George, it is one of my favourite illustrations that I use to describe the Creator's people!'

I returned her smile.

We sat there for many hours until the sky became the deepest black that I'd ever seen. Yet, at the darkest hour, the light seemed to become brighter, piercing the darkness like a sharp sword thrusts through anything that gets in its way. And, however dark the sky became, it couldn't overcome the lights on earth.

CHARLES DE GAULLE
MONDAY 27TH JULY 1992

'Have you packed my toothbrush?' Lee asked, all the while carefully arranging his hand luggage that contained six heavy cans of Grenadine syrup.

'Yes,' Kath replied.

'What about my deodorant?' He added some padding down the side to stop them rattling.

'Yes.'

'And my shampoo?' It was unfortunate that he'd not remembered to check and see how heavy it was.

'Yes.'

'Have you put them all in my sponge bag?' He jammed the last item he could in his bag and zipped up the top.

'Yes,' she paused to take a breath, 'but, it's what I haven't packed away that's more important.'

'What's that?' Lee asked.

'My patience!' and she gave a wry smile.

Lee tried to lift the lightweight hand luggage and wrenched a muscle in his shoulder with the effort.

'I think you must have packed my brains away - why, oh, why have I loaded this up with so much weight?' He thought for a moment. 'Never mind, it's your bag anyway.'

Kath ignored the remark.

I was waiting my opportunity to stowaway in their cases when their backs were turned but, so far, I'd only had a half chance when Lee went out to the toilet and Kath was distracted.

Fortunately, I hadn't tried it - I would have only got a handful of seconds before Kath resumed packing the suitcase with calculated precision. Even so, it still didn't all fit in and it had to be re-packed twice before it could be fastened. That left me only the hand luggage as an option.

'I'll go down and pay the bill,' Lee announced shortly before they'd planned to depart. 'I'll be back in a few minutes.'

'Okay.'

The door clicked shut as Kath stretched her weary arms and frame. She walked round the bed and into the bathroom to splash her face with cold water.

'Now!' I thought. 'Now's the best opportunity that I'm likely to get.' Jumping over the side of the wardrobe I landed on the bed, reaching the hand luggage in a matter of seconds. The blue bag - that I'd travelled in all holiday - would have been ideal, but both side pocket and main compartment were securely fastened and I wouldn't have been able to squeeze myself into either.

So, it had to be the green one. I dived into the open zip, taking up residence beside the camera case - Lee and Kath had already used up all their film so there was no possibility of them taking it out. I nestled down for the journey, using a couple of pairs of Lee's socks as bedding (poor Lee, he often gets told off for wearing them through so quickly - this time it wouldn't be his fault).

Much to my delight I found that my owners had packed the bag of nuts close by that they'd been given on the flight over.

Perfect!

The door clicked open, then shut.

Muffled sounds above as the zipper closed.

Darkness.

Movement.

'Now,' I thought to myself, 'I must listen carefully to all that goes on around me if I'm to avoid spending half a day cooped up in this humid bag.'

The problem with Lee and Kath is that they seem to arrive everywhere too early. This time they had five hours to spare before their flight was scheduled to take off and two hours before they were even allowed to book their luggage in.

If it'd been Heathrow Airport I would have been content to stay put in the luggage but here, in Charles de Gaulle, where there is no air conditioning (or if there is any, it doesn't work) and where (Lee assures me) there are twenty thousand passengers a day and only three seats, the least time spent the better.

As soon as my masters jumped off the Air France Bus that took them to the airport, I exited into bright sunshine and descended down the inside of a drain water pipe until I arrived 'in transit,' on the outside of the building where the planes taxi and take off.

I viewed my surroundings intently - no, this wasn't the right side.

I scurried round the back in time to see a plane take to the skies and another land - yes, this was the place. Far to my right, a queue of planes (about six) waited for clearance for take off. That was where I was headed - the end of the runway - for here, or so I had been reliably informed back in England, was where a famous hamster lived by the name of Hamdenburg.

You would have thought that the continual roar of the engines would have driven this rodent far, far away but, on the contrary, Hamdenburg had a life of plenty - no predators seeking his life and no hungry mouths competing for food.

Cadging a lift on the front wheels of a 767 that had left the passenger satellites to begin its journey, I arrived at the entrance to his nest in seven minutes, squeaking a warm greeting down his burrow before I descended into the complex maze of passages that was his home.

'Good day,' he spoke with warm affection in his voice. 'It's good to see you, whoever you are, my rodent brother.'

'It's good to be here,' I replied. 'But it must only be a short stay - my masters fly out in four and a half hours time and I must return to the departure lounge to stowaway aboard their hand luggage long before they go through the security check in an hour and a half's time.'

'No need!' He raised his hands skyward. I could tell that Hamdenburg lived for meeting other hamsters the way he made me feel so at home.

'Your masters' flight has to pass this nest before it can take off - when it does, you'll be able to sneak on board through the front wheel compartment.'

I felt terrified - it must have showed on my face.

'There's no need to worry, my friend,' he said in a calm voice. 'It's easier than shelling peanuts!' and, with that, he reached into his food store and picked up a handful of sunflower seeds.

'Let's go to a new compartment upstairs that I've just finished,' he continued. 'We can talk there.'

We ascended a steep-sided burrow, exiting into a spacious cavity that contained numerous leaf cushions on which to recline.

'Tell me,' he began, 'what brings you here?'

'Curiosity, really.' I stretched out my paw to reach for a sunflower seed, which I began to shell. 'Back in England there are reports everywhere of a hamster who lives beside the runway of Charles de

Gaulle Airport, but no-one's ever met you or could confirm the story as more than hearsay.

'So, having time to kill meant that I could see if all the rumours were true - actually, I always believed they were. A face to the legend, then....'

'Ha!' He threw back his head and laughed. 'That was a long time ago!'

'But the stories are true, aren't they?'

'They seem to change with the years! The hamsters I meet all have their own version of them and they become more incredible with the passage of time!'

'Then what is the truth?'

'Do you really want to know?'

'Of course! Besides, I write for the Sunflower Seed Press - I'm sure that, if you're willing, they'll allow me to print your story to correct the myths and fables that surround you.'

'Very well,' he said. 'Let me begin many years ago....'

...I was very young, very small and very blind. Until a hamster grows up he never really sees anything for what it really is. His eyes develop with time - not overnight.

So I had no idea that I was living on the edge of one of the major airports of the world. My parents didn't tell me either. Even if they had, I don't suppose I would have understood. How do you explain what a plane is to one who has only just started to come to terms with walking?

Anyway, this is all irrelevant - please excuse my ramblings, but I am an old hamster, full of years and experiences, and my mind occasionally wanders into side issues that have no direct bearing on the story in question.

I was the latest developer of the litter that was born that year. When the time came for mum and dad to push all of us youngsters out to fend for ourselves, I still hadn't got full vision.

Usually, this isn't too much of a problem. As you know, a hamster's smell is one of the finest in the animal kingdom - it's so highly tuned to the fragrant smells of a million subtle hues that we can tell exactly where we are by the smell of each individual blade of grass.

Our parents pointed us all in different directions, with enough food in our pouches for two days. It was just unfortunate that I got pointed toward runway two - the busiest runway in the world at that time.

Planes landed here from all over the known world - all sorts of colours they were too. Green, blue, yellow - I think my favourite are those red ones that are white underneath and the large blotchy...

There I go again, getting side-tracked - please forgive me, my friend.

Now, where was I?

Ah yes.

Because I couldn't see the dangers of living so close to runway two, I made my home here - where you are now. Over the weeks I got used to the roar of the jet engines and, besides, the abundance of fresh vegetation and absence of predators made this, for me, an ideal spot.

So that's how I got here. I hope you can put right those rumours back home that say that I flew in by plane to pioneer a new colony of rodents. Honestly! Some animals always try to make it sound like I'm a super hero or something!

But let me move on to the incident for which I'm renowned.

I frequently went on food reconnaissance missions all over the airport - nothing frightened me for the planes were easy to dodge. My favourite area was the control tower - you see, the air traffic controllers used to eat their snacks and lunches while they directed the planes to taxi, take off and land.

Pieces of food got dislodged or broken off, would fall to the ground and some would disappear into the gaps between the radar equipment. If I was careful not to make too much noise, I could search for food here among the wires that hung out the back of the controls - it wasn't an abundantly fruitful area, but it did provide me with a varied diet.

Croissants coated with jam and butter, chocolate bread (as you know a hamster shouldn't be given anything chocolate in case he pouches it - but it never lasted that long with me), toast and marmalade - one morning I even found some almond marzipan that lasted me a couple of days.

Chicken also rolled there. Other meats, too, and...

...Yes, sorry, there I go again.

It was one July evening after the sun had set that calamity struck in the control tower. All air traffic had been diverted to the other airports for security reasons as the President's plane was shortly coming in to land.

'This is flight 65934 to tower - request permission to land. Over.'

This was the pilot of the President's plane, going through the routine that had become a part of his everyday work.

'Affirmative 65934. You are clear for landing.'

I could imagine the plane descending slowly.

'65934 to tower. Are you receiving us? Over.'

'Affirmative 65934. Go ahead. Over.'

'There're no lights on the runway. Please rectify. Over.'

There was a buzz of activity in the control room.

'The console says that the lights are on,' I heard one say.

Another went to look out the window towards the runway. 'No, they're not.'

The controller picked up the microphone. 'Tower to 65934. Abort approach and circle. Do you copy? Over.'

There was a long pause.

'65934 to tower. Negative. Fuel's zero. We have to come in now. Rectify lights immediately. Over.'

The control tower went quiet. The President's plane was coming in on its final approach and it had only minutes until the wheels were to touch the runway - but it couldn't land because the pilot couldn't see where the airport was.

'I don't understand it,' one said. 'The console says that the lights are on.'

'No,' came the reply. 'The console is only telling us that there's power leaving it to activate the lights.

'Somewhere along the line there must be a break....'

'...and we haven't got the time to find out where.'

'Precisely. It'll be somewhere in here, but we can't get round the back of the controls unless we unscrew them from their fixings.'

I heard all this as I sat there in the shadows.

'65934 to tower. Over.'

'Go ahead 65934. Over.'

'What's going on? We've got to come in now. Switch the lights on! Over.'

The controller hesitated before he replied. 'Negative 65934. We have a power failure. We cannot light up the runway. We'll alert the emergency services....'

Their words came back to me. '...there's power leaving to activate the lights...there must be a break....'

'A break,' I squeaked. 'I wonder if I can see it.'

I scampered around the back of the console where the wires exited at the base before being buried under the floor. I examined each wire in turn, looking for frays or any damage that might be responsible.

Success! As I lifted a red and white checked wire I saw that it wasn't connected - indeed, there were rat marks on the end. Obviously, a family of vermin had got into the control tower and bit into anything that they could lay their teeth on.

I found the other end without too much trouble and stopped in mid-action - what could I do?

There was only one thing that made sense - I held one wire with each paw, held my breath and brought the wires together with a flash of electricity and a cascade of yellow sparks.

'They're on!' someone shouted.

They rushed over to the window 'They're on!'

In all the jubilation of that moment, they didn't hear the crackle and hum that emanated from behind the console.

A few minutes later, the President landed.

The lights went out.

I exited from the control tower as fast as my paws would carry me...

'...and since that day,' Hamdenburg concluded, 'they've put safeguards into the control room.

'You see, the problem was that the console had told them that the power was going out, but there was no evidence that it was. Somewhere along the line a disconnection had been made and it was this that needed to be rectified before the power made the light shine.

'The pilot was right - he couldn't see the evidence of what they believed to be true.

'After all, belief does you no good unless it produces light around you.'

He sat back in his leaf chair to take a rest, then jumped up as a plane taxied overhead.

'Your plane!' he squealed. 'Quick!'

We both ran through a complexity of burrows, into the bright light of day and across the tarmac to the front wheel of the jet.

'Remember what I told you about the route to the passenger cabin!' he shouted as I climbed on board. 'Give my squeaks to the hamsters in England!'

'Farewell!' I shouted as the plane turned onto runway two.

'Bon voyage, George!'

The green bag had been securely fastened in the white locker over Lee's head as I'd hoped.

I pushed the zip open with my nose, squeezed my way into the bag and closed the entry behind me.

'That was close,' I thought to myself. 'In fact, this entire holiday has been a series of close calls.'

The plane soared into the skies, leaving the earth far below.

'Next time I go on holiday,' I squeaked, 'I really must get some rest.'

An English Hamster in Scotland

A TAIL OF TWO HAMSTERS

Or

'An English Hamster in Scotland' -

an epic journey of one hamster in his masters' hand luggage

INTRODUCTION

A quick word of introduction is needed, especially if you've not read any of my previous works.

All my stories have meanings, but in my last work ('An English Hamster in Paris') I decided that I wouldn't explain them to the reader but allow him to gain his own understanding of the intended meaning.

That means that these stories are what is known as 'parables' - they aren't just empty stories, but tales with teaching.

THE JOURNEY
FRIDAY 16TH APRIL 1993

'...George was not expecting us to move him to his boarding kennels a full two weeks before we went on holiday. Beyond a shadow of a doubt, even he will not be able to work out a way to stowaway on board our car when we go north in April....'

(Excerpt from Lee's diary dated 31st March 1993)

I cannot tell you how I found myself in the back of my masters' red car as it sped up the main north/south road bound for the Isle of Mull.

Well, to be perfectly honest, I could tell you, but I won't. You see, it's not to my advantage to relate the story of how, yet again, I managed to outwit both Lee and Kath so that they thought I was asleep in my nest compartment, being looked after by some very good friends of theirs.

After all, I may need to use that route of escape again and I simply daren't let my owners on as to how one tiny rodent took on the veritable might of humankind and won.

But, needless to say, both of them knew nothing of my presence in their midst.

'I'm a little sad,' Lee said, checking his speedometer and taking his foot off the accelerator pedal, 'that George couldn't outwit us this time.'

'Yes,' Kath agreed.

She pulled herself back up from her 'crash position' that she'd adopted for the previous bend and continued. 'But poor old George didn't have a chance this time to escape, what with the dummy that you sold him.'

Kath laughed loudly and Lee giggled at the cunning of his dastardly plot.

'Let them laugh,' I thought to myself, 'they'll find out soon enough.'

If there was mention of a dummy, I knew who were the suckers - and it wasn't me.

'Are you getting hungry yet?'

'I could do with a stop to stretch my legs,' Kath replied, 'after that last place I haven't been able to get comfortable.'

The car slowed down in the deceleration lane and turned off the motorway into a local service station. The smell of freshly grilled bacon pervaded the car - how I longed for some freshly grilled bacon! Because bacon is a very salty meat I'm forbidden it at home, but every once in a while a piece of rind falls from Lee's plate and I hoover it up at night when they've long gone to bed.

It was the thought of getting my teeth round a tasty rasher of bacon that blurred my good sense and clear thinking. Instinctively, I prepared to disembark as the car slowly ground to a halt, stopping with its tail almost in the bushes that shielded the car park from the motorway.

A simple descent through the gap in the luggage compartment and I was on the inside of the bumper, leaping down into the undergrowth after a quick cursory sniff in the air for predators.

A short jog found me at the kitchen window underneath, which was an air vent that allowed me entry with a bit of force.

'Hello fellow rodent!' a low-pitched voice squeaked from the darkness. 'Table for one?'

'Yes, please,' I responded. 'Non-squeaking if possible.'

The waiter scurried away to the other side of the café, then waved to me as he pointed to a vacant two-seater that gave me a good view of where Lee and Kath's car was parked.

A menu was opened as I took the weight off my paws.

'No need,' I said, folding it in half and placing it in the rack that contained the sunflower seed ketchup. 'I'll have two large portions of bacon.'

The waiter turned to go. 'Oh, and waiter!' I called.

'Yes, sir?'

'You can leave the rind on, it will give me something to gnaw on for the rest of my journey.'

'Very good, sir.'

It was as I watched his progress into the kitchen that I noticed out of the corner of my eye a middle-aged rodent with bright ginger hair walking up and down in between the tables, looking for somewhere to sit. The diner was already extremely full even though it was barely eleven o'clock and, although I had specifically asked the waiter for a non-squeaking seat, I felt it my duty as a law-abiding rodent, to invite him to sit down at my table.

'Thanks, Jimmy,' he squeaked courteously in a broad Scots accent that betrayed his origin. 'It's good to know that there're still some gentlehams amongst the sassenachs.'

He wore a predominantly red and green tartan with a pure white sporran that jangled as he took up his seat.

'Let me introduce myself,' I ventured. 'My name is George.'

'George?' he asked inquisitively. 'George what?'

'I have no surname - I'm just called George.'

The rodent looked at me with incredulity, but obviously thought better than to pull me up on not having a surname - after all, it was an increasingly common phenomenon.

'My name,' he said after a short pause, pushing himself high in his chair with an air of dignity that was noticeable, 'my name is Hammish - Hammish McAmster - of the well-known McAmster clan who live on the Isle of Mull.'

'You're a real McAmster?'

'Aye, laddy, you seem surprised.'

'But I thought that they'd long since died out.'

'Not so,' came the reply as he lifted the ketchup to his nose to smell its freshness. 'In fact, I'm on my way to the family home in Fionnphort to take part in the New Year celebrations.'

(For those of you unfamiliar with the traditional Hamster calendar, I should point out here that, unlike humankind, we celebrate the new year at the end of winter, which is the beginning of spring. We also adopt a lunar calendar in accordance with the astronomical charts that were laid down by Alexhamster the Great so that the new year falls on a different day each year - but it's always between March and April. We domesticated hamsters don't pay much notice to the celebration of annual events, but I'd heard that the Scottish variety still kept to the traditional celebrations.)

'What a coincidence!' I said. 'I, too, am on my way to Fionnphort with my masters, but not for the celebrations - they've decided to go up there for a rest and I've hitched a ride with them.'

Hammish's ears pricked up. 'You mean you have transport?'

Before he had a chance to continue, I interrupted, 'And you are most welcome to join me. I take it that you're hiking?'

'Why, yes. It's taken me three days so far to get here.'

He thought for a moment and I could see that he was coming up with an offer that I could in no way refuse, for such is Scottish hospitality that it would have been an insult to turn down his kindness.

'Then you must be my guest at the celebrations,' he continued, 'and I will arrange to take you round the island while your masters are staying in Fionnphort.'

I gratefully nodded my acceptance.

We quickly finished our food, paid the bill and dashed across to the car park where my owners were getting into the car. It was fortunate, indeed, that Lee had parked near bushes for he never noticed our approach or boarding.

In a few moments we were away, bound for Mull.

Hammish McAmster descended back through the hole that led out into the rear bumper of the car.

'Past Glasgow, I think,' he squeaked as he picked up another rind of bacon that lay in the corner of our travelling compartment.

'That awful smell of pollution has turned into the old familiar whiff of fresh wildflowers and cool gentle streams.'

Perhaps his imagination was running away with him. After all, the speed we were going, it was surprising that we hadn't gone into orbit. But, come to think of it, there was a change in the atmosphere, now that we'd driven through the city - a certain freshness, a certain lingering shade of smell that conjured up in your mind open pastures and cattle muck.

Hammish's 'cool gentle streams,' however, was going a little bit too far.

I tossed a finished rind out through the hole and onto the road (getting rid of the evidence of occupation), then curled myself up in a ball for a short contemplative nap.

'It's a shame,' Hammish began, 'that you're not visiting us in autumn.'

'But I thought that I was fortunate to be visiting you during the new year festivities?'

'Aye, yes, you are. It just seems that every event of the islands is so important that to miss any one of them is tragic.'

He wiped his eyes with his front paws and curled up for a quick nap. But I was now awake and inquisitive, wondering what I was missing by not being in Scotland in autumn and, though I tried to settle my mind down to get some much needed rest, I found myself asking him the predictable, 'And what's so special that happens in autumn?'

He raised his head, stretching out his paws to remove the aching tiredness from his bones.

'Why, laddy,' he smiled, 'the Highland Games, of course.'

The Highland Games are truly one of the great events in the Scottish calendar, when rodents from all over the island where the McAmsters rule (and other islands that are within easy travelling distance) converge on a small plain that's specially cleared in the lowlands near the sea to compete on behalf of their respective clans or as individuals.

No one is quite sure how old the Games are - some experts put their date back as far as the ancient Olympics, but this appears to be extremely unlikely. What's more important is that they're a meeting place for the rodent communities that inhabit the islands who leave behind all differences to compete in the championships.

Among the more well-known events is 'Tossing the Carrot' - a competition requiring a good sense of balance and sheer brute force. It's usual for a water vole to win this as body building is a natural result of their continual swimming, their muscles are toned into peak condition. But it's not unknown for a giant hamster to win (as one did last year).

At the end of the Games, the festivities begin and rodents dance the night away with partners in what's known as the Highland Roll. It's said that many years ago this used to be called the Highland Fling but, because the hamsters are a bit too fat to 'fling' anywhere (especially by the field mice who are sometimes only half their weight and quite weak as well), the adaptation of this dance into a 'roll' was commissioned.

However, the field mice still fling their partners around when they get excited during a particularly fast piece of music.

But the most enjoyed of all the events through the day is the Tug-o-War, a competition for groups of five rodents who take on other teams. It's almost identical to the human version (except that the rodents' is much older and a piece of good quality string is used rather than rope), the object being to pull the opposing team across a fixed white line that begins by being in the middle of the two sides.

This particular year, all eyes were fixed yet again on the hamsters of Bunessan. They'd been the undefeated champions of the Games for the past twenty-nine years, though none of the original rodents were still in the team.

In the first round they met the water voles who proved to be no contest at all. What chance they had disappeared when they forgot to dry their hands after exiting from their natural habitation, the string slipping through their hands like butter.

In the semis they beat the field mice (who'd received a bye in the first round). To be honest they didn't actually beat them - the field mice had been disqualified for pushing (no-one had explained the rules to them).

Their opponents in the final were the MacAlpens who all shared their ancestry from Stewart MacAlpen, a cereal-eating hamster from Tobermory. The MacAlpens were fitness freaks - young and wildly enthusiastic who'd been preparing for the Games the entire year.

But no-one really believed that the Bunessan team would lose - not even the MacAlpens. They congratulated themselves on having reached the final (which they hadn't anticipated being in before they came) and set themselves to enjoy, as much as possible, their achievement.

For theirs had been an arduous road, an uphill struggle that had begun in the spring with the preliminary rounds. As they'd never entered a team before, they were automatically subject to them to make sure that only the 'cream' of the teams competed on the big day.

Having achieved the necessary standard, they met the lemmings in the first round. It was a one-sided contest, it generally being agreed that the team should never have been there in the first place as three of the five competitors had felt the call of their natural instincts since the first qualifying rounds in spring and had set out over the steep-sided cliffs to swim for Ireland.

The semi-final proved the only main obstacle for the MacAlpens but, in the end the superior weight difference they had gave them the measure of the dormice (who were always allowed seven, instead of five, competitors).

Three o'clock came, the time for the great showdown.

The teams lined up facing one another and shook paws.

'Take the strain!' the umpire shouted, the competitors bringing the mark on the rope to be level with the white line on the ground.

The rodent crowd buzzed with excited anticipation.

The umpire checked the mark one final time, raised his hand in the air to signal the teams to pay attention and shouted with a loud squeak:

'Pull!'

The crowd burst into a wall of sound that engulfed the arena.

Now I must tell you what happened the night before the Games.

Dougal, the anchorham on the Bunessan team, counted himself fortunate to have been picked to receive the honour of certain victory.

Flushed with the team's success over the past twenty-nine years of the Games, he'd become oblivious to the need for self-discipline, indulging himself in a bout of sunflower seed eating from his own private store, stashed away under the root of a local bush.

Perhaps it wouldn't have been too much of a problem had not one of the seeds been decidedly off.

The Bunessan team had had an easy route to the final as I've already mentioned and his fellow rodents had not noticed his rapidly deteriorating health since the first rounds. But, ten minutes into the final when everything within Dougal was desperately trying to get out (indeed, he was beginning to look increasingly green), the MacAlpens, sensing that all was not well with their opponents, shouted to one another to dig deep within themselves for one final pull.

The MacAlpens' effort moved their opponents' feet, gaining a few small millimetres - this was all the encouragement they needed and, taking heart that they'd found a crack in their adversary's armour, let out a defiant squeak, pulling the Bunessans over the white mark and securing the victory with ecstatic cheers from their clan who'd come to give them support.

Dougal scampered off to the nearest woodland and was sick.

'...until the victory's assured,' Hammish concluded, 'there needs to be no presumption and no resting upon the laurels of former victories.'

My attention was momentarily distracted from him as the car slowed down and muffled voices came from the driver's seat.

'I think we're here.' I turned back to face my travelling companion. 'Quickly! Into the hand luggage or we'll have to stay out here all night!'

The car boot clicked open, then shut.

We had safely arrived at our stopover in Oban.

THE ARRIVAL
SATURDAY 17TH APRIL 1993

Leopard, leopard, spotty cat,
How I wonder where you're at.
Your markings make you hard to see,
I hope that you will not eat me.

(Piece of graffiti on the wall of the café where George ate)

'Kath, look!' Lee shouted, recoiling against the wall as if he'd been struck forcefully in his stomach, a horrified grimace covering his face like an actor in a horror movie.

Kath sat up in bed in the darkness before sunrise. She reached for the table lamp, sending illuminating rays of light flooding the room as it clicked on and looking at her portable alarm - it was two thirty in the morning.

Lee stood motionless, breathless, his arms outstretched across the wall, eyes fixed downwards on the carpet near the bed that was out of sight from where Kath had sat up.

'What's the matter?' she enquired, bleary-eyed. 'You look terrible, what is it?'

'The...the...er...' Lee choked for the words. 'The floor...there...look!'

Lee pointed with his finger to a small black and white object that Kath still failed to see. Slowly, she moved across the bed to peer over the side, but before she reached the edge, Mr Duke the landlord began knocking on the door loudly.

'Are you alright in there?' His voice was panicky and there was urgency in the rapidity of his knocking. 'Is there a fire? Shall I call an ambulance?'

Distracted by the banging, Kath turned and let him in.

'It's my husband,' she said, 'I don't know what's wrong - but it must be something terrible.'

They both rushed over to Lee's side and prised him from the wall.

He was still shaking as they sat him down on the side of the bed, placing a glass of cold water in his hand as Kath repeated with much anxiety, 'What's wrong, darling?'

It took Lee a couple of minutes to calm down - then, with a tremor in his voice, he pointed down to where the object lay.

'Look!' he said, beginning to shake once more, 'look there!'

Both Kath and Mr Duke eyed the floor - nothing.

They returned their gaze to Lee. 'What is it?'

'Look!' Lee repeated, leaning over and picking up a small black and white fragment that was no more than half a centimetre long.

'This...it's the remains of an eaten sunflower seed.'

Mr Duke looked at Kath with pity.

'Shall I call an ambulance?' he said. 'I can see he's delirious.'

'No, no.' Kath tried to bring a sense of calm to the proceedings. 'He's always like...er...what I mean is he's been under a lot of pressure recently, he needs to get away for a rest.'

Mr Duke was not reassured.

Kath continued, 'I'm sure he'll be fine. Please go back to bed, I'm sure I can handle my husband's problem.'

He was only too pleased to flee - I mean 'leave.'

As he went out, he looked back over his shoulder, offering, 'If you need any help then I'm upstairs - but I'm going to securely bolt my door. You never can be too careful with some people.'

The door clicked shut as Kath began, 'Now what's the matter?'

'You don't understand,' Lee said, 'the sunflower seed...it proves... er...conclusively that George has escaped and is even now lurking somewhere amongst our luggage, waiting his opportunity to escape the confines of bondage and be free to experience another holiday at our expense!'

'Nonsense!' Kath gave a giggle. 'You know as well as I do that those shells get stuck to almost everything we put on - you must've dropped it when you took some clothes out of the suitcase. After the trick you played on George to keep him down south, there's no way he would ever be able to get up here, is there?'

Lee submitted to reason (not for the first time) slowly getting into bed to return to rest mode. Kath switched the light out and cuddled up to him.

'Never mind, dear,' she whispered. 'It'll be alright in the morning.'

I turned to Hammish and scolded him. 'Be more careful with those empty shells! You nearly had us discovered!'

'Sorry, my friend, I didn't realise....'

We exited from underneath the bed where we'd been hiding and climbed back into Lee's hand luggage.

When the alarm woke Kath, Lee was not in bed. Instead, he was on his hands and knees looking for clues through a magnifying glass that he'd discovered in the bedside cabinet.

'I've found four hairs that could possibly belong to George,' he said. 'All I need is an electron microscope and I can prove one way or the other whether he's here.'

Kath gently removed the magnifying glass from his hand. 'Now, Lee, listen to me - forget it...you're here to enjoy yourself and have a rest.'

'But....'

'No "buts" - George isn't here!'

Lee conceded, 'Okay, okay,' he said, 'I'll forget all about it.'

He got up, dressed and went downstairs to the breakfast table.

Mr Duke seemed to have forgotten about it also for he never mentioned the events of last night. Or, at least, he seemed to have forgotten it. But it did seem strange that the margarine tub had the words 'sunflower seed oil' indelibly masked out with a black felt tip - the ink was still wet, too.

Lee and Kath paid their bill, loaded the car with their luggage and drove off towards the harbour.

We sat looking out of a half-opened porthole as the ferry sailed beyond the protection of Kerrera and toward the Sound of Mull.

It was a pleasant spring morning, the gulls flying in the wake of the boat looking for food that might be dropped from the deck of the ship. We both kept well out of sight, for the birds in this part of the world think nothing of swooping down on any small rodent they spot for a quick meal.

Hammish strained his eyes westward, gazing at the shoreline of his beloved Mull. A tear came to his eye as we glided past Lady's rock, signalling our entry into the Sound.

'It won't be long now, George,' he squeaked, 'until we're on Mull.'

We both looked at the promontory of rock that jutted out from the island upon which was a building that reminded me of pictures of castles I'd seen in some of Lee's tourist information books that I'd glanced through a few months ago.

'Is that....'

'Duart castle,' he interrupted before I had a chance to complete my question, 'the home of the hamster clan known as the Macleans.'

'Is everyone in Scotland called a "Mc" something or other?'

Hammish looked at me disapprovingly but, instead of scolding, he answered, 'It only means "son of" - McAmster, which is my clan, simply means "son of the Hamster."'

This intrigued me for I hadn't heard the explanation before. I continued my questioning. 'Then was your father surnamed "Hamster"?'

Puzzled as to my logic, Hammish squeaked, 'No, he was a McAmster, too.'

'But shouldn't that make you a McMcAmster?'

Hammish laughed. 'No, you misunderstand - if we did that I'd probably be surnamed something like McMcMcMcMcMcMcMcMcMcMcMcMcMcMcMcMcAmster! It doesn't work like that!'

I was still intrigued. 'Why not?'

'Because it just doesn't, that's why! A long time ago there was a rodent who was surnamed "Hamster" and then came a clan that were all descended from him one way or another, so they called themselves "sons of the Hamster" - and all their descendants were also sons of that Hamster whether grandsons or great grandsons or whatever. But they all took the name "McAmster."'

'Oh,' I responded, 'right - thanks for explaining it to me.'

Hammish looked at me not knowing whether he detected a tinge of sarcasm in my voice or not. I'd forgotten that the McAmsters were a proud race and viewed a stranger's questions with immense suspicion - it'd all been part of the struggle for survival during the clan's early years. From then on I tried to tone down my questions to make them less offensive.

Hammish changed the subject for fear of another probing investigation.

'Duart castle was the most strategic fortress in our defence of the island against the Vikings.'

'Oh yes, I read a bit about that before I came up - didn't they set up a colony near here?'

'Aye,' he replied, 'but the McAmsters and the Macleans,' (he rushed over those names hoping that I wouldn't take up my previous line of questioning), 'defended the island from Duart castle and prevented them from ever landing.'

'But I thought there was a colony on Mull?'

'That's what the history books tell you about the human Vikings, but I'm referring to the rat Vikings that terrorised the rodents of Mull at about the same time.'

'Oh, I hadn't heard about them - who was their leader?'

'Don't you know?'

'No,' I confessed, 'I'm not too good on Scottish history.'

'His name,' Hammish spoke in a whisper as if his name was not to be used in public, 'was Ethelrat the Unsteady....'

The Epic Saga of Ethelrat the Unsteady[4]

When Ethelrat the Viking had reached the age of two, he already had a ship prepared for war,

With a thousand field mice at the oars press ganged from fields nearby, he sailed to conquer Mull, then conquer all.

He did not fear the raging sea, he did not fear the wind, but sailed boldly o'er the ocean for ten days,

'Til at last he spied a shallow port o'erwatched by Duart Castle, and set the craft to land in that fair bay.

The field mice rowed against the waves, they struggled with the tide, but one small member overboard he fled,

And having reached that northern shore upon which stood the castle, he rushed into the courts and this he said:

'For freedom! For freedom! I bring this news to you! For freedom from the power of the Vikings!

Arise bold Hams and arm for war, this day you need to fight! Be strong and heed the message of these tidings!'

This day it was a special day, it marked the fiftieth year since the time that all Mull's rodents had been freed.

'An acceptable day for fighting to the lord of both our clans!' a hamster shouted loudly who agreed.

They armed themselves for warfare, assembling on the shore, while the Viking ship came slowly t'ward the land,

But one young Ham named Nigel (who was brainier than the rest) took up his pin and t'ward the boat he swam.

'Tis better one should win for all, than all should die together! 'Tis better one should die that all may live!

'Tis better that the freedom's gained to be enjoyed by all - and so, dear friends, my life to you I give!'

'Come back!' they cried upon the shore. 'We'll fight them on the beaches!' but Nigel had gone past the point of hearing.

The Vikings failed to see him come, their attention taken up with the group of soldiers they were slowly nearing.

Pin in paw he neared the boat and sank it in the hull, the water spurted in and pulled the craft down.

'Abandon ship!' the Vikings cried. 'The vessel's doomed and sinking!' - the ship hit rock and then it ran aground.

A thousand field mice made it and were welcomed on the shore, though the rats all drowned and now the sea's their grave,

And Nigel, though they'd looked for him and had thought that he had perished, turned up alive and well on the third day.

As the ferry docked at Craignure, Hammish and I nestled down in the side pocket of Lee and Kath's hand luggage.

Although I wanted to watch the scenery flash past as we journeyed the final forty or so miles to Fionnphort, my midmorning nap was well overdue. So I closed my eyes to the world, recounting in my mind the story of Ethelrat the Unsteady as I drifted into a sound sleep.

As soon as we arrived, Mrs Haigh, the proprietor of the guest house, greeted Lee and Kath, showing them to their room.

---

[4]*The Saga of Ethelrat the Unsteady' is a folklore poem that I've translated directly from the Scandinavian hamscripts of that era. Although the memory lives on in the minds of Mull's hamsters, the extant hamscripts are in such a bad state of repair that I felt it necessary to retranslate directly from the original language. Incidentally, why Ethelrat got the nickname 'Unsteady' no one is quite sure of - there are no other events in the rodent's life that have been recorded, but it seems probable that it came from one of these, now lost, sagas.*

Hammish apologised for having to leave me, but it was important that his relatives know that he'd arrived safely. There were also plans to be made for the new year celebrations and, in the finest Scottish hamster tradition, he wanted to see to them himself.

'Stay in the house!' he warned me, 'and don't venture outside into the wilds of Mull. I'll return tomorrow afternoon and be your guide for your remaining time here, but for now....'

'Can't I wander around Fionnphort?'

'No!' his tone was emphatic, 'too dangerous. There are bogs everywhere and, besides, you're not used to the strange beasties that lurk in these parts.'

Hammish scampered off before I had a chance to further object.

'Well,' I thought, 'at least I get a day all by myself to recover!'

He swallowed long and hard as he stood there, calling up his courage to push him one more step forward into uncharted territory.

After what seemed like an eternity, his eyes opened, peering below him at the hustle and bustle of a frantic Saturday afternoon. As a frown settled upon his mind - a very worried frown at that - he folded up his wings into his body and hopped down from the coping to begin (all over again) the pacing to and fro on the roof.

'No,' he squawked fearfully, 'no, it won't do, it just won't do.'

He hung his head in shame as despair flooded his consciousness and sorrow welled up from deep within. One solitary tear came to his eye.

'Why wasn't I made like other birds?' he continued. 'Why can't I fly and soar effortlessly into the sky like I know I should?'

Not only had the pigeon continued this way for many hours, but he trudged relentlessly on, back and forth, well into the day and the early part of the evening.

Still he moaned, still he complained, as his head drooped ever lower to match his failing will.

Trepo the hamster had had a restless day trying to grab what sleep he could before the inevitable approach of night, when the energy inside seemed to get switched on and he'd dart round his territory in search of food and fun like a headless chicken.

But, as I've said, it'd been a restless day's sleep.

Trepo lived nestled around insulation that filled the cavity between the flat roof above and the ceiling beneath. An old ventilation duct gave him access to the rooms below and to the roof upon which the pigeon paced backwards and forwards most of the day.

It was this that had kept him awake for, although he was used to the occasional bird landing above him in search of food, the frequency, consistency and accompanying loud squawks were like a constantly dripping tap in his ears that dispelled sleep from his eyes and rest from his body.

In a vain attempt to eliminate the distraction, Trepo had screwed pieces of insulation into each ear and buried his head into his nesting material. But the bass of the noise could be felt, not just heard, so that any attempt was doomed to failure.

Three hours before he normally got up to groom in anticipation of the first darkness, he decided to risk a look onto the flat roof to see if the tapping could somehow be eliminated.

He poked his nose out of the ventilation pipe, taking a good long sniff. Well, it certainly didn't smell like there were any predators about.

Still erring on the side of caution, he tentatively looked over towards the coping and was surprised to see a grey pigeon pacing up and down with its head drooping with sadness, almost scraping the surface of the roof.

'Hey, gumboots,' Trepo shouted, 'can't an honest hamster get a little rest?'

'O dear,' he cooed, not hearing the squeaks that emanated from a small opening two feet away. 'O dear, dear, dear. What am I going to do?'

'This is pointless,' Trepo thought. 'So caught up with his own problems he can't hear a thing that's going on around him! Easy prey... easy prey - it's a good job that there're so few predators in these parts!'

He watched him for a full five minutes before deciding that the only course of action was to go over and sort him out. Trepo scanned the skies for gulls - there were few other dangers for him other than those most gigantic of birds, which would swoop down on unsuspecting rodents from great heights, swallowing them whole in a matter of seconds.

He'd already lost part of his tail through a close encounter and, as far as he was concerned, that was going to be the last!

But this pigeon was no threat - he was only a seed eater.

Trepo pulled himself out of the hole and paced slowly over to the edge of the roof. The pigeon was so pre-occupied with his problem that he never noticed the small tan and white object as he neared hesitantly, questioning in his own mind what an absurd scene he was witnessing before his eyes.

The bird once again peered over the coping, down into the dispersing crowds who were by now scattering for home, then resumed pacing up and down, head bent over, voice shaking whenever he squawked a few anxious words of doubt and fear.

As the pigeon began once more to pace up and down, Trepo jumped into his path and stood with teeth bared in half-threat and half-smile. The bird took one look at him and froze to the spot - it wasn't fear, only surprise, for he'd thought himself alone.

Trepo put his teeth away, sitting on his rear paws and eyeing his feathered acquaintance with a questioning stare. The pigeon returned it, baffled as to the reason why a non-predator challenged his right to pace on a piece of land - well, roof, actually.

And what was a hamster doing up here in the first place?

'Do you realise what you've done for the past day?' Trepo's tone was indignant at being kept awake the best part of the daylight hours.

The bird searched his memory. 'Done?' he thought. 'All I've wanted to do was fly!'

Before he could answer, Trepo continued. 'I'll tell you what you've done! You've been pacing to and fro, backwards and forwards, up and down, this way and that, on the roof of my nest ALL DAY LONG and I haven't yet snatched two minutes of sleep!'

The bird hung his head in shame.

'O dear,' he cooed. 'O dear, dear, dear.'

As if the burden of failing as a flightless pigeon wasn't enough, the thought of keeping this rodent awake added to the already great sorrow that had flooded over him.

After a long silence, his head drooped further downward as he whispered, barely audibly, 'I...I can't fly.'

Trepo looked puzzled. 'Can't fly? What's wrong with you that you can't fly?'

'Nothing's wrong - I just can't fly.'

The rodent thought for a moment. 'But there must be something wrong with you if you can't fly...' and, throwing his paws up into the air in puzzlement, he continued. '...All birds can fly - that's what makes 'em birds!'

'Perhaps...perhaps...' he searched for words to describe his feelings, '...perhaps I was meant to be a gorilla.'

'Gorilla?' Trepo half-laughed at such a suggestion: the other half questioned himself as to whether this pigeon might be in the process of having an identity crisis.

'Well, if you were meant to be a gorilla, you're the funniest looking one I've ever seen!'

The bird's head drooped still further. If this wasn't all-so-very serious, Trepo would have been rolling about in a fit of giggles by now.

'What's needed,' he thought, 'is some drastic action.'

'My friend,' Trepo continued, 'hop up here onto the coping a moment and let me point something out to you.'

Both animals peered over the edge of the roof, down onto the pedestrianised street that carried the last of the late shoppers.

'What do you see?'

The bird eyed the scene carefully, reeling off a list of observations.

'Very good,' encouraged Trepo, 'but you've missed one important sight. Look there!' and he pointed at a small red brick that stood out from the others. 'Do you see that ant?'

'Ant?' squawked the pigeon in complaint. 'How am I supposed to see an ant from this distance?'

'O yes, I'm sorry - I forgot that you birds don't have as good an eyesight as us hamsters,' (which was, incidentally, a blatant lie). 'Wait here a moment while I go and get you a magnifying glass.'

As Trepo scurried back across the roof, the bird strained his eyes to try and make out the insect, leaning ever more forward to see this important sight. All the while, Trepo squeaked as he went away from the bemused pigeon.

'You see, my friend, I know that you can fly because you were born a bird. If you'd been born a gorilla...' Trepo kept a tight control on his laughter, '...you'd act like one and you don't. Everything about you tells me that you're a bird - and, if a bird, then you were made to fly.'

He turned, having reached the other side of the roof, and faced the pigeon who continued to strain his eyes to see where this ant was.

'Now let me explain my final point to you...' Trepo broke off abruptly, accelerating violently towards the bird who, by now, was starting to wonder why it was taking the rodent so long.

As he neared the edge of the roof, the target firmly in his sights, he leapt upwards and made a brief but hefty impact with a bundle of feathers. Trepo bounced back onto the roof. The pigeon had disappeared over the coping.

Three days later at the close of the day when Trepo had exited from his nest onto the roof for a short drink from the rain pools that formed close to the ventilation duct, there was a clap of strong wings and the rustle of feathers as the pigeon landed on the roof, inches away from the rodent who stopped drinking immediately, looking upwards at the visitor.

'I suppose you thought that was funny!' the bird began. 'Pushing a poor, fragile bird to an early grave!'

'Grave?' said Trepo in defence. 'Pardon me if I don't see the tombstone! - you did fly, didn't you?'

Inwardly, the pigeon had been happy and smiling long before he ever landed on the roof, but had adopted a serious frown to see Trepo's reaction. His sullen face now broke into a radiant smile, cooing with glee the way only pigeons know how to, as he scratched the tarmac roof with his left foot.

'Yes,' he chuckled, 'and what an experience that was!'

The hamster began squeaking repeatedly, rubbing his nose with his paws and blinking with excitement.

'But tell me,' he squawked, 'what made you push me over the edge? Why not persuade me to stretch out my wings and fly?'

'That would never have worked! It was a desperate problem that needed a desperate solution. Pushing you over the side forced you to confront the problem that no amount of arguing would ever have done. You had to fly, you had to stretch out your wings and save yourself - and you did!'

'But what if....'

'Ha!' Trepo interrupted, half leaping into the air as if a violent sneeze had suddenly come upon him with no warning. 'Never mind the "What if" - in the confrontation you proved who you are - a bird's a bird and it's natural for him to do what birds do!'

Trepo paused and smiled knowingly at his feathered friend.

Then he giggled as the pigeon's words came back to him.

'Huh!' he squealed. 'Gorilla, indeed!'

Hammish found me late on in the afternoon, a few minutes after he'd entered the guest house.

'You're difficult to track down!' he squeaked. 'I've been following your trail all over the house! What've you been up to?'

'That's a long story,' I replied. 'Have you got everything sorted out for the festivities?'

'Oh yes - it was crucial I went myself, there were a few personal touches that are so important.'

'Do you fancy something to eat?' I asked, smelling the cooking that wafted in from the kitchen. 'My stomach's telling me it's time for food.'

'Aye,' Hammish replied. 'Let's go....'

A funny thing happened to the carrots on the way to the dining table.

Mrs Haigh distinctly remembered emptying a pan full of boiled and drained carrots into a serving dish on the kitchen work top and, even though her back had been turned, hastily preparing the other dishes, she knew of a certainty that no-one, but no-one, had come into the kitchen.

But here she was, motionless, halfway between the kitchen and Lee and Kath's table, staring down at the remnants of half a pound of carrots.

Hammish and I had been extremely careful not to leave any hairs behind - neither had we nibbled on anything that we hadn't already taken - and we'd purposefully licked up the paw prints that we'd made on the work top before disappearing behind the fridge and into our storage hole. There was nothing that could be attributed to the presence of rodents, all trace had been removed.

Mrs Haigh returned to the kitchen, opened a tin of carrots and supplemented the portion with the microwaved contents. This time she kept her eye on them throughout the entire culinary operation.

'Tell me about Iona,' I said, crunching my way through an undercooked carrot. We'd indeed been fortunate to find ourselves staying in a guest house that was almost exclusively vegetarian. 'Is it really as pretty as they say it is?'

Hammish thought for a moment before offering a reply. It seemed as if he was contemplating the length and breadth of the island to see what his words should be.

'It could be...' he paused, '...and it could not be.'

I hadn't expected such a reply, it took me by surprise. 'What do you mean by that?'

'I mean that you could find it pretty or you could not.' He had a wry smile on his face and I wondered just what it was that he was hiding from me - or was it just my imagination?

'But that doesn't tell me anything,' I complained, rephrasing my original question. 'Is Iona reputed to be beautiful?'

Hammish hesitated again before answering.

'Well?'

'Well,' he began, 'it's not that easy to answer a question like that.'

'Why not?'

'Because some people come with false hopes and are disappointed. Others go with no preconceived ideas and find it to be wonderful.' He looked me straight in the eye. 'And which one of those are you, my friend?'

This whole conversation was fast becoming like an interrogation - surely I'd asked a simple question, why the enigmatic answer? And why had Hammish always seemed to steer the conversation away from this subject every time we'd talked previously? What was it with this island that made him guard his words?

'All I'm asking,' I tried again, 'is whether the island is picturesque, whether it has any natural beauty.'

I could see that I wasn't going to get a straight answer by the look on Hammish's face.

'Would you go into a confectionery shop to buy a cabbage?' he asked.

Was I really hearing right? 'Why...er...no.'

'Or into a jewellers to get a TV?'

I couldn't see where this was leading but I decided to continue to see where we arrived.

'Most certainly not.'

'Then let me repeat myself,' he said with a broad smile on his face, 'I could tell you everything that's on Iona, but if you're going there to get something that doesn't exist then you'll come away disappointed.'

'But I'm not expecting anything, I was only asking you what I should be expecting!'

'And how can I tell you that?'

This whole conversation was beginning to make my head spin, I decided to bring it to a close. 'Then I shall wait for tomorrow.'

'Now that's the best policy you could adopt,' he squeaked. 'Why didn't you do that in the first place?'

THE ISLAND
MONDAY 19TH APRIL 1993

'Iona of my heart
Iona of my love.
Instead of monks' voices
Shall be the lowing of cattle;
But before the world shall come to an end
Iona shall be as it was.'

'So what do you reckon to that old statement that Columba made before he died?' Lee closed the tourist booklet that he'd been flicking through at the breakfast table and placed it on top of the pile of other publications that they'd been sent about the island.

'Don't know,' Kath answered. 'Perhaps we'll understand a bit better once we've been there.'

She paused before returning a question. 'What are we going there to see, anyway, some monument or other?'

'Not exactly, no.' Lee picked up another slice of toast.

'Well?' Kath began. 'What are we going to see?'

'I'm not sure exactly.'

'But you do know what's on the island, don't you?'

'Oh yes,' and he reeled off a list of geographic locations that they'd planned to visit, ranging from the mildly interesting to the areas in which certain things were reputed to have happened, '...but the main reason that we're going is to see what I'm not at all sure about.'

'A man after my own heart,' Hammish whispered, letting out a justified squeak of satisfaction as I strained at the side pocket flap to try and learn what was so special about the island.

'You're not making sense,' Kath objected - then reflected, 'but that's not at all unusual.'

Lee looked at her with humour in his eyes. 'Don't you ever feel the need to be somewhere without knowing why? That's the way it was with Paris last year - we went because I thought that that was the place we should be. It's the same with Iona - we're going cos that's where we should be, but try and get me to put it into words and I wouldn't be able to.'

Kath accepted the explanation - but I hadn't.

'What a crazy load of individuals I've made acquaintance with!' I thought. 'Is it only me who's sane?'

By this time Hammish was expecting me to concede he was right as that 'I-told-you-so' smirk covered his face. I tried not to look his way, but it's extremely difficult when you're sandwiched together in a bag with little or no room to move.

'Wait and see,' Hammish broke the silence, 'just wait and see....'

I took a long, hard sniff at the blade of grass that stood in front of me.

'Strange,' I thought, 'it smells like an ordinary blade of grass.'

It looked like one, too.

Tentatively, I gnawed at a piece and chewed it over. This was very strange - it even tasted like an ordinary blade of grass.

Hammish and I had been briskly walking round the island for near on four hours and, so far, I hadn't seen anything unusual or extraordinary. It all looked pretty much 'business as usual' as far as nature was concerned. Even the fellow rodents that we'd met were ordinary - none of them had had eight legs or three ears or twelve eyes or....

So just what was so special about this place?

'Hammish, tell me something,' I hesitantly began as we waited for the rendezvous with Lee and Kath at the quayside. Although he'd been reluctant to say what was special about Iona before we visited it, I sensed that now his mind had changed and he was willing to illuminate me.

'What would you like to know, my friend?'

'I think that you can already tell what my question is before I ask it.'

Hammish smiled. 'Nevertheless, please ask.'

'We've been all over the island,' I began, 'across it, round it (and in it); we've conversed with its inhabitants (and fled for safety from the attention of others); we've even tasted the produce of the island wherever we've gone. And yet, in spite of all this, I'm still no closer to discovering why this is supposed to be a "special" place. What have I failed to see, Hammish?'

Indirectly, he began, with a dramatic voice and an air of seriousness that fixed my attention on his every word.

'Many humans make pilgrimage to this island thinking that they'll find all sorts of things, but their hope is disappointed because they come looking for something that doesn't exist - others, more foolish than these, say that they've found what they came for when they never discovered anything.

'It's not the island that's special, George, but what the Creator did on it that's special. And if He doesn't continue to do things here then it's no longer a special place.

'It's the same the world over. A place - anywhere - is only of importance if it's a place on which the Creator is doing His own work - doing it now, that is. He's the One that makes the difference.

'Remember, my friend, that humans seek all sorts of things, but there's only One who's worth seeking wherever you go or wherever you find yourself.

'Men make bold promises about Iona but few are founded upon reality - it's better to wait and see what's there than to let another flood your expectation with lies.'

I'd listened attentively as Hammish continued to teach me about these 'special places' - he certainly knew about them, it was obvious. As he came to a conclusion I smiled and acknowledged the lesson.

Kath and Lee weren't very long in coming to the ferry. In a momentary distraction, we hopped on board their bag and made it back to the guest house safely.

THE TRUFFLES
TUESDAY 20TH APRIL 1993

In the middle of the night, Hammish decided that he needed a drink of water.

From where we'd made our nest that night, it was a simple matter of running across the bedroom floor, ascending the cold water pipe and, with one acrobatic manoeuvre, land on top of the sink that contained the regulation size bar of soap and Lee and Kath's toothbrushes.

It was my own fault that I'd not warned Hammish about the cold water tap - you see, after my masters had washed at night, the wet soap greased the side of the sink, making any walking treacherous. Even more so was the exertion needed to stretch the few inches along the tap to where the water exited.

With two rear paws on the edge and two front paws firmly grasping the spout, Hammish drank his fill to satisfy his thirst.

Not realising that the distance between each pair of limbs was growing wider by the moment, he tried to push himself back onto the top of the sink, but the pressure only forced his rear paws to slip further away until, hanging for dear life onto the tap, his hind legs ended their contact with the surface and he swung into the bowl, sliding to an abrupt end as one paw lodged itself momentarily down the plughole.

Checking to see that nothing was broken, he began pacing back up the incline but found he got nowhere - the bowl was clean and shiny and it hindered any major progress.

He took a run at it but ended up in the same place.

Then he tried to reach the tap spout, but it was out of reach and the chain on the plug was no use either as it was swung over the hot water tap.

Hammish was as stuck as a kamikaze spider that freefalls into the bath (though why spiders do this is for a totally different reason that I haven't time to go in to).

I'd heard Hammish's cry of distress as he fell into the sink and awoke abruptly to witness, in sound only, his varying attempts at an escape. Before I'd had a chance to rush over and help him, Lee sat up dozey-eyed in bed and checked his glass on the bedside cabinet - it was empty, so he got up to refill it for a drink.

I quickly calculated the speed with which I could get to the sink, rescue Hammish and return to our nest - no, there just wasn't enough time. What was going to happen would happen, I was powerless to intervene.

Lee, still bleary-eyed and full of sleep, switched on the light over the sink and gazed down into the bowl.

'Oh,' he said calmly, not sure whether this was dreamland or reality, 'there's a hamster in the sink.'

'Mcsqueak,' said Hammish, embarrassed at his dilemma.

'Now, little hamster, you really must stop playing in there,' and he gently lifted him up in both hands, placing him on the carpeted floor and instructing him, 'Run along home and snuggle into your nice warm nest.'

He returned to the sink, filled his cup and took a long drink.

Hammish, by this time, had fled for his life to the safety of our nest situated underneath the wardrobe.

'All's well that ends well,' he said.

'It's not over yet,' I corrected him.

Lee returned to bed, put his empty glass back beside him and settled down to sleep. Ten seconds later he sat up abruptly, looked over at the sink through the gloom and darkness and let out a deafening, 'There's a hamster in the sink! KATH, THERE'S A HAMSTER IN THE SINK!!....'

Kath jumped out her side of the bed forgetting the wall, then reached over to the bedside lamp to illuminate the room.

'Calm down,' she said. 'Calm down!'

Lee sat shaking on the bed. 'There's a hamster in the sink, I tell you - it's George, it must be!'

She got up, all feeling of sleepiness banished, and gazed into the bowl.

Nothing.

'Have you been dreaming?' she asked.

'No, no, it was real - I went to the sink to fetch a glass of water and there was this hamster looking up at me with a Scottish accent.'

Kath observed the tumbler beside the bed. 'But the tumbler's empty. Wet, yes, but empty - that's the way it was when we went to bed. You must have had a dream.'

'But I can't have done - it all seemed so real.'

Confused by his wife's persistence and certainty, he lay back on the soft downy pillow.

'A dream? Was it a dream?'

He thought for a moment before concluding, 'Must have been, yes, a bad dream.'

The light was put out and they drifted back into a deep sleep.

Mrs Haigh, the proprietor, still had her finger hovering over the nine button on the phone, ready to press it for the third time.

When morning came, Kath woke up before Lee and gently got out of bed without disturbing him. The ginger hairs that remained stuck on the soap and around the plughole, she washed down with some cold water before climbing back into the comfort of bed.

'At least,' she said to herself, 'Lee won't be able to claim his own hair is certain proof that George is with us!'

Nevertheless, Lee was disappointed that the sink was clean when he got up to brush his teeth.

Before leaving for the day, Mrs Haigh reminded them of the guest house rules and emphasised the point about excessive use of noise during the early hours of the morning.

Wisely, we avoided all possible contact with Lee and Kath that day, but out of necessity we joined them for the evening meal. A little later, we followed them, so to speak, into the residents' lounge for a warm.

'Do you think we could train George to hunt for truffles?' Lee jokingly asked Kath as they sipped a hot cup of tea. Inspired by a conversation Lee'd had with a local about the training of pigs to hunt these delicacies, he'd let his mind work overtime and now made an observation about our incredible sense of smell.

'If we could bridle and refine George's natural talents, we could become millionaires almost overnight. Just think, Kath, of the simplicity of the procedure - an ordinary piece of string tied around his waist to pull him up out of the soil whenever he found a truffle, and an endless supply of sunflower seeds to give him as a reward....'

I was about to raise myself above the shelf of books that we were hiding behind and protest with the loudest possible squeak I could, but Hammish had already noticed my annoyance and had placed his paw on my shoulder to prevent me.

'Humans are strange,' he whispered as I turned to complain at the restriction. 'Besides, I wonder how your master would envisage teaching us to hunt for them.'

'Weren't you listening?' I squeaked. 'He said that with modern techniques, it should be possible to train pigs to teach us to do their job!'

'Well that is silly!' Hammish laughed and he repeated the phrase. "Pigs to teach us." Ha!'

He paused momentarily before exclaiming loudly, 'But everyone knows that it was us hamsters who taught the pigs to hunt for truffles in the first place!'

Furlock Holmes, that most celebrated of all Victorian rodent detectives, and Doctor Flotsam, his beloved assistant, plodded gingerly along the coastline at the base of towering cliffs that stretched skyward immeasurable distances, making them both dizzy when they gazed upward.

'This scenery is breathtaking, Holmes!' Flotsam spoke enthusiastically, 'I'm so glad we chose Mull as the location for our holiday this year.'

'Yes, indeed.'

Flotsam was drawn to the cliffs, impressed by their grandeur and magnitude. 'Tell me, Holmes' he began. 'You're well up on geology and all that - what type of rocks are these?'

Furlock didn't have to look, he'd already made a mental note of their classification. He turned to his colleague. 'Sedimentary, my dear Flotsam,' he squeaked.

Just then, a squeal of panic echoed off the hard-faced cliffs and they spun round to see a small, grey rodent - the proprietor of the guest house at which they were staying - race into view, rapidly arriving where they now both stood.

'Tragedy!' he squeaked, 'tragedy! And double tragedy!'

It took Flotsam a moment to calm the breathless messenger, sitting him down on a small pebble until he regained his composure.

'Mr Holmes, you've got to help!' he begged. 'You're the only one who'll know what to do!'

'And what dilemma brings you here that couldn't have waited until our return?'

'It's Larry,' he was taking deep breaths, trying to calm himself, 'he's been kidnapped by the rats. Oh, it's terrible, Mr Holmes, you've got to help, you're the only one who can....'

Doctor Flotsam once again calmed the messenger down.

Furlock, in a voice of tranquillity, offered some advice. 'Now, my friend, it's better that you take your time and tell me the entire story - and begin by telling me about this Larry, the name means absolutely nothing to me.'

'Larry,' he began, 'is the brother of Harry' (that still didn't mean anything to either Furlock or Flotsam). 'They're twin brothers in the island truffle trade.'

'Ah yes,' Furlock remembered, 'I recall seeing their names in a number of articles.'

'Well, Larry has been kidnapped by the rats and news has just come that they're demanding one million sunflower seeds ransom to be delivered by the paw of his brother Harry at the site of the secret truffle tree in three days' time.'

'And where is this "secret truffle tree"?' enquired Doctor Flotsam.

'That's the reason it's secret - only the brothers know. It's why they've done so well in business cos they don't disclose the source of their products....'

'...and the problem, therefore,' concluded Holmes, 'is that Harry can't divulge the location of the secret truffle tree and thereby rescue his brother with a band of hamsters from the village, otherwise their empire will crumble as everyone will know the tree's location....'

'That's right!'

'...so he's forced into paying the ransom to both save his brother and protect his livelihood. But,' concluded Holmes, 'I fear that the rats won't stop at the ransom price....'

'You don't mean, Holmes?' Flotsam looked horrified.

'Why, yes, my friend. What's a million sunflower seeds in comparison to the knowledge of where an endless supply of costly truffles are? The rats could finance an evil empire, the likes of which has never yet been seen - if they alone know that secret.'

The messenger spoke again. 'And Harry refuses categorically to do anything but pay the ransom. He trusts...' that word was particularly unpalatable with the next phrase, 'he trusts the rats.'

'But tell him that he must reveal the location!' Flotsam objected.

'Not so fast, Doctor,' Holmes interrupted. He put his paw to his chin and gave it a brief scratch as he thought through the dilemma. 'You say we have three days?'

'That's right, sir.'

'Then tell thirty of the bravest of your village's hamsters to arm themselves for war!'

'But Holmes, how can....'

'We have much to do.' Furlock turned to the messenger. 'Please excuse us.'

He bowed politely as they walked off.

'Now listen carefully, Flotsam, this is what we will need....'

Deep in the heart of the wood stood the secret truffle tree - one tree amongst many others, but special to the trained nose of the connoisseur. A few yards away, a series of bramble bushes rose to a height of two and a half feet, providing ample cover for the four rats and one hamster that sat underneath.

'So what do we do with a million sunflower seeds then, Rufus?'

'Nothing!' came the barked reply. 'We're not interested in sunflower seeds, you numbskull, it's the location of the truffle tree that we're interested in!'

'But I thought the ransom was for sunflower seeds?' another queried.

'No, no, you don't understand!' Rufus was beginning to lose patience with his band of imperceptive rogues-in-fur. 'The ransom only brings out the other hamster who knows the location - with them both in our power, and with them both "disposed" of, all the profits of the business will be ours!'

The rats squealed and cackled their delight at their leader's intelligence.

'You'll never get away with this!' Larry spoke up. 'Even now, I'm sure, my brother will have a trained band of guerrilla fighters prepared nearby to liberate him should anything go wrong.'

'Rubbish!' Rufus derided. 'Your brother is as gullible as an old rabbit!'

That was an insult that Larry squeaked his displeasure at.

'Gag him!' Rufus ordered. 'It's nearly time for the rendezvous.'

A few minutes passed as the rats sat anxiously awaiting the arrival of the victim. From a long way in the distance rustling was heard, growing louder by the second, approaching faster than they were expecting. The rats cowered fearing a predator.

'Grunt, grunt!' A wild pig burst his way through the foliage on the other side of the clearing, his left flank facing the small band. He sniffed through a pile of leaves that had nestled in a small hollow before continuing his rummaging as he trotted over to the truffle tree.

'That's all we need!' Rufus whispered. 'A stupid pig!'

He sniffed round for a few moments before continuing his motion to a small elm that grew far away on the band's left, not quite out of view but a fair distance from where the ransom was soon to be dropped off. The pig stood motionless for a couple of minutes, rummaging through some twigs that had fallen from the tree's overhanging branches.

Then, as quickly as it had come, it disappeared, squealing and grunting as it went. The rats listened as the sounds faded in the distance and were replaced by the step-step-step of a small animal that they knew to be Harry.

His head darted out of the bushes, surveying the scenery with an innocent gaze.

'Hello?' he whispered.

There was a long silence.

'Hello?' he squeaked louder.

Still nothing.

'Hello?' he strained his voice to its full volume.

Rufus answered from the cover of the brambles, 'I'm glad to see that you made it. Have you brought the ransom?'

'As we agreed, I've hidden it in the location that you told me. Now where's my brother?'

Larry was thrust out, bound and gagged, into the open. He rolled around in the dirt, trying to loose his mouth to shout to his brother to run, but it was too late - Harry ran over to where he lay and began tugging at the bonds.

'Larry, are you okay?'

The four rats broke cover and grabbed the hamster tightly.

'What?' He was surprised. 'What about our agreement? Hey, let me go! Let me go!'

'No chance!' Rufus grinned. 'You stupid hamster! Fancy believing a story like the one we told you! Looks like we've bought your shares out, hammy old chum!'

'Not so fast!' a strange voice boomed from behind them. Rufus felt it was familiar, but he wasn't sure he could put a face to it. They turned just in time to see a multitude of mighty hamsters bearing down on them, matchstick clubs in their hands and hazelnut shields covering their bodies.

'Run!' Rufus shouted. 'We've been tricked!'

The rats dispersed as fast as they could, the hamsters giving chase with a mighty roar and a defiant shout of victory that sunk deep into the rats' bravery.

As the chase sped off into the more remote parts of the woodland, the parts where no hamster had ever boldly gone before, Furlock Holmes and Doctor Flotsam emerged from the brambles to stand in front of Harry who, by now, was untying his brother.

'Mr Holmes!' He smiled. 'But how did you...I mean, when did...I just don't understand!'

Furlock began his explanation:

'You see, my friends, we knew that these rats wouldn't keep to their side of the bargain - rats never do - and so we began to plan ahead for this day since the moment the hotel proprietor came and told us of your dilemma.

'For the past three days, we've been training a local pig to hunt for truffles. Now you didn't see his arrival, but shortly before you came, he trotted into this clearing and discovered the secret location of the tree. Keeping his left flank at all times to the probable hiding place of the rats, he ran to another tree and gave us time to get off. You see, we'd been tied to the right flank of that pig - all thirty of us - and, as soon as we alighted, we disappeared under the tree's cover until an opportune time!'

'Now here's a lesson to learn, my friends - and mark my words well. Just as the secret of the truffle tree was your downfall, so now your deliverance has come from the secret that the other tree concealed.'

Both brothers stood speechless.

'And one final thing,' Furlock concluded. 'We came to this area blindfolded. No-one knows the location of the secret truffle tree except the pig but, of course, he can't talk - what you thought you'd lost, you've regained.'

Doctor Flotsam and Furlock Holmes turned to sniff a route out of the woodland, but the brothers motioned with their paws and led them by a shortcut into the brilliant sunshine of day.

THE CELEBRATION
WEDNESDAY 21ST APRIL 1993

O mister spider go back home,
Your wife and kids are all alone.
The bath is not the place for you,
Nor is it floating down the loo.

(From an anonymous seventeenth century
poem in the British Museum)

It was the new moon and the evening was to see the beginning of the new year festivities.

Hammish busied himself most of the day with last minute preparations, darting in and out of the guest house as he remembered first one thing, then another, that needed to be done.

It was better that I let him get on with it, for he knew what he was doing and needed no help. I settled myself down to rest - all this fresh air was causing me to be extremely tired.

Mrs Haigh was not sure what to make of Lee and Kath.

True, they seemed like a nice couple - very pleasant and courteous whenever she'd had dealings with them. But here she stood in their room doing her household duties, looking down at an array of sunflower seed shells that were scattered over the face of the carpet.

The dilemma was a complex one. Even though she didn't mind guests eating food in the rooms, she was a little put out that the remains of this feast were strewn over the floor. But, there again, how could one conceive of two adults ever wanting to consume one - let alone this vast quantity - of these seeds?

She stood there for a couple of minutes, contemplating her course of action - this was difficult. Although she didn't want to offend her guests, she knew that she had to bring it to their attention without too much fuss.

Perhaps a word at the evening meal table? No, too confrontational.

Or some pointed comments about tidiness? Again, no - they might not take the hint.

Then Mrs Haigh had a flash of inspiration in a brief instant that made her smile.

'Yes,' she said under her breath, 'that's what I'll do,' and she began collecting up each tiny fragment, each shell, into the palm of her hand until she had a fair pile of debris. Then she placed them on the bedside cabinet underneath the lamp with a short note that read:

'Dear Mr and Mrs Smith, you appear to have dropped these valuable items and I was reluctant to hoover them up in case you should still want them.'

I watched Mrs Haigh's movements from my vantage point on top of the wardrobe, knowing that something had to be done about that pile of shells - they'd be a certain giveaway that I'd stowed away successfully and was, even now, located somewhere in the room.

Mrs Haigh left after completing her tasks and I descended onto the floor via the rear panel that was next to the wall. It was important to sort this out as quickly as possible for the weather had turned decidedly nasty and Lee and Kath could return at any time.

I stood at the base of the bedside cabinet and looked up at the summit. There was no way I could scale it - there were no footholds and the sides were too slippery. But between the bed and the top edge there was only a gap of a few inches. If I was careful, I might be able to reach across to pouch the shells.

With difficulty I climbed the outside of the duvet and scurried over to the gap - it was wider than I'd first thought, but not impossible.

I firmly grasped the bed with my rear paws and stretched out in mid-air for the side of the cabinet, my front paws landing on the edge with a dull thud.

But I couldn't move - either forwards or back - for I was as long as I could make myself and had no way to push myself to either side. All I could do was let go with one set of paws (when I decided), and swing to collide with a hard wooden surface or the soft, downy duvet - I'd already made my choice as to which option to go for.

The sunflower seed shells rested on Mrs Haigh's note and there lay my one hope. If I could grip the paper in my teeth and pull gently, I might be able to drag the shells over the side and onto the floor, then hoover them up when I descended back down.

I extended my neck as far as it would go and attached myself to the note, but my paws were perspiring so much that I was fast losing my grip on the cabinet. With a sharp tug on the paper that sent it floating downwards, I lost hold with my front paws and swung into the duvet.

Having pulled myself up I surveyed the scene. The note had fallen under the bed and was now out of sight (when I finally went back onto the floor I found that it'd come to rest in a place where even I couldn't reach), but the sunflower seed shells hadn't moved a millimetre - just like those tricks with a table cloth and crockery, I'd successfully removed the note but hadn't disturbed my real objective.

I sat there trying to work out another plan, but there was just no way that I could safely get onto the cabinet top. I had to resign myself to the fact that, when Lee and Kath finally returned to their room, questions would be asked in the house....

'That was a good day apart from that horrendous downpour at lunchtime,' Kath said as they both walked in through the door, 'but at least we were under cover the whole time.'

They took off their walking shoes and stretched out on the bed for a quick five minutes' rest. The events of the day flashed through their minds as they discussed their experiences.

'How long have we got 'til dinner, Kath?'

She turned toward the bedside cabinet to look at the clock.

'There's about twenty sunflower seed shells left,' she said, then sat up abruptly and slammed her nearest hand onto the cabinet to cover the pile from view.

Lee jumped up with shock. 'What's wrong?'

He was startled, Kath's previous words being dispelled from his memory.

'Nothing, I'm fine.' She smiled, trying to bring some order to the proceedings.

She certainly didn't look fine, stretched over, as she was, with one hand on the top of the cabinet and the other firmly grasping the headboard to prevent her from falling off the bed. One foot touched the floor to give extra support, while the other had dug into the duvet.

Lee sat up on the bed and looked at his wife. 'Are you comfortable?'

'Er...yes,' she replied.

'Well, you don't look it - are you sure you're alright?'

'Oh yes, it's the only way I can get some relief from that muscle pull.'

'You didn't tell me you'd injured yourself.'

'Well, I don't like to worry you.'

However, Lee was not convinced.

'When did you do it?'

'Er...a little while ago...er...could you see if Mrs Haigh has got any muscle liniment?'

'Yeah, sure,' and with that he went out of the room, down the corridor and into the kitchen.

Kath jumped up, scraped the shells into her hand and threw them out of the window, then looked round the room briefly for any more signs.

'George?' she whispered in a voice that couldn't be heard outside the room. 'If you are here, then kindly remove the evidence of your occupation and be a bit more careful with your rubbish!'

There was the sound of voices in the corridor so she jumped back onto the bed to assume the same position as she was previously in.

'...I think she's pulled a muscle in her back,' Lee was telling Mrs Haigh, 'she needs some cream to rub into it.'

They came into the room. From where they were stood, Kath's position looked even more precarious than it had previously.

'Actually,' Kath began, 'I think the spasm has subsided. If you'd like to help me up I might be alright.'

Mrs Haigh took the side that was nearest the cabinet, supporting her underneath the arm. She couldn't help notice the lack of both note and pile on the surface.

'I see you got the message I left on the side,' she began, 'was it alright?'

Kath looked surprised. 'So it was you?' she laughed. 'I thought it was our hamster that'd done it! That's a relief!'

Not for Mrs Haigh, it wasn't. Neither was it a relief for Lee, he was totally in the dark over this whole incident.

'Your hamster?' Mrs Haigh asked.

'Oh yes, it's really very simple. You see he's ever so clever and I thought that what you'd left had been put there by him.'

'A hand-written note,' Mrs Haigh turned it over in her mind, 'written by their pet hamster? I knew there was something not quite right with this couple.'

She smiled politely and excused herself at the earliest possible moment.

Kath related the entire story to Lee - at least he saw the funny side of it.

And, what was more important, they still didn't think that I was there.

During the early part of the evening, Hammish brought me to a large underground cavern a short jog away from the guest house.

As I entered the scene laid out before me, I was taken aback by the beauty of it all.

Flaming torches hung in almost every crevice in the rock, casting their yellow flickering light onto the dancers below who twirled and span to the rhythm of the musicians located at the far end of the cavern where the sound bounced off the wall behind them.

The table to the right was arrayed with all manner of goodies - not just the normal staple diet of sunflower seeds and various nuts, but fruit and delicacies that I'd never heard mention before (let alone tried!), from places that I'd not heard existed.

The entire cavern was decorated in the most beautiful colours of glittering metals that acted like spotlights on everyone who was present.

And there, standing on a table all by itself, was the traditional Hammis - a daffodil trumpet stuffed with fresh wild seeds from the glen and previously roasted over an open fire to cook it to perfection.

This whole scene was a dream come true - I was indeed privileged to find myself as a welcome guest of the McAmsters.

But there was still an unanswered question in my mind that I needed answering - admittedly, the future of the world didn't depend on it, but I was intrigued to know the answer.

You see, I knew that most people celebrated the new year at the end of December though I'd also read somewhere (the source escapes me) about groups that started the year sometime during September. But I knew of no civilisation, no people, no race that celebrated the occasion in the month of April at the first new moon.

Intrigued by this anomaly, I turned to Hammish to question him.

'Why April?' I squeaked. 'Why begin the new year in the middle of it?'

Hammish smiled at my lack of tact - it was purely a bad choice of words, no offence was intended, but he couldn't help replying half-jokingly, 'We begin the new year at the start, it's the other people who celebrate it in the middle!'

'Touché!' I thought. 'I asked for that!'

If there was one thing I'd learnt about Hammish over the week, it was that he always prompted me into thinking for myself. The problem for me was what my next question should be. If I asked him, 'Why is this the beginning of the new year?' he'd probably answer me something like, 'Because it's the end of the old one!'

I thought through my options and chose the one that seemed to be less ambiguous than the others.

'What does the new year mean to you and your community, Hammish?'

I could see that he was pleased with the question.

'Well, now,' he began, 'I think the main problem is the misunderstanding that the phrase "new year" conjures up in people's minds. For all of us here would consider our time together as a celebration of the new beginning, not simply the new year.'

'The new beginning?' I repeated. Hammish nodded. 'What is this "new beginning"?'

'To explain that to you,' he replied, 'I'd best tell you the event that sparked off these festivities....'

In the dim and distant past, when dinosaurs walked the earth and small rodents had to dodge the monsters' footsteps, there lived a band of hamsters in northern climes who had aspirations to be sabre toothed tigers.

It wasn't that they disliked being hamsters, but they were fed up with being forever trodden on by the bigger and greater animals that inhabited the earth.

Rarely would a day go by without some rodent or other dropping his head to stare at the ground with a melancholy sigh and a depressed half-whisper that summarised the entire band's heart.

'If only I was a sabre toothed tiger.'

And, if any other rodent was near enough to hear that sad noise, that pitiful squeak, that plaintive cry, he also would spend a few moments in quiet reflection at the dream that each one bore of being one of the most ferocious and strong of all the animals on earth.

Fortunately, these hamsters were rodents of action - it wasn't for them to sit around in depression forever, bemoaning their fate until they lost all hope of achieving their target. And so, when a wise old hamster visited the band's burrowed home early one summer, they approached him as one ham to ask him if, perhaps, he knew how they might become sabre toothed tigers.

'That is not an easy question to answer,' the visitor began after mulling the problem over in his mind for a long while, 'but seeing as your hearts are set on it, do this: make a resolution to change - you are strong hamsters, masters of your own destiny, decide on this matter that you *will* become tigers and you shall!'

The rodents squeaked with delight - now, after all these weeks of longing, they could actually become what they'd always wanted to be.

Early the next morning they began to resolve to be tigers.

Shortly after sunrise, the community huddled together under a small bush and started chanting (very quietly at first), 'We *will* be sabre toothed tigers! We *will* be sabre toothed tigers!' gaining strength and belief all the while as the wise old rodent encouraged them to raise their voices to a crescendo of determination.

Some began to growl, still others tugged at their teeth in order to make them grow faster, while still others painted their fur with the different coloured muds that lay near their burrow to resemble a tigers' markings.

If any band of hamsters *could* have become tigers, then they *would* have done. But two months later, when another visitor stayed with them, morale was at an all-time low - not one hamster in all that time had started to become a sabre toothed tiger.

'We've done all that the last hamster told us,' they squeaked, standing before the new visitor with sorrow in their eyes, 'but we still aren't changed!'

This hamster, who was obviously more wise than the previous one, didn't take long to answer.

'You are not changed,' he said, 'because you are only confessing what you *will* be, not what you *are*. "You will be" has no limits to it. It could mean tomorrow, next season or a thousand years' time! No - affirm that you *are* tigers, never doubting in your heart for one moment, and you'll see that you are who you confess yourselves to be!' The crowd of rodents erupted into a scream of delight. With one voice they chanted, 'We *are* sabre toothed tigers! We believe it, we receive it!'

Many months passed and the jubilation of that evening waned in the memory until it became barely a whisper upon the lips of the community.

Just when they were on the point of giving up hope of ever achieving their objective, a third hamster arrived on their doorstep with much expectation being kindled in the hearts of the community.

'We've confessed that we would be,' the spokesman said, 'and we've confessed that we are, but it never made any difference - we're still hamsters through and through!'

'You foolish hamsters!' the wise rodent began, 'both these former messengers have not told you all the truth. While it's quite true that you must have that desire to press on to be tigers and have that confession that you are in embryo now what you will be then, these two things aren't sufficient in themselves, for how are you going to change with words?

'No, my friends, you must live like sabre toothed tigers *now!* Whatever they do, you do - and then, by your actions, you will find that you grow into everything that you desire to become.'

This time, they thanked their visitor for his kindly advice and, after saying a fond farewell to him early the next morning, they went about applying this liberating truth.

The younger hamsters formed themselves into a pack and went out hunting. For the time being they decided not to try for a gazelle until their strength grew along with their stature, so they made for the seashore and stalked a crab that they brought back to the others - unfortunately, they were none too sure how to kill the thing and after many valiant attempts to subdue it, they were forced into letting it go.

The older hamsters, meantime, had decided to forsake their burrows for a loftier nest in the trees. After all, everyone knew that sabre toothed tigers lounged sleepily about on strong branches that offered them a shade from the dazzling sun. I'm sure that in a couple of years they may well have mastered the skills needed, but for now they kept rolling off each time they had a particularly vivid dream about chasing a runaway hazelnut.

All in all, the experiment was not a success. Even though they continued to affirm both what they desired to become and what, they believed, they already were, not even one of them seemed even the slightest bit changed.

Then came the fourth visitor.

He looked different to all the others in that he didn't have any wise hamster's clothes on him - no, he looked incredibly ordinary.

THE OBSERVATORY
THURSDAY 22ND APRIL 1993

We'd been walking on the island of Erraid for a couple of hours, using the rocks as cover from predators and sampling the delightful wildflowers that grew in patches almost everywhere we went - I just hoped that they weren't endangered species.

The previous evening's celebrations had continued well into the early hours of the morning, the last of the hamsters dispersing shortly before sunrise.

It had been a most enjoyable experience, but we were both weary and, after making it back to the guest house, settled down to catch several hours' sleep before waking shortly after noon to visit Erraid.

It was a pleasant day, the sun shimmering off the water and making us both squint from the glare.

'Where's this observatory then, Hammish?' I asked.

He looked puzzled. 'It was that building we saw when we first got here.'

Now *I* was puzzled. 'That wasn't an observatory, it was a signalling post.'

'No, no,' Hammish began. 'I concede that it may be described as a signalling post observatory, but that still makes it an observatory.'

'But I've been looking forward to get a chance to use a telescope and look at the stars! You mean to say that it isn't a real observatory?'

'It *is* a real observatory! But your concept of what an observatory is, is obviously amiss. From there they observed,' Hammish emphasised the word to draw my attention to it, 'the two light beacons farther out to sea and signalled to them.'

I was disappointed that what I thought it was, it wasn't.

'That's the problem with labels,' Hammish added philosophically. 'Unless you define what you mean by them, they could conjure up all sorts of concepts in the minds of those who hear you speak.'

'But I thought it was common knowledge what an observatory was!'

Hammish tried to explain. 'It's the same as the label "hamster". If you know what one is then the label is adequate, but if you don't then you might as well not use one....'

In a far-off land that's no longer the way it used to be, there once lived a hamster who didn't know what he was.

He certainly knew who he was, but not what - that was his dilemma, for although his parents had given him the best upbringing any pair of hamsters could, they'd failed to give him that one piece of vital information - namely what kind of animal he was. Perplexed and troubled, he'd tried to resolve the matter early after he'd left the nest, but comparison with the other animals didn't help for there were none in that region that looked like him at all.

And he'd also forgotten his route back to his parents' nest so he was unable to return to ask them for this vital piece of information.

Lonely and distressed, he found a clump of grass that provided shade from the rising sun and settled down to bewail his ignorance.

'It's not fair!' he squeaked indignantly. 'If only I knew what I was, I could get on with being what I'm supposed to be! But instead I have to sit around with no purpose and no way of finding out what I am!'

Just then, a passing giraffe heard sad squeaks coming from the thick grass that lay at his feet. Intrigued by this phenomenon, he bent his long and slender neck until he was able to poke through the greenery with his nose to find what was making these peculiar sounds.

The giraffe's gaze met the two beady eyes of the hamster.

'Hello,' said the giraffe. 'What's wrong with you, my friend?'

The hamster, unconcerned for his own life, looked at the head that absorbed his vision.

'It's not fair!' he said. 'My parents never told me what I am and I can't be what I'm supposed to be cos I have no idea what that is!'

'Don't know what you are,' the giraffe summarised. 'Mmmm, let me see - we've had this problem before with the parrots. They were so busy imitating other species that they clean forgot what they were created to be. Let me go and get some of my colleagues-in-fur and I'll be right back. We'll find out what you are in no time at all.'

The giraffe was gone only a few minutes, shouting to whomever he saw, 'Hey, there's a thing down here, doesn't know what it is.'

Very soon a vast array of wild beasts gathered round the small bundle of fur that sat with its head drooped.

'Let me see,' the giraffe began, 'do you have a name?'

'Oh yes,' he replied, 'my name's Hector.'

The other animals looked at one another blankly. He heard them whisper, 'I've never heard of a Hector before,' and, 'Is this a Hector? It doesn't seem like the right name, surely.'

'No,' ruled the giraffe, 'that must be who you are, not what you are. Anyway, that was only a guess, we'll begin by comparing you with each other then we'll see what you most resemble.'

Each animal looked at the hamster, then at one another, trying to distinguish any characteristic that was common. Apart from fur, eyes, ears and a mouth there wasn't too much that made it stand out - except, perhaps, its size. But then all the other animals were so large in comparison to it that it couldn't possibly be anything to do with what they were.

'We don't seem to be having much success,' the giraffe admitted, 'let's find out what type of things you do, that might give us a clue.'

He turned to the other animals and encouraged them to ask questions.

'Where do you live?' the lion asked.

'Nowhere,' he replied. 'I haven't got a home because I don't know what I should build to live in.'

'What do you eat?' That was the antelope's question.

'Well, I've been eating seeds and green plants,' he began. 'I tried eating some red substance that had flies buzzing round it but that didn't agree with me at all.'

'Now we're getting somewhere,' one said, 'that means you're a herbivore.'

'A herbivore?' The hamster began to get excited. 'You mean I'm a herbivore?'

'Oh yes. But it only means that you eat plants and things like that - it's not the type of animal you are.'

The hamster's head drooped over once again.

The snake eyed him over a couple of times before asking, 'Are you edible?'

Quickly, the lion grabbed the serpent's neck in his mouth and gave him a gentle reminder that now was not the time to be thinking about lunch.

'Perhaps I'm an elephant,' the hamster said. 'They eat plants, don't they?'

'But I also have a tail on both ends of my body which you don't,' said the elephant.

This was getting pointless. The animals were no nearer getting to know what their distressed friend was than they were when they first met him - apart from knowing he was a herbivore, but that was more than obvious even before they began their questions.

Disappointed, the hamster squeaked, 'Look, can't I just have any name?'

'No, no,' the owl replied. 'Your name tells you what you are. If you were called "tiger" you'd catch gazelle, or if you were named "chimpanzee" you'd swing in the trees - you can't put a label on yourself if it doesn't represent what you are.

'I mean,' he continued, 'there'd be no end to it - we'd have lions wanting to be called moles and mice wanting to be called badgers. Where would that get us, apart from totally confused?'

Hector sighed as the owl took a deep breath before speaking once again.

'But, fortunately, I know what you are - I've met your kind once before, a long time ago in another part of the land. You're a hamster.'

The pig looked at him in case this was some sort of joke - no, he was serious, this really was a relative of his.

The hamster squeaked with delight. 'A hamster!' he shouted.

'I'm a hamster! A hamster!'

The other beasts joined in the rejoicing. After a couple of minutes, the owl motioned with his wing, calling for silence - he had something further to say.

'There are many in this world who take a label upon themselves that's not theirs to possess. Be careful who you meet, my friend, for many will claim to be your relative when they will really be your enemy.

'You will know them by the things that they do. Just as a hamster is a herbivore, so too will all your relatives be herbivores. Do not be deceived by those who would come dressed in fur such as yours but who inwardly would devour you for their lunch.' He looked at the snake as he hooted his instructions.

The hamster was elated, except that he wasn't quite sure what a hamster was supposed to do - okay, fine, he had a label, he knew what he was, but that didn't help him when it came to knowing how that was to be translated into conduct.

The owl could see the questions on his brow. Before he asked the question, he gave him the answer.

'Do you remember all that your parents used to do?' he asked.

The hamster nodded. 'Then these are the things you do - follow their example and learn from them. Besides all this, you'll know both what's right and wrong to do, because all you need is written on the inside: you'll be all that you are from within.'

And with that, he spread out his wings, caught the breeze and took to the sky while the other animals gradually dispersed.

Hector the hamster sat alone thinking.

Then he ran for cover and began digging a burrow as a nest.

I'll kill for a piece of melon.

Well, okay, I don't mean that literally, but I think that you understand how much I love that fruit. Whether it be a water or honeydew melon, a charantais or a galia, it makes no difference to me - they're all worth getting out of my nest at home and descending to my food dish for a quick snack as soon as I'm aware that I've been given some.

I'm like that with apricots as well. Lee used to get worried when I'd eat nothing else but that fruit during the brief period that they're in season, but now he's resigned himself to giving me a whole one each day.

Roast chicken is a particular favourite, too. According to Kath, one minute twenty-seven seconds is the all time record from the moment a piece is dropped into my dish until I get my teeth into it after being sound asleep. I've been quicker, I know I have, but they couldn't've had the stopwatch going when I broke the sixty-second barrier. One day I'll surprise both my owners and emerge from my nest in under thirty.

These, then, are my three favourite foods.

You can imagine what my natural instincts were doing when Lee and Kath sat down at the dining room table with melon as the starter, the subtle smells of roast chicken floating around the guest house as it was being browned in the oven for the main course and apricot crumble with custard for afters - hot apricot crumble, that is, the aroma mixing itself with the chicken.

'What's the matter?' Hammish asked as I paced to and fro in our make-do nest for about the seventy-ninth time in the past four minutes. 'Is there something troubling you?'

Hammish, unfortunately, did not understand my dilemma as I explained it to him. Not only is he not susceptible to the presence of any of my three favourite foods, but he's not got any special dietary preferences, just so long as it's edible and there's plenty of it - he's certainly no fan of nouvelle cuisine.

'I'm going for a walk!' I announced grumpily and scampered off across the floor to exit the room under the door.

Being meal time, it was safe to wander the house as any guests would be in the dining room. I intended exiting the building to sit in the fresh air to regain my composure and control but, instead, my paws went the other way against my better judgment until I found myself in a place where I could see into the dining room.

I could just make out Lee's voice as he talked quietly to Kath.

'If only George was here!' he giggled. 'Melon, chicken and apricots - boy, oh, boy, he'd've been going bananas by now!' and then he laughed loudly as he realised his unintended pun.

Of course, it wasn't their fault, they didn't know I was there - if they'd known then they would have saved me a few scraps, they always did.

But I was hungry, desperate and capable, in that attitude of mind, of anything.

I slowly paced over to the kitchen door, beginning to allow a snarl to come to my lips, just like a sharp shooter approaches his opponent in those westerns before he shouts 'Draw!' and guns down the enemy.

Yes, I was feeling mean and nasty and look out, Mrs Haigh, cos here I come. It's either you or me, baby, I ain't gonna take no pris'ners....

There was a loud scream and a tumultuous clatter of crockery that emanated from the kitchen. The peas on Kath's fork scattered across the dining table and floor, rolling under adjacent furniture. Lee almost choked on his drink, but wiped the liquid up as it flooded down his nose.

Mrs Haigh reeled into the room, her face ashen and her legs barely able to support her weight. She grabbed at a chair and sat down heavily.

Kath was still trying to find the eighth pea that had launched itself off her fork as Lee said, 'Are you alright, Mrs Haigh?'

It was obvious that she wasn't but, in the circumstances, it seemed like the best thing to say.

Mrs Haigh pointed into the kitchen.

'A mouse,' she said. 'It frightened me half to death.'

Kath, still on her hands and knees in search of the lost pea, saw a bundle of fur dart like lightning across the doorway with its pouches full and with an apricot in its mouth.

She stopped what she was doing and stared blankly ahead.

Could that have been? No, surely not!

She kept her eyes fixed firmly on the doorway as she took up a seated position under the table, finding the last pea as she did so.

Lee was still comforting Mrs Haigh - it wasn't that the owner was frightened of mice, she was just shocked.

This time two hamsters went past the door, unladen and going the other way.

Kath saw them both.

'I'm alright,' Mrs Haigh said. 'I'd best get back to the kitchen - I've left half the crumble in the oven and it needs to come out.'

'I'll come with you and give you a hand.'

The same two hamsters, heavily laden with full pouches, walked briskly across the doorway as Lee and Mrs Haigh went back into the kitchen.

'Well I never,' Kath said under her breath. 'I was right after all - George really did make it up here!'

'Do you think they saw us?'

'No, never, we moved far too quickly.'

THE RIVER
FRIDAY 23RD APRIL 1993

'Kath?'

It was the early hours of Friday morning and Kath, like most of the inhabitants of Fionnphort, was sound asleep. Lee shook her arm as he repeated, 'Kath? Kath, are you alright?'

She rolled over, taking a deep breath and half-opening her eyes.

'Have you got a piece of carrot for me?' she asked.

Kath sat up in bed, turned to look at the clock and realised where she was.

'Did you just wake me up?'

'Yeah. I couldn't get to sleep with all the noise you were making. You were...' he paused before he broke the news gently to her, 'you were squeaking.'

'Oh,' she said nonchalantly, 'I was dreaming - can't remember what it was about now.' She thought long and hard. 'No, it's gone - couldn't've been important.'

She rolled over to settle back down to sleep.

'Goodnight,' she said.

'Goodnight.'

'Kath?'

It was still the early hours of the morning, but a little later than before. Lee was rubbing both his eyes with his hands after he'd yawned quietly.

'Kath? You're dreaming again, wake up!'

'Nonsense,' she replied, 'I know where I left my walnut, it must have sprouted legs and walked off.'

Lee shook her arm once again and she sat up in bed.

'What now?' she asked. 'What was I doing this time?'

'Sniffing,' he replied, 'and then you said "It was here somewhere, I remember the place."'

'Really strange,' she whispered. 'Can't think what I was dreaming about - never mind.'

And they both settled down to slip back into sleep.
'Goodnight.'

'Kath?'
Lee lovingly poked his wife in her rib cage to bring her gently round.
'Wobb?' she asked. 'Wobb ob I dumm now?'
'Sorry?' It was Lee's turn to sit up in bed. 'What did you say?'
Kath repeated her sentence.
'Are you alright?' He reached over and put the sidelight on. Kath squinted with the sudden brightness.
'Wobb's wonn?' she complained.
Lee stared at her.
'I think you're coming down with something, your face is swollen and your...what's that white stuff hanging out your mouth?'
'Wobb wibe stub?'
Lee pulled on the white substance - he pulled and pulled. In all, sixteen tissues had been pouched by his wife - it was just as well that the box on the bedside cabinet was empty or there may have been more.
'Are you sure you're alright?'
'Yes,' she assured him. 'It was only a dream - I think - I can't remember what it was, but I'm sure it must have been a very vivid dream.'
Lee was tired and wanted to get back to sleep so he dispelled any doubts from his mind, settling down in the warm bedding as Kath switched out the light.
'Goodnight, again,' he said.
Kath replied, 'Squeak.'

Hammish had promised me a ride down one of the local streams in the area, but he'd left it until the last day as he said it would be one of the highlights of my time in Fionnphort and he wanted to save the best until last.
It was only a short jog to the river bank, but being a sunny morning we took our time whenever possible, stopping to try different flowers as we stumbled upon them. The warm sunshine made everything come alive with colour while the brief shower that had fallen through the night brought the fragrances of the plants into an almost overwhelming array of smell.

We arrived at the river bank around midday and immediately set about constructing a raft from various twigs that had fallen from the trees. Using the stems of the toughest grass, we tied them together to make a craft that was, I considered to be, far stronger than we would ever need to gently float down the river to the sea.

Thoughtfully, Hammish had also sewn some paw straps into the raft so that we could both secure ourselves - but this was only a precaution, Hammish assured me, for hamsters have such wonderful balance that it would be extremely unlikely that we should fall off into the gently flowing stream.

We pushed the raft out into the water and boarded it before it got too deep to leap onto. It slowly glided out into the middle of the stream, then caught the main flow and began its slow descent towards the sea.

'Now put your paws in the straps,' Hammish instructed me. 'I don't want you to go falling in and spoiling it for yourself.'

I obeyed without question, even though I knew that on this calm day there was simply no danger of me losing my balance. Besides, Hammish had often travelled this stream as a youngster and it was best I follow his instructions just in case there was a sharp bend en route that would flip me off the raft.

This was the life, it was beautiful! Tranquil, serene, calm. The sun beat down on the river making it twinkle with all kinds of flickering light. The birds darted from tree to tree in search of food, squawking and tweeting their merry tunes at each other.

And the occasional fish would leap out the water with the excitement of spring in his lungs (do fish have 'lungs'?).

I must admit that I hadn't noticed the raft speed up, I was too busy taking in the rich grandeur of my surroundings, but Hammish turned his head and spoke to me in calm, even tones.

'You know, George, riding a river is like life - you never quite know when you'll meet the rapids.'

If there was ever a sentence that dispelled security and well being from my heart, it was this one.

I looked in front and saw the water turn white with foam. Rocks also appeared above the level of the water and I realised that the paw straps were no 'optional extra' - Hammish knew full well that this gentle stream became a veritable monster in its lower courses and he'd made provision ahead of time for my well being.

'Well being?' I thought to myself. 'If I'd've known what this river became later on in its course, I'd never have allowed myself to get on!'

The raft twisted and turned as water splashed over our heads soaking our fur and filling my ears with liquid. I squealed a number of times with fear as I saw rocks come straight towards the raft fearing that we'd be dashed against them, but each time the flow of water took us away from danger into another channel.

Then, almost instantaneously, there were less rocks - and less foam. The roar of the water was predominantly behind us and the craft reduced its speed.

'Isn't that just like life, George?' Hammish squeaked.

'You mean how it suddenly becomes calm?' My voice quivered.

'No, no,' he replied. 'How just when you think that the worst of it's over and that you'll never go through anything as difficult again, the going gets even worse and the ground seems to disappear from under you.'

I couldn't believe what I was hearing - but I turned to face the flow of the stream.

Sure enough, not ten yards away, there wasn't anything - absolutely nothing.

No water - I mean no water!

I grabbed hold of the straps even tighter than before (if that were possible) and let out a terrified yell as we sailed out into a void where the water fell vertically for some twenty feet.

It seemed like we hung there for ages and I braced myself for impact as the raft rapidly descended picking up speed with each passing moment.

Splash!

I don't know how far we sank under water, but the raft pulled us back up to the surface. Using the straps as support I pulled myself onto the raft and took a deep breath.

We were suddenly becalmed in a pool of water that lay at the foot of the waterfall. There was peace yet again - except this time it was a stillness that I appreciated more than the previous one because of the torrent I'd just come through.

Hammish continued, '...and then life seems to calm down to something we can really appreciate!'

I would have replied (in no uncertain terms) but I wasn't sure that I had any voice left in me. He pointed to a grassy bank across the pool and began paddling with his paws to direct the raft.

'That's the thing about life, George, it's so important to know that throughout it we have a secure craft on which to travel. Otherwise, when our head sinks below what we know we can cope with, it won't be able to pull us back up because it'll have disintegrated in the trial we've just been through.'

We reached the bank quickly, Hammish disembarking first and holding the raft steady for me to get off - but everything seemed to be continuing to move.

I summoned my strength and leapt onto the bank, but my legs were shaking so much that I didn't stay upright very long. It took me awhile to recover in the warm sun.

'Are you okay?' Hammish asked me after a long time.

'Yes, I...er...think I'm back in control of my limbs.'

'Splendid!' He smiled. 'Let's go back up and do it again!'

THE DEPARTURE
SATURDAY 24TH APRIL 1993

Kath had inspected every article of clothing as she packed it away on that Saturday morning. She'd looked in every pocket, every sleeve and even felt the lining of every garment that had one. Although she found a number of loose hairs, their origin couldn't be determined.

Then she went through the case feeling down every crack, gently exploring with her hand areas that she didn't want to have to repack.

She stood upright and scratched her head.

'He's not there,' she thought, closing the lid and locking it securely.

It was the rucksack's turn for inspection - each pocket was delicately opened, examined minutely, then resealed with the fastener. The contents of the main compartment were removed and subjected to a similar treatment to that of the contents of the now-locked suitcase.

A few more strands turned up but all the evidence was, so far, inconclusive.

All the other carriers were similarly scrutinised - nothing.

She sat on the bed puzzled and rubbed her eyes.

'Have you lost something?' Lee asked. 'Only I can't understand what on earth you're doing.'

'Oh...er...' she thought quickly, '...nail clippers. I can't remember where I put them.'

'You haven't, we left them at home, remember?'

'Oh yes, silly me!'

Lee looked at her as she eyed each corner of the room, then lifted the duvet and felt all over the bedsheet.

'Now what?' Lee put his book down, unable to concentrate with all the movement and interruptions. 'The soap was by the sink when I last saw it!' he said jokingly, then paused before continuing. 'Are you alright, Kath? Ever since Mrs Haigh saw that mouse you've been acting really weird.'

'Yes, I'm fine.'

'Only it's a bit ironic that at the beginning of the holiday you were worried about me but now the roles are reversed.' Lee smiled.

Kath didn't hear him, she was on her hands and knees looking under the wardrobe. She found a few more hairs but these were definitely human - no doubt. They were tossed into the bin.

'I've already paid the bill,' Lee observed. 'It's too late to think of a reduction for cleaning our own room.'

Kath sighed, there was still no evidence. She decided to confess - well, sort of....

'I was thinking,' she began, 'about George and all that....'

Lee laughed. 'I thought we'd decided that he couldn't possibly be here?'

'But supposing he had made it - just suppose - one small hamster desperately trying to stow away aboard his masters' luggage before they leave for home, finding it difficult to know where to hide....'

'...cos you keep uncovering every hidey hole....'

'He could be, even now, in some remote part of this guest house, trapped by circumstances over which he has no power...' it was a very impressive dramatic voice, '...imprisoned to be forever a guest in a house in Fionnphort with humans that don't understand him.'

Lee looked at her, appealing to reason.

'Okay,' she said, 'I concede - I won't say another word about it.'

They both took the luggage to the car, locking it in the boot.

I had to dodge the suitcases as they came into the car, they weren't too careful how they put them in.

Still, I'd had no other choice but to say my farewell to Hammish earlier that morning before sunrise, and conceal myself in the boot of the car. He'd decided to stay on for a few weeks - being a wild hamster, he had the freedom to choose, but I wasn't at liberty to do so.

The car started up and we moved off down the road, back the way we came.

It had been a most enjoyable week's holiday.

Appendix

APPENDIX
FOR A FEW PEANUTS MORE

While this book was being typeset, I decided to go through a series of notes that I'd put to one side after George had passed away. I can only imagine that I must have chosen to save them for posterity's sake (although the reason now escapes me) because, over ten years on, I fail to see any importance of all these 'first drafts' and 'incomplete hamscripts' that have already been extensively recorded for analysis.

However, in the file marked 'Hamster Histories,' I discovered the hamscript below, which appears to have been compiled by George for a fourth volume of stories that never came about - the large characters 'HH4' appear in the top right hand corner of the opening sheet of lino along with a personal note at the very end that reads (italics added) 'Dr Leaf, please put this one aside *as well* and we'll compile the work just as soon as I can find some time to get away.'

The hand-writing seems to be that which is regularly attributed to his 'Scottish' period and may well yet show us that, had George not gone the way of all hamsters, another great work would have been forthcoming early in 1994.

It may also prove that there really does exist a fourth volume of Hamster Histories that has yet to be discovered.

The publishers have been kind enough to allow me to include it here as an appendix seeing as the importance of the text will be immediately apparent to all first-year degree students who've just embarked on their three-year literary course of critical study.

FOR A FEW PEANUTS MORE

for Jaron Plasencia

Montmorenci was suffering from amnesia.

At least, he thought he was - he couldn't remember.

He looked round the dimly lit room trying to make out blurred forms that were defying his struggle to bring them into focus.

Then he noticed the throbbing on his head and, reaching up a paw to feel for its source, encountered a large bump that pulsed with pain as he gingerly felt for an explanation. His mind raced to plumb the depths of his memory but he barely scratched the surface - until he could dig deeper, it was going to remain a mystery.

The one clue he had as to who he was lay in the contents of his pouches that he now emptied onto the floor, examining each object in his fingers.

Sunflower seeds - three of them. That made sense - it's what he was half-expecting to be there but, when he found two halves of shells with their edges sharpened, he sat up with surprise.

Then there was that small black object that seemed to be made of a silky-like fabric and which, when unrolled, showed itself to be a small black mask only sufficient to cover the eyes.

'Perhaps I was at a fancy dress party?' he thought.

He repeated the phrase to himself, trying to summon up an image, a flashback, a face.

But nothing came.

Just a void where he knew something must be that would answer him as to why he sat, head throbbing, in a dark compartment alone.

Or was he alone? True, he hadn't checked but he couldn't hear the sound of anyone's breathing save his own. He moved about the room feeling for walls, stopping to recover his composure when the pain overwhelmed him.

No, no one else - and a wire door that was locked on both sides with a metallic smelling security device that prevented the normal means of escape.

Normal means of escape? That was strange! Why was his mind speaking of a normal means of escape? Had he done this before? He had an overwhelming sense of déjà vu in that instant as if where he now was was where he'd been before - but it didn't make any sense.

That was the problem - nothing made sense.

As if in answer to his inner panic and remembering nothing, his own voice burst into his mind, a voice from the past that shot like a bolt from the blue. Almost deafeningly, he heard his mind recall the slow, calculated statement, 'Tell them they stink. And tell them I said so.'

'What?' he squeaked quietly. 'What's that supposed to mean?'

But nothing more came - no context, no image.

Nothing.

He marvelled in what context the words could ever have been used but all to no avail. He might as well have started life as a new born hamlet with a clean memory and a desire to learn, but this present state was plain baffling.

Just then, he heard movement - a faint scratching noise that stopped almost as soon as it'd begun.

There, again.

It was coming from the door, there was no mistake. He crept over, trying to make as little noise as possible and sniffed at the entry.

The scratching seemed to be echoing off the sides of walls - was his room but one compartment in a hallway full of them? - that slowly changed to the crackle of a sunflower seed being opened.

'Hello?' he squeaked, his voice bouncing back off the solid panels in front. The cracking stopped.

'Hello?' he shouted again.

'Morenci?' came the reply. 'Is that you?'

'Morenci?' he thought. 'Is that me? Is that who I am?'

'Perhaps,' he whispered back, 'I...I can't remember. I appear to have been hit on the head and now can't remember too much about who I am or how I got here.'

'It certainly sounds like you, Morenci! I thought I was the only one left! Hang on! Let me pouch my things and I'll be right over.'

And, with that, he heard rustling and scraping, scampering of sharp claws on stone floors and the creak of the metallic door as it swung gently open to reveal a small, black rodent, barely an inch tall but sniffing him to make sure it was who he thought it was.

'Morenci! It *is* you! Don't you remember me?'

He contorted his face to summon from within something that he couldn't find, breathing out deeply as he shrugged his shoulders and lifting his paws into the air while he confessed, 'You'd best tell me - the name just isn't there.'

'Fabian!' he near shouted. 'It's me!'

Montmorenci stared at him with empty eyes, still oblivious to the reason for his presence in what he'd thought - until five seconds ago - was a secure cell and uncertain as to how he now found himself in a place that his mind was telling him he shouldn't be seen dead in.

'You really don't remember me? Or what happened?'

'Not at all,' he squeaked back.

'You poor thing.' He sounded shocked. 'Let me tell you how we got here....'

Scratchville had been a small, quiet town, pioneered by settlers moving west from the relative safety of the east coast, travelling light under the wagons of those humans who'd felt the call to explore strange new worlds, to seek out new life and new civilisations, to...

...you get my drift, anyway.

Perhaps they should've seen it coming - or, rather, them. They always came wherever there was hope and new life, where there was a cheap killing to be made and control to be exerted over hamsters who lived peaceably amongst themselves.

And they came in force, too.

It was then that a stranger came to town. Hearing of the reports from hamsters and mice alike who'd fled the safety of the town and abandoned possessions for their own personal safety, he'd come to stand against the darkness and death that had oozed across the streets and homes that once supported life.

His name - as every rodent knew it - was the Lone Hamster.

'Lone Hamster?' thought Morenci. 'I know that name! Why do I know that name?'

There was something vaguely familiar that caused sweat to appear on his brow and, although he was sure that he knew him better than anyone else he was ever likely to meet, he could neither summon a face before him nor describe those things about him that Fabian was now relating.

The first battle had been almost a non-event.

Arriving anonymously and in heavy disguise in town, the Lone Hamster had hired a room in the central hotel and sent message to the rats to meet him. Not realising the hamster's identity, they'd unwittingly decided on an open confrontation and stood, their ranks displayed like a mighty army, in front of their challenger.

But that was their mistake.

In a cunningly sly move, the Lone Hamster threw them into confusion and chased them out of town, removing himself from Scratchville before there was a chance for him to be idolised.

Round one over, the townsfolk settled back to another life of tranquillity not perceiving that, even though they'd been defeated, the rats were planning an even more dastardly plot to regain control of Scratchville.

But, for the time being, the place grew, hamsters and mice attracted to the place, thinking themselves secure from attack.

'That's when you came,' Fabian squeaked, 'highly recommended from the headquarters of the Furs National. Don't you remember? You were Chief Banker for months.'

Montmorenci tried to summon his past life but it just wasn't there, the bump on his head bearing witness to his friend that his memory might take its time.

'It doesn't matter,' he half-whispered, 'I just thought you might make the connection....'

The rats had attacked while the rodents were gathered together as one hamster to discuss the celebrations for the harvest, surrounding the place and out-numbering the inhabitants three to one.

Resistance was futile - or so everyone seemed to think.

In blind panic, rodents rushed out through holes in walls, cracked floorboards and wind-moved roof tiles, fleeing for their lives to anywhere their tiny paws would carry them.

Just twelve of us were left and they descended upon us like a pack of wolves, jabbing at our heads and pushing us to leave...

'...that was when you must've got that blow to the head,' Fabian concluded.

It still helped Morenci little in his quest for memory but he nodded agreement and encouraged his new friend to finish the story.

'Well, I found a hole in the floor and came down here - I never knew this place existed and probably neither do the rats. I just kept quiet until the scampering of their feet faded to silence. You must've found the same hole and fled for safety here, too.'

Still nothing.

All Morenci knew was what he'd been told and that strange double sentence that, even now, was reverberating round his head.

'Tell me,' he began, 'I have these words in my head and they're the only things I recall. Do they make any sense to you?'

Fabian listened carefully as if there was some clue that needed to be solved that would unlock his friend's memory. These were strange words indeed. He repeated them slowly, carefully, scratching his head in bewilderment as he repeated - now for a third time - 'Tell them they stink. And tell them I said so.'

His eyes bulged widely.

'Beats me,' he squeaked, 'I've never heard them before in my entire life.'

The next few hours passed rapidly, Fabian intermittently tiptoeing over to where the small shaft of light cascaded a few rays of sunlight into their otherwise darkened hole. He sniffed as deeply as he could without making any sound that could be heard above ground until that final lingering odour of rat disappeared from detection.

'Look,' he squeaked to Morenci, 'if we can get up there and sneak out into the back yard, we can take for the hills and flee for our lives....'

'What did you just say?' he interrupted. But Fabian, struck dumb by the intrusion, also forgot his train of thought. Morenci repeated it with a twist that rang a bell in his head that identified it as a saying from his past.

'Take for the hills,' he stammered. 'Flee for your lives. I've heard that before, Fabian, I know I have!'

But his friend wasn't impressed.

'I'm sure you have,' he squeaked indignantly, 'but now's not the time for you to recover from your memory lapse. Now's the time to turn tail and run when we get the first opportunity!'

Fabian was right - he had to be. Morenci agreed and shuffled silently behind him as they both made their way to the crack and, as they hoped, freedom.

'Look!' he whispered, 'I'll go up and check the coast is clear....'

'How far are we from the coast?' Morenci interrupted. 'Can you see the ocean from here?'

'No, no, no! I was speaking figuratively!'

'Oh.'

Fabian exhaled deeply with exasperation before continuing, 'I'll scratch on the opening once I've made sure it's safe. You got that?'

Montmorenci nodded.

With his nose twitching for the first sign of oncoming danger, Fabian pawed silently through the hole into the now vacated room, his rear end disappearing from the safety of darkness after a few short, hesitant stops.

As soon as he was fully above ground, he extended his frame vertically, poking his nose as high as he could while he smelt to all four points of the compass.

Nothing.

Peering through the window, he eyed an empty street, houses carelessly open and debris from the raid lying all about the well-used thoroughfare that'd been his home just a few short hours before. He walked carefully over to the crack and scratched at the edge, Montmorenci exiting into the light with squinting eye and suppressed cough as the dust cascaded into his breath.

'All's clear,' Fabian whispered.

'Is it really?' a rat cackled.

Trapped!

It was impossible to say just how long they stood there, frozen in fear as rat upon rat congregated before them, swelling their ranks until not an inch of space was left. It seemed like an hour but it was probably only a few short seconds; such is the deception of fear when it controls the mind.

Montmorenci couldn't help think that he'd been here before - but he also couldn't think why. It didn't seem to make any sense.

Unprovoked, a walnut found itself catapulted from the rear of the crowd, striking him violently between the eyes and knocking him unconscious to the ground.

The lights went out faster than if someone had flicked a switch....

Morenci was drifting on a soft, downy cloud with stars in his vision no matter where he looked - up, down, it made no difference. The concussion was playing tricks on the receptors in his eyes and his mind was masking the stress with images of floating that inspired peace and calm.

Some way into the distance a bird squawked, flying with speed directly to where he drifted, landing close by with an inquisitive eye that gazed into his own.

'Hello? Anyone home?' it squawked. 'There's work to be done, wake up!'

Morenci stared at the raven with an almost comatose glaze.

'Sure, sure,' he squeaked back.

'Wake up!' commanded the bird. 'You've a message to deliver to the rats!'

That snapped him awake - he'd lost conscious memory of the danger and now the scene in the room flooded back. But where was he? This wasn't the place! This was...where? He wasn't sure, it was strange, weird. As if he'd turned round to look inside his own mind to discover the truth he'd been searching for since he first lost his memory.

'What's the message?' he drowsily asked.

The raven turned his beak to face him and, tapping firmly on the protruding bump, said precisely, 'Tell them they stink. And tell them I said so....'

That was it!

The answer!

He heard the scuffle of approaching rat paws and felt the clammy feet of Fabian dig into his frame as he backed away, pressing himself against the wall. With incredible speed and agility, Morenci flashed out the mask from his pouch, slapped it across his eyes and jumped to his feet, stretching himself to his full height.

'You've calculated the victory without the Lone Hamster in the equation,' he squeaked defiantly. 'At your service, my little enemies-in-fur!'

Jaws dropped open, eyes widened and weapons fell from hands as the Lone Hamster raised a lip to reveal a toothy grin that gave the rats no hope. Panicking, they edged backwards, slowly at first then with increasing speed as they ran at full pelt out of the room, into the street and away, their last squeals being heard as the rabble disappeared into the distance.

Fabian's legs were shaking furiously as he pushed on the wall and raised himself up to his full height.

'You've saved the town!' he squeaked. 'Lone Hamster, you're a genius!'

His thankfulness was cut short as he started looking about the floor for Morenci.

'What?'

'Don't worry, your friend's safe.' The Lone Hamster's mind was working overtime. 'Your friend slipped down through the crack in the floor just as I was ascending to do battle. I'll go get him for you.'

Without a moment's hesitation, he scampered into the hole shouting, 'Montmorenci!' and answering himself, 'Yes, I'm here! Over here!'

In a couple of minutes Morenci exited the crack into daylight, Fabian pulling his fur from the abyss while dancing with the excitement of the victory snatched from the jaws of defeat.

'You should've seen it, Morenci!' he began, squeaking with delight. 'One hamster against the vast array of ratdom - it was incredible!'

He paused to look round before he asked, 'Where's the Lone Hamster?'

'Oh,' Montmorenci answered, 'he said he had other work to do...in another town a long way away.'

He thought for a couple of moments before adding, 'He apologised for being late. Only, he couldn't remember how to get here....'

THE TEXAS CHEESESTRAW MASSACRE

'Mmm,' squeaked Larry the Hamster, 'those cheesestraws were delicious!'

'Yes,' agreed Gertrude, 'and we ate the whole packet too.'